DIPLOMACY

ZAHRA OWENS

D0168300

Published by
Dreamspinner Press
4760 Preston Road
Suite 244-149
Frisco, TX 75034
http://www.dreamspinnerpress.com/

This is a work of fiction. Names, characters, places and incidents either are the product of the authors' imagination or are used fictitiously, and any resemblance to actual persons, living or dead, business establishments, events or locales is entirely coincidental.

Diplomacy
Copyright 2007 by Zahra Owens

Cover Design by Mara McKennen

ISBN: 978-0-9801018-6-7

Printed in the United States of America
First Edition
December, 2007

eBook edition available
eBook ISBN: 978-0-9801018-7-4

Author's Note

A writer doesn't exist in a vacuum.

Although we tend to be loners, happy to spend time with just ourselves for company, we can't live without other people to interact with. We need others so we can borrow a look, steal a character trait, use a quirky insight from them. It's other people that help us write fleshed out characters, interesting people and intriguing situations and that interaction starts early on in life. Without other people in our lives, our imagination would be sadly limited.

Some people are more important than others in that respect.

My mother raised an open-minded daughter and showed her, in a very matter-of-fact way, that relationships come in all shapes or sizes and that some of them involve two people of the same gender. Thank you Mom, for being one of my most avid readers and for not even blinking when a passage turns a little explicit. Also, thank you for saying that my book was every bit as good as the romance novels you devour at a pace of three a week, even though I know you're biased.

On the internet I met many kindred spirits and one who became my regular editor. Silv, thank you for correcting my strange European sayings, my wonky spelling and weird sentence structures and putting up with my sometimes very American way of putting things. Also, thank you for having the guts to tell me when things don't work and the tact to tell me in such a way that it doesn't damage my delicate writer's ego.

Nancy, you persuaded me to send this story to a publisher and here I am!

To all my internet readers, thank you for encouraging me to write more. Every single one of your comments was devoured and appreciated. Feedback keeps a writer not only on her toes, but also keeps her motivated.

Elizabeth and all the lovely people at Dreamspinner Press, my professional editors, Lynn West and Willa Canter and my cover designer, Mara McKennen, thank you for giving me a voice.

From behind her desk,

Zahra Owens

Introduction

JACK took a deep breath. He hated his job.

Well, not exactly his whole job, just the pomp and circumstance that came with it. Far away from the official engagements, he actually adored it. He did what he had always longed to do, ever since he was a child. He did what his father had always done, and as soon as he was in high school, he knew he wanted to follow in his father's footsteps and become a diplomat. Thanks to the fact that he grew up all over the world, he spoke quite a few languages, and he was learning another one now that he was in a new country. All his life he had wanted this, and now he had it.

Only tonight was one of the nights when he hated what he did. Because he was helping his President host a banquet in honor of his visit, he was dressed to the nines in an Armani suit that was especially cut for him and a designer shirt underneath with gold cufflinks that Maria, his wife of more than fifteen years, was helping him fasten.

"Will you just...hold still for one second?" She wasn't smiling when she asked. He figured she was as nervous as he was, if not more so. When it came to banquets, he was the host in name of the President, but all eyes were invariably pointed towards 'the wife' because it was understood she always made all the practical arrangements. He smiled as he realized how lucky he was to have her.

Maria was also the child of career diplomats with an upbringing similar to his own.

The reason why he had gotten his first ambassador posting before the age of forty was undoubtedly in large part thanks to the fact that she was an impeccable organizer. Tonight would be no different. She had arranged a banquet for 112 dignitaries with a five course meal and speeches, and it would all flow together seamlessly, no doubt. He would get all the compliments tonight, not in the least about his wife's radiant beauty. And a beauty she was, her medium length blond hair pulled back and pinned up with the diamond hair pin he had bought her in Antwerp for the wedding anniversary they had just celebrated, her slim body and delicate breasts enrobed in an elegant burgundy red strapless dress that flowed over her body as if it was molded onto her and made her smooth lily-white skin stand out. As she reached up to brush some stray hairs off his shoulders, he rested his hands on her waist and leaned in to whisper in her ear. "You look absolutely eye-poppingly gorgeous tonight. You'll knock 'em dead out there." Maria just smiled her knowing smile. She was more than aware of the heads she would turn this evening.

One of the Secret Service men stuck his head inside the room. "Mr. Christensen, Ma'am, POTUS is ready to go inside."

They both knew the jargon. POTUS was the name used for the President of the United States. They would need to be by his side as he walked in.

While Maria straightened his tie one more time, he leaned in to give her a quick kiss on the mouth.

"Oh, Jack." She ran her finger over his lip to erase the tiniest red mark her lipstick had left. Jack could see the worry lines on her forehead.

"Just smile, Maire, you look much nicer when you smile."

This was their little ritual before these occasions; their own way of getting ready to face their guests. Maria loved it when Jack called her by her nickname, which was the Irish version of her Christian name. Her father had called her that and after his death, Jack had adopted the practice. It would inevitably make her relax, a shy but warm smile appearing on her face.

Jack took her hand as they headed towards the next room where they would join their President.

Preliminary Negotiations

Chapter One

AS Ambassador, Jack Christensen was the representative of his Head of State in the country he was assigned to. That didn't mean he always agreed with the man, it just meant he had to pretend he did. So he was not exactly a member of the current President's fan club. In fact, he had always been a fairly eloquent Democrat, so he was quite surprised when he was appointed to replace the Ambassador to Belgium who was retiring.

Even though a large part of his job was to translate his President's policies for that country, the assignment excited him. This was a small country indeed, but a well trusted one. Not to mention it was interesting diplomatically, since its capital housed not only the Headquarters of NATO, but also the seat of the European Commission, and was considered the de facto capital of the European Union. The north of Belgium also housed a major international seaport that was often used by the United States for military transport, making it an ally to be pampered.

On the other hand, Belgium was known to be a headstrong country that did not follow the pack blindly. On more than one occasion, the former Ambassador had needed to smooth out wrinkles in the transatlantic relationship, so Jack knew he had his work cut out for him.

Tonight had been his baptism of fire. He hadn't even had the occasion to officially present his credentials to King Albert II yet, as was the custom for new ambassadors, and now his President was visiting and he had a house full of government officials and Secret Service personnel.

The visit would last three days, and Jack knew that with all the receptions and banquets it was going to be the longest three days of his life.

The banquet went by perfectly, even though the United Kingdom's Ambassador went home early with a bad case of the flu. At least that would be the official explanation. Just after the main course, Maria had noticed he was rather inebriated, and after she alerted Jack to this, he was discretely removed and sent home in his chauffeur driven car.

Since the President and First Lady were guests at the Embassy, Jack and Maria were required to stay in the private quarters of the Embassy instead of going to their home just outside the city.

"Tonight was perfect." Jack was in his pajama bottoms, leaning against the doorway watching Maria take off her make-up. He knew she would understand that as 'thank you for a great job'.

She rolled her eyes. "We came close to a small diplomatic incident, though. Luckily, our Brit didn't object too much to being sent home."

Jack moved behind her and rested his hands on her slender hips. "Judging from his reaction, his assistant wasn't surprised." He was watching her elegant figure in the large bathroom mirror.

As they had greeted their guests before the banquet he had seen quite a few men's eyes travel across his wife's body. Some of them had even looked at her lustfully, not bothering to hide it while he was talking to them. So why had she never conjured up those feelings in him? He loved her, of course. She was beautiful, that he could see too, but he had never felt the uncontrollable need to just have his way with her on the top of the table. Even in the beginning of their relationship, making love had been tender and caring, but rarely unashamedly passionate.

He kissed her neck tenderly. Luckily they were great friends. "It's going to be a long day tomorrow as well, starting bright and early with a private breakfast with our honored guests."

She turned around and brushed her finger along his jaw. "Yes, we'd better turn in."

THE following evening there would be a reception where the Americans living in Belgium would not only get a chance to meet their

President, but also their new Ambassador. Even though it was a much more relaxed affair compared to the banquet, Jack and Maria would have to make their rounds and shake a lot of hands, leaving very little chance to actually have a decent conversation with anyone.

Jack was talking to a Presbyterian minister and his wife who had lived in Belgium for more than twenty years. As always, he had one eye on the entrance where the guests where greeted by his Protocol Officer. Just as Jack politely declined the minister's dinner invitation, his eye was caught by a young man entering. He was tall, dressed all in black, and instead of a tie he had on a black silk cravat, wrapped loosely around his neck. His hair was long and wavy, and Jack realized that he was probably the only one in the entire room who could get away with that look and not seem underdressed for the occasion. On his arm was a beautiful, fresh looking young blond woman, who smiled nervously and clung to him like wrapping paper.

"Oh, but you and your lovely wife must come to our church, Mr. Christensen. Antwerp is just a forty-five minute drive, you know," he vaguely heard the older woman say.

As if emerging from a daze, he excused himself, "Mr. and Mrs....Wallace, I'm sorry but I need to attend to a minor emergency." He quickly made his way through one of the side doors.

Just seconds later Maria entered as well. "I almost felt like I should come and rescue you."

"Huh? What?"

"I saw your eyes glaze over. She *is* a little pushy, isn't she? Now let's go back in before our guests start to wonder why the new Ambassador and his wife disappeared together."

She smiled as she gently nudged Jack back into the room.

Both the President and the First Lady, closely watched by the Secret Service, worked the room like consummate professionals, trying to cover as much ground as possible in the shortest time. Jack and Maria were well experienced in doing the same, but as he emerged, Jack realized he was scanning the crowd for the dark haired young man. Even though the reception was at its height, he quickly found him and his twinkling companion, animatedly talking to the First Lady, who was clearly very taken by the confident young man. Jack could tell he was in no way fazed by the First Lady's notoriety and seemed totally at ease, something Jack had never achieved in all his years in the diplomatic corps. Just as he was ready to make his way over to him, sensing the First Lady was ready to move on, he was engaged by an older businessman, a newcomer to this country and clearly eager to meet his Ambassador. They exchanged courtesies, but Jack was relieved when another older couple joined in the conversation, giving him a chance to take his leave.

"Your Excellency?"

A fairly low, confident and very British voice made him turn around, and he found himself looking into the most beautiful chocolate brown eyes he had ever seen. There was a moment of awkward silence between them that seemed to last forever. Jack knew he had to respond, but his mind was an absolute blank.

"You Excellency, my name is Lucas Carlton, Assistant Information Management Officer for The Right Honourable Marcus Boyles, and this is my fiancée, Lucy Marsh." He indicated the young woman who disentangled her arm to shake his hand. "Nice to meet you, sir."

Glad for the forwardness of the young man, he first shook her hand, then his. Lucas's grip was firm and his hand soft and dry. The familiar protocol helped Jack recover somewhat. "Ah, yes, our esteemed U.K. Ambassador. How is he feeling today?" They exchanged knowing looks.

"Still a little uncomfortable, but nothing that can't be remedied," the young man responded with a conspiratorial smile.

Jack had a hard time breaking eye contact with Lucas, but it was only polite to address the young woman as well. "Miss Marsh, you are American, I believe?"

Lucy smiled at him, clearly ill at ease. "Yes, from Boston."

"And you decided only a Brit was good enough?" As soon as the words left his mouth, Jack wished he could take them back. That was awfully forward as a conversation starter.

Lucy smiled, a little unsure of how exactly she was to respond, but Lucas rescued her. "We met at Stanford, where I was studying International Relations. She made a foreigner feel very welcome." He smiled at her reassuringly.

"Was it you I spoke to last night?" Jack asked Lucas, relieving Lucy of being the center of attention.

Lucas raised his eyebrows. "Ah, yes, we were expecting a call, so I stayed to co-ordinate. His Excellency was…'ill' already when he was dropped off, but he was determined to attend. I could only hope that you or your wife would save him from embarrassment, as you so kindly did."

The understanding glances between Lucas and Jack were totally lost on Lucy, who clearly didn't have a clue that the U.K. ambassador was not really sick.

"Well, we won't keep you much longer, your Excellency. I simply wanted to introduce myself, since the U.S. and the U.K. have always been close allies, and I expect we will be meeting again very soon. My boss has informed me I will become his liaison officer with your Embassy since I have strong interests in that area anyway."

Jack expected Lucas to look at his girlfriend to acknowledge exactly where those interests were situated, but he did not, instead captivating Jack with his gaze for what seemed like forever.

Lucas finally nodded as he took a step back and guided Lucy further into the room.

Jack sighed, releasing a breath he'd apparently been holding. He then took a few deep breaths, trying to calm down his racing heart.

IT wasn't until later that night, when he was alone in the bathroom of his private quarters in the Embassy, that he had a chance to think it over. What was it that made Lucas so special? Why had this young man awakened feelings he had buried long ago? He let his head fall into his hands and tried to ban the thoughts that kept creeping into his mind when he thought of the young Brit, of his chocolate brown eyes and his radiant smile, of his firm handshake that went straight to his groin.

He got up and threw some cold water on his face while he looked at himself in the mirror. *Forget it Jack, he's got a girlfriend and you have a wife. You're both successful heterosexual men. It's pointless to let your pecker take over.*

After drying his face, he walked into the dark bedroom, trying not to wake up Maria.

"You don't have to sneak around," he heard her say, just before he slid under the blankets. She wrapped herself around him as he lay down on his back and rested her head on his shoulder. "Well, you seem to be happy to see me."

Chapter Two

ONE of Jack's functions was to coordinate his staff and make them work to their full potential so they could be of service to the Americans that lived in Belgium, but an Embassy was more than that. Jack and his staff were considered 'legitimate spies', since it was also their task to be informed of the policies and politics of their host country and be specifically alert to what that meant for America as a country and for the Americans living under their wing.

As with every new Ambassador, Jack had a lot to learn, and he knew by now that every country was different. His staff briefed him extensively about the communities and regions of this small country and the sensitivities that lay in the fact that not only the North and South spoke a different language, but that their culture was also quite disparate. Jack knew that speaking French would not be a problem for him, but when he was told in no uncertain terms and by his secretary, no less, that almost sixty percent of Belgians spoke Flemish, he asked her to arrange for him to learn the language. She was a no-nonsense Belgian woman in her early fifties, and the fact that he answered her rant with this request almost made her blush. Jack realized this had gained him her undying respect and he made a mental note never to assume everyone spoke French around there.

Home life had by now returned to normal and the Christensens were no longer required to live at the Embassy. A comfortable and spacious house was provided for them in Tervuren in the green belt around the capital. Maria was all too used to packing up, leaving, and settling down again in another part of the world without too much advanced notice and made it her personal goal to make each house still feel like home.

"You know Jack, we should ask that young Englishman with the American girlfriend to dinner one night." Maria was buttering a piece of toast in their kitchen.

Jack looked up from his newspaper. "Why?"

Maria gave him an 'I don't know how you've achieved what you have with that attitude' look. "He's charming! Even the First Lady couldn't stop talking about him after they met at the reception and they spoke for...what? All of three minutes? I just figured he's an up and coming guy and his girlfriend could use a little help."

Jack raised his eyebrows.

"I mean she's a nice enough girl, but if she ever wants a chance at helping her future husband's career, she's going to need to be educated a bit. Did you know this is her first time outside of the States?" Maria was hugging a cup of coffee by now, settling down next to Jack, and stealing the New York Times from his stack of different newspapers.

"Well, he did tell me he was going to be the liaison officer to our Embassy, so maybe we should get better acquainted. Mind you, we will be talking shop all night, so it may get a bit boring for you girls," Jack answered without looking at his wife.

Maria rolled up her Times and playfully flogged him with it. "Well, I'm sure 'us girls' can retreat upstairs and paint our toenails while the men do business."

Jack looked up and realized he'd just offended his well-educated wife.

LATER that morning, Jack's secretary stuck her head inside his office as he reviewed the new financial sanctions the Belgians had imposed an all non-EU imports.

"Mr. Christensen, security has Mr. Lucas Carlton downstairs. He's the liaison from the..."

"I know who he is, Mrs. Claessens, just send him on through and..." he called her back just before she left, "...arrange with security to let him through next time? He's C.D. like the rest of us, just U.K. instead of U.S."

She nodded as she closed the door again to relay her boss's request.

Just minutes later Lucas strolled confidently into Jack's office, a small folder under his arm, wearing virtually the same clothes as Jack had seen him in at the reception. The ever present smile on his face, he leaned over the impressive oak desk littered with papers to shake Jack's hand.

"Mr. Christensen, I'm glad…" Lucas stopped mid-sentence as Jack raised his hand.

"Please, call me Jack. If we are going to have to work together on everything that concerns both our countries, then you are going to drive me crazy with all that 'Mister'ing, so just… Jack."

Lucas smiled broadly. "Okay, Jack. But it was still nice of you to see me without an appointment. I'm usually better at sticking to protocol, but I wanted some fresh air and these papers needed to be delivered, so…"

"So you walked from your Embassy to mine? With…" Jack quickly leafed through the folder, "…three pages on the U.K.'s view on the import sanctions?" He realized he was amused by this as he watched the young man loosen his scarf while not quite settling in one of the chairs across from him.

"It's only about a five minute walk and like I said, I needed the air. Taking a car would have been utterly useless." His voice trailed off as he admired the rather opulent decoration of the office.

"So how's old Boyles?" Jack asked, understanding that the young man wasn't going to indulge him with a straight answer.

Lucas was still looking around at the intricately carved borders near the ceiling, giving Jack the chance to stare at the young man. "He's had a bit of a…relapse, so we're expecting that he'll go home to England for an extended…rest, pretty soon."

Jack chuckled. He had met the U.K. Ambassador only once and they had taken an instant dislike to one another. The man was notoriously inept at keeping his alcohol consumption to an acceptable level and always managed to insult a few people before he needed to be escorted out. Not Jack's favorite kind of diplomat.

"Can I get you anything to drink? Since you walked… I thought you might be thirsty," Jack asked a little hesitantly and not quite at ease.

Lucas jumped up. "Why don't I get us something? Tea, coffee, water?"

"Lucas, sit down, you're my guest here, Mrs. Claessens will get us something."

The young man turned around. "What's her first name?"

"Who?"

"Your secretary," Lucas answered, stating the obvious.

"Oh, ehm...Gurdy or something. Something I can't quite pronounce, it seems." Jack watched the young man chuckle and walk out the door like he owned the place. As he looked down at his papers again he realized he couldn't focus. He decided that working with this bubbly Englishman was going to prove more difficult than he thought, because looking at him sitting across from his desk made him think of lots of things, none of them even remotely connected with work, and those thoughts made him uneasy. So he started clearing up, putting papers in neat little stacks, trying to keep his mind on placing them in the correct order and...

"It's Gertje." Lucas pronounced it carefully, Jack hearing at least three sounds that were unfamiliar to him, "but she says it's okay for her to be called Mrs. Claessens. That way you don't make a fool of yourself, and it shows a healthy respect."

Jack hadn't even heard him enter the room again.

"I can't believe she said that," Jack rebutted with a smile, trying to hide his unease behind a little humor.

Lucas set the two cups down on the table and raised his hands in surrender. "I don't know you well enough to lie to you yet, besides, what do I gain? She's a feisty lady, and she told me you want to take Flemish lessons, so I told her I'd take you where I go for Dutch class. Then she kissed me and I always want to be at least on a first name basis with the people I kiss."

"You were gone... two, three minutes? And you talked about all that?" Jack was quite amazed.

Lucas nodded as he sat down and took a sip of his cup of tea. "Oh, and she's a cat person."

Jack chuckled. "No, I'm sorry I don't believe you."

"Seriously," Lucas answered, clearly not easily put off. "You should get your own coffee more often. There's a picture of her and two tabbies in the little nook where the coffee maker is and her paperweight is a Siamese." He pointed his cup at Jack. "Now drink your coffee, because she doesn't seem to me like the kind of woman who would like her boss to waste a perfectly good cup of coffee."

Jack couldn't help but smile as he reached over his desk for the steaming cup, sat down again, purposely not looking up at Lucas, and took a sip. "I suppose she told you how I like my coffee too?"

Lucas shook his head as he swallowed some clearly still hot tea. "No, she actually poured it for me. Wouldn't let me do it. She's very protective of you, you know. Says you're the best boss she's had so far."

"Smart woman," Jack murmured as he thought how totally irresistible Lucas was. They continued to drink their beverages, making small talk about the importance of learning the local language as part of their job, and Jack relaxed as he enjoyed the effortless conversation.

"Well, I better leave," Lucas stated suddenly, as he got up. "They may start wondering where I am pretty soon, and since I haven't told them I'm liaising with my American Ambassador... Well, they're clueless...in more ways than one."

After Lucas was gone, Jack let himself sit back in his chair, still a little dazed by the whirlwind visit. *My American Ambassador.* He shrugged. *MY American Ambassador? You're going nuts, Christensen. And reading things into someone's words that aren't there. It's just a manner of speech.* Still he felt like he had just been made a pass at, like the beautiful Brit had just laid himself wide open to him. *Take me, I'm yours.*

Jack shook his head. *You're married and he's almost married. Get your mind out of your pants.* Oh God, and he had to invite him over for dinner.

"Mrs. Claessens? Can you get Lucas Carlton on the phone for me, please? U.K. Emba... Yes, I know he just left. No rush, just sometime today please?" He put down the phone and glanced at the clock. Mrs. Claessens was right. There was no way Lucas could have made it back to his desk yet. The young man was surely getting to him.

Damn.

Chapter Three

AS Lucas walked out of the U.S. Embassy, he tightened his scarf and tucked his hands in the pockets of his trousers. It was early summer, but the freakish European weather made it a bit nippy. At least it wasn't raining.

It was about a ten minute walk to the U.K. Embassy, if he took his time. The most annoying bit was the fact that he had to walk quite a way to the nearest zebra crossing, but he wasn't about to risk his life trying to cross the Avenue that was part of one of the busiest inner city roads in Brussels any other way. He didn't really mind the walk, it would clear his mind.

Why did he put himself in this situation? Why did he get himself smitten with a man again? And a married one at that. Even if there was a remote possibility that Jack was interested, the man had even more to lose than Lucas did. He had climbed to the highest ranks in diplomacy. A U.S. Ambassador. And Lucas had seen his wife; she was the perfect Ambassador's wife. He even had to admit he liked her. She was obviously a strong woman, and there was no doubt that even if Jack was a first class diplomat, he was not the one who was boss in that relationship. He almost felt sorry for Jack, but then he knew the value of having a strong woman to lean on. His own mother had been like that too, though when his parents were young, a diplomat's wife was a trophy. She had to be beautiful and a good organizer, but she also had to be silent and no one ever acknowledged her strength.

In the past few years it had become painfully clear to Lucas that without the right woman on his arm, he could kiss a diplomatic career goodbye. Even in the lower ranks, the invisible masses, you needed the perfect background to push ahead. In the three years that he had been working for the U.K. Foreign service he had been sent from one menial job to the next, every senior officer telling him he was sure to get ahead because of his pedigree, but being brushed aside every time.

Until he brought a girl to one of the Embassy's receptions. They weren't even really dating, but she was the daughter of the new Economic Counselor and had actually asked him out.

He never realized that one date would get him noticed. Then coming back from a trip to California with an American girlfriend got him promoted to Assistant Information Management Officer, and now that same girlfriend seemed to be the basis for making him the liaison with the Americans. And she was nowhere near the perfect diplomat's wife.

So going back to dating men was out of the question. He'd have to put his U.S. Ambassador out of his mind. There. Done.

He took one last breath of the crisp morning air and entered the U.K. Embassy, opening the service entrance by sliding his security badge through the reader. He went straight to his broom closet of an office and had barely hung his coat on the hanger when his phone rang.

"Mr. Carlton, this is Gertje, Mr. Christensen's assistant. Can I put him through to you?"

Lucas felt a rush of blood to his head. *Fifteen minutes after I leave he's already calling me? Calm down, mate, and answer the woman.* "Sure, Gertje. Thank you."

He heard the click of the transfer and then a slightly hoarse voice. "Hi, Jack here."

Lucas swallowed as he heard Jack clear his throat. "Yeah, I know," he chuckled. "You have a very efficient secretary, remember?"

"Did you get back okay?"

Lucas smiled at Jack's attempt at small talk, but he had to admit he liked listening to his voice. "Yeah, the lunch hour traffic was murder, but I made it here in one piece."

He heard the older man clear his throat again. Was this a nervous tic with him or something?

"What I forgot to tell you, well, to ask you was…Maria suggested that I invite you and Lucy to come over for dinner. On Saturday, if you're free. If not, then next Thursday maybe, because the Saturday after that we have a function to go to so…"

He heard Jack sigh and didn't quite know what to think of what he was hearing.

"I'll have to check with Lucy, but as far as I am aware my calendar is blank. Is it okay if I call you back tomorrow and let you know?"

"Yeah, sure, I'm sure Maria doesn't mind last minute changes." Another sigh. "That didn't quite come out right. What I meant is, sure, tomorrow is plenty of time and if you need more, the day after is fine too. Maria is good at improvising."

Lucas smiled. What more could he ask to keep hearing Jack's voice? "Will it be just the four of us or will there be other guests? Just so I know what the dress code is."

He could hear the American smile, "No… just the four of us and please, wear something casual. On occasions like this, I refuse to wear a tie, jacket, dress pants or anything remotely close to what I have to wear at work. It's taken me a number of years, but I've finally persuaded Maria that it's okay to wear jeans around your friends."

Why was this eloquent, thoughtful man rambling? Yes, this was a social call, but what was the problem in asking someone to come over for dinner? No problem at all, unless his first impression was right. There was a reason why Jack seemed uncomfortable around him, and Lucas was determined to find out if that reason was mutual attraction.

"I'm sure I can persuade Lucy to come, but I'll call you tomorrow to confirm. What time do you want us there?"

"Why don't we start unfashionably early, say around five? We have a fabulous garden and Belgian weather permitting, we can enjoy it a little before we start dinner. Oh, and you'll need the address?"

Lucas jotted down the Ambassador's home address on a piece of official Foreign Service notepaper. "So we'll talk tomorrow, yeah?"

"Yeah, tomorrow," he heard from the other side, just before the click signaling the end of the conversation.

Lucas sat there for a while holding the telephone and smiling.

The man was definitely an enigma, and the way he was feeling about him was a complication he could do without in his life right now. Finally his career was on track, and Lucy was a large part of the reason why. She made him… normal. Not the secretive guy with no discernible private life, but an ordinary guy with a beautiful blonde on his arm.

It wasn't like he was totally faking it. He loved Lucy; she was nice, full of life, with a naïve outlook and not too many ambitions of her own. They knew each other from the six months he had spent at college in America, and even though he had a boyfriend at the time, they had become friends. The first time they slept together was about two months before he was supposed to leave for the posting in Brussels, and when push came to shove, she came with him, just to be away from her overbearing family.

They were doing remarkably well in their one bedroom apartment in the European district, from which Lucas could walk to work and Lucy could take the metro to the Vesalius College where she was taking Communications and International Affairs classes. Lucas found Lucy easygoing and undemanding, and even the sex was okay.

Despite all that, Lucas never stopped longing for the touch of another man.

He had kept his urges in check for almost a year now, and up until a week ago, he'd found the desires easy to live with. The benefits greatly outweighed the occasional wet dream and the use of a little imagination went a long way while he was making love to Lucy, especially as her wiry frame lacked the usual curves of a woman.

That evening, after she had come on to him while watching TV, they made love in the darkness of their bedroom. The only reason Lucas lasted long enough to make her come was that he had tried hard not to think of Jack. Once he heard her cry out his name and felt her spasm beneath him, he could no longer control his thoughts and, imagining how he would touch and kiss the older man and thrust inside him until Jack too would shout his name, he came just moments later.

As he rolled over onto his back, panting heavily and trying to catch his breath, he could feel Lucy wrap herself around him.

She looked up at him with glazy eyes. "God, Lucas, I don't know what got into you tonight, but it was just amazing."

Lucas kissed her hair and closed his eyes, feeling guilty about the deception.

"They want us to come over for dinner on Saturday," he spoke softly.

"Who?" Lucy asked, now more awake.

"The Christensens. The U.S. Ambassador and his wife, remember?"

"Oh, I hope you said yes!" Lucy exclaimed, now sitting upright next to Lucas. "Oh, my God, Lucas, what will I wear?"

Chapter Four

IT may have been uncharacteristically cold all that week, but Saturday turned out to be a wonderful day. Most Embassy personnel lived in the European quarter around the European Parliament and the Embassies, so hardly anyone had a company car, but Lucas had arranged to borrow one of the Smart cars the embassy had on standby, much to Lucy's contentment.

"Don't tell me you're going to wear *that*?" Lucy asked as she passed Lucas while he was checking himself out in the bathroom mirror. "Lucas, we're going to Saturday night dinner at the house of a U.S. Ambassador. *That* would not even get you invited to the dinner table at my parents' house." She gave him a once-over and then retreated to the bedroom.

"Well, Jack said no ties, jackets or dress pants, so…" He looked happy in his faded jeans and green shirt.

Lucy gave him an amused look while she was slipping into a soft yellow sweater. "Oh, it's Jack now, is it?"

"Yes," Lucas answered, a little annoyed it had slipped out so easily. "You can't expect me to call him Mr. Christensen all the time when we're working together, now can you?"

"Oh, I don't know. You're a junior assistant and he's an ambassador, of course you're on a first name basis. Here, try this." She threw him a midnight blue silk shirt and black jeans.

He sighed as he sat down next to her on the bed after taking his favorite pants off. "He asked me to call him Jack, all right?"

Lucy got up and kissed him on the forehead. "No need to get defensive… and I just want you to look nice. It's not like those clothes aren't comfortable." She turned around and disappeared into the bathroom.

Lucas let himself drop so he was lying on his back on the bed. She didn't deserve being snapped at, but for some reason, she was getting on his nerves these past days. He knew, of course, why she did. The past year had been easy, but now that the genuine article was right in front of him, he was no longer content with second best.

Tonight was not going to be easy, though. He was probably going to be confronted with Jack being fussed over by his perfect wife and Lucy trying hard to impress everyone. He didn't know which thought he hated more.

SINCE Brussels traffic was notoriously difficult to predict, they arrived at the villa in Tervuren according to Belgian custom: a very fashionable ten minutes late.

Lucas had missed the rather well hidden entrance the first time they drove past and had to turn a little further up the street. Once they entered the narrow driveway, it took a sharp turn to the right and they were stopped by two Secret Service men.

"Can we see some identification, please?" the man on Lucas's side of the car demanded.

Lucas handed over his passport together with his diplomatic pass and Lucy's papers. "Lucas Carlton, Lucy Marsh, to see Mr. and Mrs. Christensen."

"Very well, sir. I'm afraid we will have to take a look at your car. Could you step out of the vehicle and open the trunk, please."

It was not a question, so Lucas complied. The guard flicked on his flashlight and checked the empty boot. He then nodded at Lucas, allowing him to close it. The second man looked around the inside of the car.

Once Lucas was back in the driver's seat, the guard gave him back his papers. "Mr. Carlton, Miss Marsh, thank you for complying with our security regulations. You may drive along this road to the house without stopping and park to the left of the main building. We will inform the house that you have arrived. We wish you a pleasant stay as guests of our Ambassador."

Lucy was annoyed they were late, but Lucas figured he at least had something to talk about with his hosts, explaining just why they were held up, but his fears of the whole setup being uncomfortable were unjustified as they neared the house. Maria was walking up from the front of the garden towards the house with some hydrangeas in her arms and she looked absolutely radiant in a simple white dress. She smiled at them invitingly.

"Drive on up to the house, you can park at the side, and I'll let you in."

The house itself looked like it had been featured in "Homes and Gardens", but the inside was cozy and nice, clean and tidy, but not to the point where you felt uncomfortable. There was a table filled with magazines and newspapers and lots of flowers everywhere.

"Come on through," Maria urged as she walked in front of her guests into the house. "I just want to put these in a vase. Did you find the house easily?"

"Yeah, Jack's directions were good. The traffic was just a little busier than I predicted," Lucas answered, looking over at Lucy. "So I guess we honored a Belgian tradition and arrived a little late."

Maria smiled warmly. "Don't worry, Lucas. Since everything in our lives is so meticulously planned, we try to keep home life a little more chaotic and unplanned. So I apologize beforehand if things seem a little 'unrehearsed' tonight. We like to keep things relaxed when we have friends over. Jack's elbow deep into preparing dinner, so come say hi in the kitchen and I can get you some drinks there."

Lucas and Lucy exchanged looks at being considered friends, even though they had only met briefly, but followed Maria nonetheless.

She wasn't kidding about Jack being elbow deep into cooking. He had his shirt sleeves rolled up and was wearing an apron, which was a good thing since he was kneading dough.

"Lucy, Lucas, you found the place!" Jack smiled broadly. "Welcome! As you can see, Maria takes care of the house, but the kitchen is my domain, so forgive me for the informal greeting."

"Oh, the man does the cooking around here. Lucas, you could pick up some pointers from Jack, then," Lucy teased.

"Yeah, well. I'm afraid growing up with a live-in cook didn't do my cooking skills any good, so I had to find myself a man with hidden talents," Maria was quick to answer as she put her arm around Jack and stole a kiss.

Lucas felt himself go pale and hoped it wouldn't show. What was he thinking? This man was clearly in love with his wife, and why shouldn't he be? She was perfect, a charming hostess, complete with a sense of humor. He watched her reach up for glasses to put the home made iced tea in, but more clearly noticed the way Jack looked at her, letting his eyes ghost over her perfect female form.

LUCY and Maria retreated to the garden, leaving Lucas in the kitchen with Jack.

"You're unusually quiet," Jack inquired softly, breaking the rather uncomfortable silence.

"So you make your own bread?" Lucas replied, since he didn't want to answer the question.

Jack smiled. "Yeah, that's my party trick," he shrugged. "Maria loves to boast to our guests that I can make bread, so she makes me do it every time."

"Must be quite an ordeal. Being made to perform like that..." Lucas answered, trying to crank up his sense of humor.

"Well, what can I say, I'm a henpecked husband," Jack snorted, still smiling. "At functions, she's my sidekick, so at home I'm a good boy and I do what she asks."

Lucas could almost see them in bed together, Jack on his back and... He turned around when he realized it would never be Maria bent over Jack in his fantasies.

"So, Lucas, I could use a hand, if you don't mind?"

The young man turned to face his host again. "Ehm, sure, but as Lucy said, I'm not a great cook."

"Well, wash your hands, and I'll tell you what to do."

Jack could tell Lucas was nervous, but nowhere near as nervous as he was himself. It helped that he had things to do. Things that kept his eyes from wandering over the flowing, slightly on the large side silk shirt Lucas was wearing. Things that kept his hands busy (and dirty) so he wouldn't be tempted to grab the young man as he passed behind him to wash his hands in the sink. *Bury it, Christensen,* he told himself as he kneaded the dough once more before it was ready for the oven.

Lucas looked at him expectantly after returning to the counter where Jack was working.

"Okay, we need to divide this dough into smaller pieces to make individual rolls and then shape them into little balls. Can you do that?" Jack felt the young man's heat next to his arms as they were standing quite close to each other.

"Ehm?"

Jack gave him a small chunk of dough. "Just knead it gently, don't knock the air out of it. Think of it as a woman's breast."

Lucas chuckled, "Which in my case will make us end up with very small buns."

Jack knocked him playfully with his elbow, and they both laughed as they continued making the rolls.

Jack looked up through the kitchen window towards the garden, where the two women walked through the rose garden, clearly in animated discussion.

"They seem to be getting along just fine," Jack tried after silence had fallen between them again.

"Yeah, look at that… our women."

Jack wondered if he was just dreaming the tone of Lucas's voice at that statement. He realized he had seen Lucy clinging to Lucas, but they were not close physically otherwise. It felt like a one way relationship, but then he was hardly the one to make an objective assertion of that.

"Things a little difficult between you two?" Jack offered, only to be met by a frightened look from Lucas. "I'm sorry, I didn't mean to pry, it's none of my business, of course," Jack was quick to add after he averted his gaze. "Can you open the oven for me, please?" he asked Lucas, pointing at the large stove underneath the gas burners. After Lucas complied, he put the bread in the oven and moved back to the counter.

"It's not easy, Jack," Lucas eventually whispered.

Feeling the tension in the air again, Jack tried to rescue the situation. "It must be hard for her, leaving her family like that to move to a foreign country."

"Yeah." Lucas nodded, not entirely convincingly.

Damn, now the moment was lost. But what could he do? It's not like he could ask Lucas straight out. Straight, yeah, funny…

"Now I literally need a hand," Jack stated, trying to lighten the mood.

"Sure," Lucas answered, "a hand, two hands, arms, shoulders, whatever you need, Jack."

Jack could feel Lucas looking at him and for a moment the brash, forward young man he knew from the office was back. He was at a loss for words momentarily, but recovered shortly afterwards.

"I need to wrap this salmon in phyllo pastry and then tie it up with string, so I need a third hand to help tie the knot."

They worked together silently and Jack felt Lucas stealing little touches. Was he just imagining the fact that Lucas was standing very close to him, their arms brushing and purposefully making their hands touch as he put his finger on every knot Jack tied? Was the young man lingering a little longer than he should?

"There," Jack stated as the eight small packages of pastry wrapped salmon were arranged on the baking tray.

Suddenly he felt Lucas's hand rest on his, fingers curled loosely around the side of his hand. As he looked up, Lucas was staring at him, his eyes soft, expectant and a little fearful, too. He didn't want to move his hand, didn't want to let go of the warmth that was spreading through his entire body and making something jump in his stomach.

Chapter Five

THE dinner was absolutely delicious and the two women hit it off together so well, it was hardly noticeable that the men were barely speaking unless they were dragged into the conversation by Lucy or Maria.

Lucas noticed, though. He felt the tension could be cut with a knife. And he was sure Jack realized it, too, as he was steadily avoiding Lucas's gaze.

Why had he touched Jack's hand like that?

They had been in the kitchen, the atmosphere relaxed, as Jack was showing him all kinds of cooking tricks. Simple things he could probably have come up with himself, if he had ever ventured in there for more than frying an egg or putting a pizza in the oven.

Lucas had moved closer to Jack, stealing occasional touches as his elbow grazed Jack's naked arm, the silk of his shirt transferring the body heat. He had studied Jack's hands as they delicately wrapped the salmon in herbs and then in pastry, and had helped by adding his finger so Jack could tie the strings. They made a good team, Jack had said so himself.

And then all of a sudden, the small touches weren't enough anymore for Lucas. What he really wanted to do was put his arms around the man, hold him tight, kiss him, feel their bodies come together.

Instead he put his hand on Jack's. Where the older man had carelessly put his hand on the counter, Lucas covered it with his and curled his fingers around it, his heart racing a mile a minute.

He expected Jack to pull his hand away. Not that the older man had given any indication that Lucas was crowding him, even though it was a large kitchen and they had been standing close together. But this time he let his hand linger a little longer than the other times, and as he looked up, he saw Jack look at him, too. From the look in Jack's eyes, Lucas could see that he understood this was a deliberate attempt at physical contact.

And to Lucas's surprise, he didn't retract his hand. The look in his eyes was another matter, though. What was it? Surprise? Disgust? Jack's breathing had become a little faster, a little more pronounced and then Lucas saw it, the mixture of regret and something that looked suspiciously like fear. Was he afraid Maria would walk in? Was he telling him that he wanted this, too, only not now? Or was he too nice to freak out?

Lucas removed his hand and averted his eyes. At that precise moment, Maria walked into the kitchen, Lucy in tow, both of them holding roses they had cut from the garden. Lucas took a step back, creating some distance between them.

"So how's dinner coming along?" Maria asked as she filled a vase with water and started arranging the flowers.

"I love kitchens that smell of freshly made bread. Reminds me of my mother's kitchen at home," Lucy commented brightly. "Don't tell me you make your own bread as well?" she asked Maria.

"Yeah," Lucas answered, looking over at the older man, "Jack's a man of many talents."

Jack didn't answer. He simply turned to the oven and checked on the bread. Eventually he smiled faintly at Lucy. "Almost ready, won't be long now."

So here they were, the four of them sharing a comfortable, slightly chaotic dinner table, their stomachs full, wine flowing copiously, the two women chatting animatedly and the two men sitting in silence, staring at the wallpaper or Maria's beautifully arranged flowers.

Lucas wanted to break the ice, but had no idea how to do it without drawing attention to the way they were behaving towards each other and therefore having to explain what happened in the kitchen. The strange thing was, even Lucas wasn't quite sure what had happened. It would have been easier for Jack to just take his hand back and continue without letting on that anything even remotely intimate had passed between them. It was not as if he had kissed him! Still, Jack didn't seem to be able to place his feelings either, or at least it seemed he wasn't fully in control of the situation.

All Lucas knew was that he would have to make amends. After all, they would still have to work together after this, and if they couldn't talk about their differences, how would their countries work well together? He had to make the first move and show the older man he could set aside his personal feelings for the greater good. He would have to do what was expected from a diplomat.

Lucas was shaken out of his reverie when Maria got up from the table. He could hear her tell her husband, "Jack, why don't you take Lucy and Lucas into the living room, I'll clear up here."

Lucy jumped up too. "I'll help, Maria."

"Oh, no, I couldn't let you do that," Maria told her. "You're our guest. The rule when we have guests is: Jack cooks, I clear up."

Lucy helped anyway, so when Jack excused himself, Lucas was left to his own devices. He picked up some of the empty plates and brought them to the kitchen where he was met by Maria.

She was smiling warmly. "Oh, no, not both of you in this kitchen! Did Jack leave you alone?" She rolled her eyes. "Typical! Listen, Lucas, I bet he's on the porch smoking a cigarette. I'm sure he won't mind some company, if you can stand the smell of cigarettes, that is."

Lucas nodded and smiled at her.

She handed him two tulip glasses of brandy. "Why don't you take these out to him?"

"Surprising how warm it still is out here, after this cold week." Lucas started as he found his host sitting on the bench outside, leaning against the brownstone wall of the house.

Jack took a long drag of his cigarette and simply answered, "Yeah," without looking at the young man.

"I thought all Americans had given up smoking by now," Lucas tried to tease as he handed Jack one of the glasses he was holding.

Jack shrugged, his gaze still out towards the garden. "Well, I can quit anytime, just never know for how long. Maria keeps asking me to, but I guess that's not enough of an incentive."

Lucas sat down on the opposite side of the simple wooden bench, careful not to come too close to the other man. He leaned forward and rested his elbows on his knees.

"Nice garden."

"Yup, the last Ambassador had a wife with green fingers."

"Well, Maria seems to know her way around pruning shears as well."

"Yeah."

There it was again. Lucas couldn't help feeling that every time Maria's name came into the conversation, Jack went silent. Or was it just his imagination?

"I'm sorry, Jack."

"No, you're not," Jack rebutted without hesitation.

"You don't even know what I'm apologizing for." Lucas sat up straight and looked over at Jack, who was still reclining, staring out to the horizon where the sun was setting.

"You were apologizing for almost getting caught."

Lucas stared at the American for a long time, searching for confirmation, wanting to know if he understood Jack right, but his stare was not returned.

"Actually... I'm not sorry," he found himself saying, deciding to be brave for now.

"Thought not," Jack answered and a small smile spread across his lips. He took a swig from his brandy, got up from the bench, and walked around Lucas on his way back inside.

As he passed the young man, he let his index finger brush lightly against Lucas's jaw and then squeezed his shoulder, before disappearing again into the living room.

Lucas was dazed by the gesture as he let his head fall to the side, in an attempt to recapture the feeling of the older man's hand against his face.

He replayed this evening's events in his head over and over again and kept coming to the same conclusion. That was not the way a man behaved if he wasn't interested.

Jack walked inside the house again, a smile on his face as he raised his hand to his nose, catching the faint residue of Lucas's aftershave left there by the brief touch.

Despite his resolution to not get carried away, the young man had invaded his heart, and he knew it was not going to be easy to work with him from now on. Even though there was no way he could ever give in to these feelings, a part of him still enjoyed them. And why couldn't he indulge himself? Lots of men had affairs, slept around behind their wife's back.

From the dimly lit living room, he could see Maria in the kitchen with Lucy. Could he be unfaithful to his wife? Lucas clearly wanted more; Jack could practically see the lust in the young man's eyes when they were pointed at him. He knew the ball was in his court. He didn't think that Lucas would ever make a bold move towards him, because the young man knew that Jack had the power to get him fired. Goodbye dreams of diplomacy. Come to think of it, Lucas had the same power over him. If he ever let their relationship develop, they would have to be on their toes constantly, always afraid of being exposed. Having an affair behind your wife's back was almost considered natural. You apologized, kissed, made up, and promised never to do it again. But an affair with a man would cost him his commission; he knew that and had always known that. His credibility would be shot. He would come to the bargaining table with empty hands, while his adversaries would be laughing behind his back.

Jack shook his head to get the thoughts out of his mind and took one more deep breath before entering the kitchen.

"Dessert almost ready, Maire?" he asked his wife affectionately.

Maria looked up at him with loving eyes and then looked over to Lucy. "He doesn't trust me in the kitchen." She put her arm around his shoulder and pulled him close. "But we're making my specialty, aren't we?" Then back to Lucy, "Blueberry pie with ice cream."

"Sounds yummy!" Lucy exclaimed.

"Not to mention so easy to make, Lucas could probably do it," Jack told her after playfully nuzzling his wife's neck.

Jack relaxed his grip on Maria as he saw Lucas walk into the kitchen. He could tell the Brit was trying to look cheerful.

"I could make what?" the younger man asked.

Jack curled his index finger at him. "Come here."

As Lucas moved towards him, he grabbed his apron, came around Lucas's back and slipped it over his head, making bold gestures like a magician at a kid's birthday party. He could see Lucas smile, a little unsure of the situation and how to react, but the women were clearly enjoying the spectacle.

Jack flew around the kitchen grabbing an assortment of things and showing each one off to Lucas and then the girls. "We need... one egg... one small and one large bowl to separate them. Can you do that, Lucas? Separate an egg?"

Lucas took the egg and the bowls from him and gave him a doubtful smile. "Well, I can try?"

The American continued. "We also need one box of fresh blueberries, very much in season right now. The sugar. Maria, dear, would you be so kind..." He pointed at the cupboard behind his wife, at which she reached up into it and handed him what he wanted.

"Lucas, I see you've managed to split the egg. Young man, you have hidden talents!! You're going to make this pie for me, while I whip up the egg white." Jack reached into the fridge. "But first, my dear spectators, this is something I prepared earlier." He took the cling film off a carefully rolled up circle of dough already on the baking paper.

"Lucas, take the blueberries, put them in a bowl, add three tablespoons of sugar and the zest of one lemon." Maria was already getting Lucas the lemon and the zester. He raised one eyebrow as he turned to the young Brit. "Don't tell me I have to show you how to use a zester?"

Lucas gave him a desperate look. "Okay, you mix the ingredients, I'll zest the lemon. Lucy? Can you whip up the egg white, please?" With hands that were clearly more experienced than Lucas's, Jack proceeded to use the curious implement to take off tiny strips of the outer layer of the lemon peel.

Jack turned to check if the oven was hot, then clapped his hands and looked at Lucas, who was enjoying this even though he didn't look completely at ease.

"Okay, chef, let's assemble this pie. Baking tray, pie crust. Use a fork to punch little holes in the center."

Lucas followed the instructions after which Jack turned to Lucy. "Bottom is a layer of whipped up egg white. Then add the berries."

He waited until Lucas emptied his bowl. "Now comes the hard part."

He winked at Lucas, standing close to him, like they had been standing before in the kitchen, only now he put his arm around the Brit's shoulder while he pointed at the full baking tray. "We have to close the crust around the berries. Make a nice pouch." Jack looked up at the two women and their amused faces as Lucas proceeded to fold the sides of the dough over the berries, sealing them in. He felt how tense Lucas was and figuring the women's eyes were trained on what Lucas was doing, lowered his hand, gently stroking down Lucas's back. Jack could see the young man look at him hopefully and smiled. He then pointed at the pie again. "Make sure there are no holes, otherwise the juices will flow out and that would be a pity."

Lucas playfully patted the dough here and there to make sure.

"Now 'le moment supreme'. To give it a nice color we brush some of the yolk over the top and then put it in the oven. In about twenty-five minutes, we'll have the best blueberry pie Lucas has ever made."

Chapter Six

WORK was incredibly busy that week and by Friday afternoon, Jack was happy that he could finally go over his correspondence in the peace and relative quiet of his own office. In fact, it was the first time this week he was in his office long enough to actually sit behind his desk. There was an opening of an art exhibition he would have to attend tonight, but for now he was content to just sit there going through the many letters and documents that required his attention.

His secretary quietly entered his office carrying a tray of coffee and cake with a folder under her arm.

"There you go, Mr. Christensen. Nice of you to drop by the office." She smiled at him cheekily. Since she was the one keeping his appointment book, she knew exactly what he had been up to all week, and she knew he had spent most of it in the back of his chauffeur driven car being taken from one meeting to another.

She handed him the folder after she had put down his coffee tray. "This is the draft of the legislation on same sex marriages they are trying to get approved in the Chamber and Senate and an overview of debates preceding it, complete with any polls I could dig up on how the Belgians feel about it. Frankly, I don't know what all the fuss is about, but I don't suppose my opinion is important here."

Jack was amused. She was a deadly efficient secretary and sometimes he felt she could read his mind. This case was no different. He had asked his legal team to get him the draft, but it was Mrs. Claessens who had added the debates and polls, knowing he would be interested in more than just the new law. Her professional demeanor meant she could not give her opinion, but since she was Belgian and therefore a citizen of only the second country in the world to consider allowing same sex marriage to become legal, he was interested in knowing what she thought about a subject he knew was a very sensitive issue in his own country.

"Come on, Mrs. Claessens, I'm sure in the confines of this office you can tell me what you think? I promise I won't hold it against you." He smiled at her and took a sip from his coffee.

She stared at him suspiciously. "You may not agree with me, but I think this is a very sensible law. I don't know what took them so long."

Jack dropped the papers down on his desk and took another sip, still looking quite amused, so she continued. "I'm sure you as an American don't see it that way, but I mean... these people live together, share everything, house, kids, car, you name it. But if the wrong one dies, the one left behind may end up on the street or see his child taken away simply because his bond with his partner isn't recognized by law. It's barbaric. And you can tell that to your President."

Jack laughed as he saw her tug at the front of her jacket to stress her point.

"I totally agree with you," he answered.

"You do?" She seemed to blossom all of a sudden.

"Yes, I do. Don't tell my president that, because of course it's not U.S. policy, but here in the confines of my office I can tell you that I agree. It would just take a little explaining to our own citizens living here that if they are of the same sex and want to get married, their marriage would not be valid in the States."

Mrs. Claessens sighed. "And I suppose that won't change anytime soon?"

Jack gave her a pained smile.

"Mmmh, I didn't think so. Can I take these papers back now?" She was indicating the stack he had already sifted through.

"Sure, thanks," Jack answered as she walked over to the door.

Just at the last moment, she turned around. "Mr. Christensen, I almost forgot. Mr. Carlton has been trying to get in touch with you. I've had about three phone calls, but he would never leave a message and he didn't want me to patch him through to your cell phone. Of course I wouldn't give him your number... and he's been to the office twice. I have his cell phone number, shall I call him for you and patch him through?"

Jack's heart leapt as he heard Lucas's name. They had not talked yet about what happened between them on Saturday. In fact they hadn't seen each other for almost a week now.

He probably thinks I'm trying to avoid him.

"Mr. Christensen? It may be important. He didn't say it was urgent, but, I mean, five times...?"

This woke Jack from his thoughts. He looked up at her as she was standing at the door with a compassionate look on her face. It seemed the young Brit had gotten to her as well.

"Why don't you just give me his cell phone number and I'll call him myself."

Just moments later she returned with a small Post-it note containing Lucas's number.

Once he was alone in his office again, he held the note and looked at the number. Should he call? If Lucas had tried to reach him on official business, he would have left a message. So this was personal.

It was not like he hadn't thought about Lucas this past week; he had just been too busy during the day. Nights were another matter, though. He had woken up more than once in the middle of the night realizing he had dreamt about running his hands down the gorgeous Brit's back again, but the dreams didn't end there. He woke up with a persistent hard-on, demanding some form of release. The third time it had happened, he had gotten up and walked downstairs, not wanting to wake up Maria . In front of the TV, watching the twentieth rerun of some eighties TV series, he had settled himself on the couch and closed his eyes. The images of Lucas were easy to conjure up as he let his hand slip into his baggy pajama bottoms. He just had to think of the young man's radiant smile, of the tight black shirt he always wore, outlining his nicely shaped form, of the feeling of Lucas's hand on his....

It was easy to imagine kissing Lucas's shapely lips and pressing their bodies together. Jack stroked his rock hard cock and could almost feel Lucas's hands all over his body, stroking his belly, his mouth on his hips, thighs, licking his nipples. He could almost see Lucas's mouth take in his straining member until, until...

Jack fisted himself hard and came with Lucas's name on his lips. In the aftermath, shivers still rippling through his body, he went limp on the couch. He realized he had said the young man's name aloud in the otherwise silent house and strained to hear if he had maybe awakened Maria, but everything remained quiet.

Behind his desk at the office, Jack knew there was no denying his feelings for the young man. He would have to talk to Lucas. All he could hope for was that he had misread the signs and that Lucas simply looked up to him. Maybe that was it, maybe Lucas just saw Jack as an example, something to aspire to. Only time would tell.

BEHIND her desk outside the Ambassador's office, Gertje Claessens sorted through the stack of papers she had brought in from her boss's office and wondered about the conversation she had just had with him. Had she done the right thing giving him Lucas's phone number? Of course, it was none of her business why Lucas seemed so desperate to contact Mr. Christensen. She liked the young Brit. He was a charming young man, very polite too, without being too shy, and she could see a warm glow appear in his eyes whenever she took him into her boss's office.

She liked her boss, too. He was warm and generous with her, never ordering her around. In the few months since he had taken up his post, he had always treated her with respect and had more than once not only asked for her opinion, but had also taken it into account. It was something she was still getting used to.

How he could end up with Mrs. Perfect Ambassador's Wife, she would never understand. The woman might be nice to have on his arm, but having overheard Maria tell her husband that she couldn't understand why he had been given 'one of those motherly types' as a personal assistant, Gertje had classified her immediately. Of course she would always be polite to Maria, but no more than was strictly necessary.

Giving Jack Lucas's phone number was right, she concluded, no matter what Lucas's intentions were. Besides, Jack Christensen was a grown man. He hadn't made it this far in his career at such a young age by making the wrong decisions. She closed the filing cabinet in a determined fashion, just as Jack walked out of his office and handed her another stack of papers on his way out.

"I think this is the last of them. I'm off to celebrate the 20th anniversary of the day I met my wife, so you know how to reach me, but only if you have to." He rounded the corner and then turned back. "Once I'm at the art exhibition, feel free to call a national emergency."

They both laughed.

"Come on, Your Excellency, it's art," Gertje mocked.

"It's not the art that's boring; it's the politicians who feel they have an opinion on the art who drive me up the wall!" Jack rolled his eyes, before he waved at her and walked away again.

LUCAS sat in his broom closet of an office in the U.K. Embassy with his cell phone in his hand. He wanted to call Jack, listen to the man's soothing voice and arrange to meet him somewhere to talk, continue where they left off that night of the dinner at his house. Only it was abundantly clear that Jack was doing his best to avoid him. His secretary had given him a lame excuse every time he had called, and the times when he had walked over there on his lunch break, he hadn't been able to get past her, either. No doubt she had been given instructions not to let him in. Since he didn't have Jack's direct number, he would have to go through the guard dog again.

He knew he had taken it too far, but he was so sure that the older man had not only acknowledged his feelings, but had also given some indication that they were mutual. Only now, reality had kicked in, and since they were not together, it was probably easy for Jack to deny the feelings were there and choose his easy, comfortable life with Maria.

But Lucas couldn't forget the way Jack had slowly run his hand down his back, deliberately taking his time to feel every bone, every muscle. Slowly torturing Lucas, who couldn't even acknowledge how good it felt to feel Jack's warm hand caressing him, because the eyes of both their women were on them.

Lucas had jacked off every single morning in the shower, thinking about what it would feel like to really touch Jack, to kiss him, and to make love to him. This morning he had almost gotten caught when he had failed to hear Lucy enter their tiny bathroom. He had obviously not been silent during his release since she asked him if he was okay. He had mumbled something to her, afraid if he stuck his head outside the shower curtain, she would see his flushed complexion.

"Damn!"

Lucas got up swiftly and grabbed his jacket from the peg on the door. One more time. One more time he would go to Jack's office and demand to be let in.

"HE'S not here, Lucas, I'm sorry." Gertje Claessens was compassionate, watching how disappointment took hold of Lucas's face. "Listen, sit down for a moment and let me get you a cup of coffee. Or tea, you drink tea, right?"

Lucas shook his head. "Did you give him my phone number?"

"Yes, dear, I did."

He tried to smile. "Thank you, Gertje," then turned around to leave.

"Lucas..." As he turned back he could see she was clearly hesitating. "Go to the Palais des Beaux Arts tonight. It's the gala opening of the American Indian Art Exhibition. Here..." she dug into her drawer, "...is Jack's spare invitation. I always ask for one, in case he and Mrs. Christensen can't arrive there together."

With a big smile on his face he took two steps forward, grabbed her head in his hands and gave her a smacker on the lips.

"Don't do anything I wouldn't do," he heard her call after him, when he ran out of the office.

MARIA had spent her day at a spa in Grimbergen. It had been her welcome to the American Women's Club of Belgium, and even though it was not exactly her goal in life to spend her time there the way most expatriate women did, she enjoyed the pampering just as much as the next person.

She wore a cream-colored cotton undershirt, skimpy panties and no bra, and admired herself in the gigantic bathroom mirror that lined most of the wall. She didn't look any different from this morning. Still fairly bony, missing the curves of a true woman, she feared, and not enough bosom to properly fill a bra. Thank God for Wonderbras. She had some muscles though, in all the right places too, she thought, because this is how Jack liked her. Her skin did feel nice and soft after all that peeling and mud packing they had done to her in the course of the day.

As she was lightly stroking her flat belly, she noticed Jack standing in his usual place, by the doorpost.

"So stranger…you like what you see?" she asked him seductively.

Maria could see Jack slowly take his shirt off and move behind her. As he wrapped his arms around her, he moaned appreciatively. "Hey Maire, you smell like roses and your skin feels like silk."

His touch was light and soon made her skin tingle as she leaned back to feel him closer to her. He was kissing her neck and slowly grinding his growing erection against her ass as he slipped his hand down her belly and into her panties. Maria enjoyed this new side of Jack she was seeing. He had never been the most adventurous bed partner, but there was something to be said for a dependable husband. Only now she stared at herself in the mirror while he kissed her shoulder and used his finger to slowly stroke circles around her clit, making her wet.

She reached behind her back to unbutton his pants. To feel his fingers on her was amazing, but to actually see him do it as well made her heart race. She wanted to feel him inside her, wanted to bend over the sink and let him pound into her, all the while watching him do it to her.

"Come on Jack, show me what you got."

This made him look up at the sight in the mirror, his cerulean blue eyes a little glazy, his lips red and moist from kissing her neck. Her hair was coming undone, and he smiled as she pinned it up again so it stayed out of her face. He let his pants and boxers fall to the floor and stepped out of them and then crouched to slip her panties down.

"I want to see you fuck me, Jack, here in front of the mirror. Would you like that?" She inhaled sharply as he pushed her down over the sink and roughly inserted two fingers.

As she looked up, he was smiling widely. "You're absolutely soaking wet, Maire."

"Well, what did you expect?"

She moaned as she felt him entering her right after pulling his fingers out. He felt good inside her, and she knew all too well he was the most unselfish lover she had ever had. She only hoped that the intoxicating sight of the two of them joined in front of the mirror wouldn't make him come too quickly; she wanted this to last. But then again, he wasn't really looking. She could feel his hands on her hips and his heavy breathing on her neck.

As he slowly started to move, she realized she wanted more, she wanted to be in control, which was a lot less unusual than the fact they were being adventurous enough to fuck in front of the bathroom mirror they had both hated from the moment they entered the house. All of a sudden it became an asset.

Maria pushed herself and Jack with her away from the sink and down onto the closed toilet seat. He clung to her and gasped as they came down on the hard surface. She realized that from where they were sitting, she had a full-length view of the two of them, between the two sinks. As she slowly spread her legs and leaned back she could see him buried deep inside of her, his cock shiny and wet with her juices. With his arms wrapped around her waist, she bent forward again so she could put her hands on his knees and use them as support as she started to ride him. Slowly at first, she found it easy to vary the angle a bit until he was hitting just the right spot, just the right amount of friction to make her pant and moan. "Oh, Jack, so good, Jack."

He moved his hands to her ribs to support her movements as she increased the speed and he started thrusting upwards. The sight in the mirror was exhilarating as she could see herself riding his beautiful, rock hard cock. She knew she was going to come like she hadn't come in a long time as she felt the tension build in her belly. Jack spread his legs too, pushing hers even wider apart. It made her lose her leverage, but as she looked up, she saw his eyes, dark with passion looking at the two of them in the shiny surface of the mirror, and this sight pushed her over the edge, convulsing around his hard cock. She could feel him burying his head in her neck, murmuring something that sounded like 'yes, yes, you can now' as his movements too became erratic and convulsive.

She slumped down onto Jack's now limp body and realized through her haze that they hadn't even kissed. His body was hot and sweaty beneath her.

"Are you okay?" she whispered.

"Yeah," he croaked. "Just give me a minute."

As she got up from their uncomfortable position and felt him slip out of her, she decided they would both need a shower before they could go anywhere.

And they had an art exhibition opening to attend.

Chapter Seven

JACK and Maria arrived late at the Argentinean restaurant where they had booked a table for dinner, and thanks to the Friday night traffic, they would undoubtedly arrive even later at the exhibition opening.

Jack was clearly in a wonderful mood, and over dinner they reminisced about how they had met at an Embassy party in Argentina, where Maria's father was the Information Officer and Jack had been sent on his first overseas posting. That was twenty years ago and Maria was glad she could still look at her husband and say that marrying him was the best decision she had made in her life.

"So tell me again why it took you almost a year and a half to sleep with me?" she teased him.

Jack wiped the corners of his mouth with his napkin and ticked off the reasons she'd accept. "I was a gentleman, what can I say? Besides, I didn't know where my life was going. You knew I could be posted anywhere with almost no notice, so I guess I wanted to be sure you were right for me. And I wanted to get my master's degree first, so if I took you abroad with me, we would at least be able to live off one salary."

"Well, it was nice of you to leave such a good impression with my parents. I think that was the only argument I gave them that stood any ground when I told them I wanted to move to Denmark with you before we were married." She put her hand on his and played with his wedding ring. "I have to say this afternoon made up for the eighteen months of waiting for you."

"I thought I made up for that a long time ago, Maire," Jack answered a little shyly.

"Well, I don't know *what* you were making up for earlier, but by all means do it again!" She rolled her eyes as she took another sip of her wine.

Jack grew silent until he realized this was probably making him look guilty. "So do you want dessert?" he asked lamely.

LUCAS walked into the Palais des Beaux Arts with Lucy on his arm. He had tried to go without her, but after seeing her eyes light up when he told her where he was spending his evening, he didn't have the heart to tell her she couldn't go.

Even though it was a large museum, the reception was in one of the smaller halls and consequently, it was fairly packed. Most of the guests were older, stuffy men with bored looking women by their sides, and very few people were actually looking at the objects on display.

Lucas scanned the room for Jack, but couldn't find him, so he guided Lucy towards a large tapestry covering most of the wall nearest to them. He didn't want to venture too deep into the crowd in case he would miss Jack walking in.

Tall, elegant, but stern looking young men in tails walked around the room carrying trays with drinks and Lucas was quick to scoop up two glasses of champagne, handing one to Lucy.

"We should mingle with the crowd, Lucy, there are a lot of important people in this room," Lucas suggested, but he saw panic overtake his girlfriend's face. "Don't worry, I'll be here," he offered with a smile, though it meant that it would be virtually impossible to talk to Jack alone tonight.

Just at that moment flashbulbs went off at the front entrance and all eyes turned to the couple that walked in.

Jack wore an elegant dark suit and tie, and Maria looked absolutely radiant in a powder blue two piece. They were greeted by the curator of the museum and quite a few of the other guests flocked towards the entrance to shake their hands.

Lucas knew he and Lucy would have to bide their time before going over to them. This function required far more protocol and their status of personal friends would not carry far here. Jack would probably open the exhibit or at least observe that opening, and many more 'higher ranking officials' would want to talk to him before Lucas and Lucy could greet him.

Although Lucas knew this, he still wanted the American to be aware of his presence, so he casually led Lucy into Jack's range of view. He still had the feeling Jack had been ignoring him all this week and he wanted it resolved tonight, one way or the other.

"Why can't we just get in line with everyone and go say hi?" Lucy asked.

"Because there are other people he needs to meet first, Lucy," he shot at her, then sighed, "I'm sorry, but we can't just…" Lucas didn't finish his sentence, because Jack was staring him straight in the eye, his expression blank. After an almost imperceptible nod, Jack's eyes turned to an older lady in traditional Indian costume, who was clearly introducing herself. The surrealism of the situation made Lucas wonder if the nod of recognition had really been there, or if he had just wished it.

As one of the waiters passed with another tray of drinks, Lucas replaced his empty champagne flute with a full one. Jack was ushered towards the passage to the exhibition where he would have to cut a ribbon to open it officially, so with Lucy still on his arm, Lucas followed the stream of guests into the hallway. He made his way to the front of the crowd that formed a large semicircle to listen to the short speeches and official words of welcome.

Lucas couldn't help but admire the natural ease with which Jack acquitted himself of his task and the grace with which he turned the focus away from himself and his presence here to place it on the plight of ancient culture in today's global society and the importance of the preservation of indigenous culture and art. His short and concise speech even contained humor as he added that Belgians were particularly adept at understanding this, since they had been conquered by so many nations in their past before becoming a country in their own right.

Lucas was wondering if Jack wrote his own speeches when their eyes met again. Once more Jack's expression was unreadable and he turned away almost immediately, leaving Lucas with a hollow feeling in the pit of in his stomach. He couldn't just stand here; this was driving him crazy. If Jack didn't want to have anything to do with him ever again, he wanted to hear the man say it himself.

After the ribbon was cut, the crowd was allowed to enter the exhibit and it dispersed quickly. Lucas and Lucy were finally able to make it over to where Jack and Maria were still being greeted by all sorts of people.

"Lucy, Lucas!" Maria greeted the young couple warmly with a kiss on the cheek. "What a surprise to see you here! Lucas, I didn't know your liaison duties extended to art exhibit openings?"

"They don't," Lucas answered trying to come up with an excuse, but drawing a blank. "I was just… interested." *But not in the art.*

"Lucas, would you mind very much if I stole that lovely fiancée of yours away for a moment? There are some people here I'm sure she will want to meet, and I have to turn her into the perfect diplomat's wife for you, right?"

That was obviously a rhetorical question, because as Lucas was trying to form a witty answer, Maria carted Lucy off to a group of middle aged women standing together at the other end of the room, so he was left to his own devices, only a few steps away from Jack.

Lucas hadn't even been able to say hello yet, as Jack was still busy with a number of Americans and Belgians. Lucas could hear him speaking English and French, occasionally even Spanish, seemingly effortlessly switching between the languages. Lucas knew he should be building his network, talking to people and introducing himself, but what he really needed to do was talk to Jack. Unfortunately, the American might as well have been on the other side of the world.

Eventually Lucas took a walk around the hall, admiring the very diverse artwork, hoping that Jack would take his continuing presence at this function as the sign it was meant to be: a cry for contact.

People started to leave as the waiters stopped coming around with their drinks trays, and Lucas found himself almost alone in a corner of the hall. He had seen Maria and Lucy talk to numerous people, and they were now sitting together in the foyer talking girl talk, judging from the excited expressions on their faces.

"It always strikes me how effortless art is with indigenous people," Lucas heard a familiar voice with an American accent say. "They use it in everyday objects, like this rug for instance, and they depict ordinary daily occurrences." Lucas closed his eyes and a smile broke on his lips. He was afraid to look to the side, afraid that he would break the spell if he looked, and the voice continued. "Art is also a collective thing. The ego of the artist is not important, in fact, you may have noticed that on a lot of these works, there is no artist mentioned, because the name or names are not known." Lucas could listen to this voice for hours and searched for the right question to keep him talking.

Eventually he dared to look sideways, only to find there was no one there. He could see Jack walking out towards the hallway. *Oh no, he wasn't leaving!*

Lucas looked around to see if it would be deemed suspicious if he followed suit. Realizing the hall was almost deserted, he practically ran in the direction where he had seen Jack disappear. Once inside the hallway he only just saw Jack slip into the men's room. There were more people standing around here, and he noticed some of them looking in his direction. He tried to look inconspicuous and took a deep breath to calm himself while he walked over to the side where the toilets were.

As he stepped inside, Jack was washing his hands.

"Now can you tell me why you're avoiding me?"

Jack looked up, giving the young man a stern look. He took a paper towel, dried his hands and then proceeded to open all the stall doors to check if anyone was inside. Luckily they were all empty. Lucas understood he had been careless, and his shoulders slumped.

"I'm sorry…"

"No, you're not," Jack answered, with clear amusement in his voice.

When Lucas looked at the older man he saw Jack was smiling. "Why do I feel like we've had this conversation before?"

"Well, if you stop apologizing for things you're clearly not sorry for, then we can stop having this conversation."

Lucas took a step closer to the American. *Come on, you're both adults, can't you have an adult conversation about this?* "I tried to contact you, talk about…" Lucas's voice was unsteady all of a sudden, "…things."

"I've had a very busy week, Lucas. First time I was at the office for longer than it took me to change my jacket was this afternoon. I…"

"You had my cell phone number. Gertje did give it to you?"

Jack nodded, but since Lucas was still looking at the wall over his shoulder rather than at him, he added, "Yes, but not until a few hours ago. I was going to…"

"You were going to call me on Monday, right?" Lucas sighed and then looked defiantly straight into Jack's eyes. "You probably figured this was business?"

Jack shook his head, taken aback a bit by Lucas's aggressive tone.

"Fine, let's treat this as a negotiation. Negotiations always work best when both parties are open and honest towards each other. So why don't we call a spade a spade, then. Why don't you explain to me what happened in your kitchen?"

Jack shushed him "Keep your voice down, we are in a public place."

"Is this what you and Maria get off on?" Lucas answered now in a much lower tone. "You seduce young men in front of her and then she needs to win you back?"

"I wasn't seducing you!" Jack rebutted, also trying not to talk too loud. He pointed at Lucas, "*You* put your hand on my hand. *You* made the first move." The American stepped back and leaned against the partition between two stalls.

Lucas, having regained a bit of his composure, was a lot calmer now. "I couldn't help myself. I wanted to show you that you mean a lot to me." He averted his eyes and slightly shook his head. "I wanted to tell you that I couldn't stop thinking about you. I didn't have any hope that you would return the feelings. I mean you being married and all… But then you didn't take your hand away and you looked at me with those eyes of yours and…"

Lucas looked up at Jack, who was now looking at him, his face soft and his eyes wide, his hand reaching out. He took a tentative step forward and then slowly lifted his hand to touch Jack's.

Jack cleared his throat. "When you were finishing the dessert, I couldn't help but touch you. You were so close to me, smelling of peppermint and wine and… I was glad there was a counter in front of us, because I would have given away some things our women wouldn't have understood. It wasn't until later that I realized that if you had reacted to my touch, we would both have been in a lot of trouble."

Lucas could feel Jack's hand pulling him closer. Instead he turned into the cubicle and pulled Jack along with him, pushing the older man with his back against the partition. With his free hand, he snapped the latch on the door, giving them a semblance of privacy. He then leaned forward to whisper, "I was glad for the counter too, because what you were doing to my back with that hand of yours..." He lightly kissed Jack's temple then leaned his head against the older man, pressing his body against him as well. He could feel Jack's free hand tentatively moving across his back, just like that first time in the kitchen, and Lucas almost moaned when that hand retraced their first real touch.

Lucas's right hand and Jack's left hadn't parted since their first contact here in the men's room, but now Lucas could feel Jack moving his hand to gently cradle his head. Their lips were almost touching. He could feel Jack's heat radiating off him and his breath ghosting across his face. There was a moment's hesitance when they looked into each other's eyes, and then Lucas felt himself being pulled into a kiss. Chaste at first, just their lips touching, he could feel Jack open up to him slowly but surely. He could feel the hunger rising in the older man and responded by eagerly sucking on the American's lower lip.

At that moment, Jack pulled away as much as he could, pinned between Lucas and the partition, panting.

Lucas, feeling confused, somewhere between rejection and awkwardness, tried to give him a bit more space, but Jack wrapped his arms around his lean frame and pulled him close to his chest. "Oh God, Lucas, I didn't mean to push you away, I'm just... please tell I'm not making a huge mistake here, that what I feel is real and not some delusion."

The Brit ground his body against Jack's. "Does this feel real enough to you?" He felt some of the tension flood away under Jack's tight grip so he pulled his head back and smiled. "Ever since that night at the embassy... I just never figured you..."

Jack pulled him into a desperate kiss again, this time hungry and unbridled. Lucas could feel the American's tongue in his mouth and gave into him completely, pulling away after what seemed like forever, partly to catch his breath but also because he felt his body reacting to the other man's growing arousal. "If we don't stop now, I don't think I could stop before..."

Jack let go of the Brit, chuckling. "Yeah, I know…"

They were standing, leaning against opposite walls of the cubicle, still holding hands, almost afraid to let go, but eventually they ended up moving away from the wall together to step outside.

"I'll go first," Lucas offered, "See if the coast is clear."

"Yeah…" Jack said softly, close to him. "I hope no one walked in here, because I don't know how quiet we were."

First Lucas and then Jack stepped out of the cramped stall and checked their appearance in the mirrors on the opposite side of the men's room.

Lucas looked over at Jack. "Hang on…" He moved behind the American and pulled at the bottom of his jacket, then wiped his hands across Jack's shoulders.

"Thanks, Maria…" Jack's quip startled Lucas. "She always does that too, I'm sorry…"

"No, you're not," Lucas answered, now smiling lopsidedly as he straightened his tie and tucked down his own jacket.

Both men smiled as they walked out into the outside world again.

"**OH**, and I thought it was just us ladies who couldn't go to the little girl's room alone."

The two men turned upon hearing Maria's mocking tone and saw the women standing against the outside wall of the men's room.

"Lucy saw you two disappear in there and so we decided to wait here to tell you the news."

"Yeah, and you two took forever," Lucy added, rolling her eyes.

"So what's the news?" Jack asked.

"Lucy and I are going to spend next weekend in Amsterdam. It's about time she saw a bit of Europe. She's been here almost a year, and I can't believe, Lucas, that you haven't taken her anywhere."

Lucas felt his heart leap out of his chest. A weekend alone with Jack. He looked over at Jack who was staring back at him, giving him one of his poker faces.

Maria slid her arms underneath her husband's. "Don't look so worried, dear, I won't max out my credit card." She stretched her arm out to Lucy who came closer as well, in turn taking Lucas's hand. "And I promise I'll keep Lucy away from temptation as well. Besides I'm sure you two have some guy things to do which, now, what was it you said the other night? 'Which us girls would find boring'." She was feigning innocence but Jack knew the comment was anything but that.

Lucas saw a smile break on Jack's face. "Yeah, I'm sure we can keep each other occupied."

Chapter Eight

WITH the President declaring they were no longer at war, the work for the Embassy in Belgium was really only just starting. The Belgian government had always been rather vocal in their opposition to the war, and now that a peace-keeping mission was being assembled to help rebuild the ravaged country, this stance was by no means toned down. Together with France and Germany, they blatantly refused to add troops to the International Armed Forces, and Jack almost felt like he was constantly meeting with the Prime Minister and the Defense Minister on this matter. The whole situation didn't look good, since NATO headquarters were situated in this country, and Jack had been given precise orders: make them take America's side in this conflict.

The fact that Jack didn't agree with his government's point of view didn't help. It wasn't the first time this had happened, and he knew very well that his own feelings on the matter were completely unimportant.

There was one upside to this, though. The British Prime Minister had stuck his nose in and had promised British help. Normally this would fall on the shoulders of the British Ambassador, but since he had been given an extended vacation, his Deputy Head of Mission was in charge. As taking on both jobs was a little much even for a competent man like Sean Gallagher, Jack hoped he could ask for Lucas's help on this.

In the car on his way from SHAPE, the Supreme Headquarters Allied Powers Europe, going back to the Embassy, Jack couldn't keep his mind on the papers he wanted to review. The crisis at the European Union over the war had kept him busy all weekend, but now for some reason, his mind kept wandering to what had happened at the exhibition opening on Friday. Kissing and touching Lucas had felt good, for sure. But was it the right thing to do? The young Brit clearly had less apprehension about the encounter then he did. Lucas was probably more experienced or felt less guilty about being unfaithful to his girl.

Jack kicked himself for thinking too much, but was it right for him to lust after a man? He had denied these feelings in himself for most of his adult life, so why was it so hard now?

Maria loved him, in her own no-nonsense, no-frills way. He didn't doubt that for even a moment. She was a wonderful wife, the kind of strong woman that he needed, someone who took care of all the decisions in the relationship when Jack was tired from all the choices he had to make every minute of his working life. It was nice to come home to a warm house, to a partner who had her own life, who never nagged him for working late or forgetting to make time for her, but who was somehow always there for him.

The only thing missing was passion. She never made his blood run faster, never made his heart skip a beat. In fact, he could probably do without sleeping with her, and if it wasn't for her seducing him from time to time, they would probably have a nonexistent sex life.

Then Lucas walked into his life and he was smitten. From the first moment he laid eyes on the beautiful young Brit, something had happened inside him that he couldn't explain. He clearly remembered Lucas's firm handshake, the bright look in his eyes, and the overt confidence that could so easily be mistaken for arrogance if it wasn't for the disarming smile and boyish nonchalance.

Somehow he couldn't keep his hands off the man, and even though they had only kissed (*And what a kiss!*) he truly lusted after Lucas. Even before that exciting first contact, Jack had imagined what it would feel like to have him in his arms, to feel their naked skin touch, to make love to him…

Jack asked his driver to close the partition between them. He wanted to call Lucas on his cell phone and that clearly required a little privacy.

It took a few rings for the call to be picked up.

"Hey there. Can you talk?" Jack asked in a subdued voice.

Lucas's voice sounded bright, but a little strange. "Mr. Ambassador, how nice of you to call!"

"Lucas?" Jack asked a little taken aback. "Listen, I'll call back if…"

"Oh, no sir, we were just talking about how close our embassies would have to work together on the European situation and…"

Jack smiled, there was clearly someone in the room with Lucas who had to be made aware of what a good job he was doing liaising with the Americans. In all likelihood, it would be Gallagher. This made him smile wider, since he knew the British second-in-command quite well from a rather traumatic year when they'd both worked for their respective Embassies in Beirut. Now Jack wanted to know how well Lucas could think on his feet.

"Well, I was thinking about our plans for the weekend…" Jack tried, his voice soft.

"Yes, of course sir, I was thinking about the very same thing." He could almost see Lucas nod at his boss and fidget in his chair.

"Were you thinking about what you were going to do to me on the two nights our women will be gone?"

Silence. *Talk to me Lucas, I want to hear your voice.* Jack's voice was soft and seductive. "Come on, Luke, show me what you're made of. Can't tell me what you want to say, eh?"

"I would if I could… sir," Lucas answered in a strong voice, "but it's not British policy."

"Not British policy to talk about sex or not British policy to tell your boss, who's obviously in the room with you, that you've gone a bit overboard liaising with the Americans?"

Again a short silence, before, "I'm afraid, sir, I will have to discuss this with my superior before I can give you a conclusive answer on that."

Jack could almost hear Lucas smile and was glad he hadn't taken his last comment too seriously.

"I didn't think we went too far on Friday, Lucas, I hope…"

"No, sir, I agree we didn't overdo it. I think the other party showed the appropriate response to my overture."

"So how do you want to play this weekend?" Jack asked, amused at how professional Lucas sounded.

"I think we should up the stakes, sir. Test the waters a bit first, of course, see how the opposing faction reacts. Small steps at first, until they bite, and then I'll reel them in. How does that sound... sir?"

Oh dear, Lucas was truly good at this. Jack never realized he could get turned on by a young man calling him sir and by talk of negotiations, even though he knew that wasn't really what the Brit was saying.

"Why don't you drop by the office this afternoon? With a little luck I'll be there for the rest of the day," Jack asked hesitantly.

"Yes sir, I agree we should talk strategy as soon as possible. I will join you this afternoon."

LUCAS closed his cell phone and looked at the stern fair-haired man at the opposite side of the desk.

"Christensen?" Gallagher asked, looking at Lucas over the top of his rimless glasses.

"Yes, sir," Lucas answered, hopeless at hiding his smile.

"Competent chap," the consul-general admitted, "but remember your place, Carlton. We Brits are there to lend support, if necessary guide the Americans, but not dominate them. You are by all means his subordinate and you should act accordingly. He is a much more experienced player in this game and there's a lot you could learn from him."

I'm sure the feeling is mutual, Lucas thought.

A smile appeared on the more seasoned diplomat's face. "We go way back, Christensen and I. Got bombed out of the hotel we were running negotiations from in Beirut. Was a close call, that." Sean Gallagher was obviously remembering those times with some fondness. "Now, back to business. Carlton, even if these negotiations with the Belgians about the war fail, don't forget that although it may be a small country, we have important trade relations with them and we can't afford to lose those, so make sure you leave the table as friends, okay?"

Lucas nodded, his thoughts about a ten minute walk away.

ABOUT an hour later Lucas walked past the American security guard and up to the Ambassador's office.

"He's been expecting you," Gertje told him with a wink as she walked around her desk to open the door for him. "Tell him I'll hold his calls."

Lucas kissed her hand, which made her blush terribly, and entered the office.

Jack sat behind his desk, papers literally everywhere. There were deep lines on his forehead and he was frowning incessantly. "This is an asinine country. They're one of the world's biggest small arms dealers, but they're against going to war."

Lucas moved a stack of papers and leaned against Jack's desk. "Yes, makes it interesting, doesn't it?"

Jack couldn't help but smile. It never ceased to amaze him how calm and collected the young man could be, unless of course, Lucas felt he was being watched. Then he could turn into this fidgety, stammering teenager who didn't know where to put his hands. Not now though. While they were alone, in the privacy of the office, Lucas was effortlessly calm and this rubbed off on Jack. He gently placed his hand on the young man's thigh.

"I missed you this weekend. I'm glad you could come by."

Lucas smiled as he looked out of the window behind Jack. "Well, I had the perfect excuse. Sean thinks we should plan strategy, and who am I to argue with my boss?"

Jack loved how the summer light played with his lover's olive skin and chestnut curls. Was this real? Was this young man becoming his lover? Or was the kiss just a tease, a trial thing that wasn't to be repeated? He hoped not, so he got up from his comfortable chair and moved in between Lucas and the light. "I'm still glad you could come by, excuse or not. I played our kiss back over and over again in my mind."

Lucas simply smiled, uncrossed his ankles and spread his knees, inviting Jack to move closer to him. Just as Lucas moved his arm around Jack and touched his lower back to pull him closer, a short double knock on the door made Jack step back and away from Lucas.

Gertje walked in, her eyes on the contents of a folder she was carrying. "I found another bit of information from your predecessor, Mr. Christensen. Memos and minutes from meetings he had with the French

Ambassador and with our Ambassador to France about arms dealing to the Middle East."

Jack walked over to her and accepted the folder, nodding to her, "Thank you, Mrs. Claessens," and then, hoping she would take the hint, "You are holding my calls, yes?"

"Of course, sir," she answered, smiling enigmatically as she exited his office.

Jack walked back over to where Lucas was still sitting patiently on the edge of the desk. "Now, where were we?"

Lucas grabbed him again and pulled him closer, this time a little more forcefully. There was nothing hesitant about how their lips locked now. Jack could feel his heartbeat speed up as he was turned on by the determination of the man he was kissing. Lucas's hands pulled their bodies close together, and he could feel the other man's arousal grind against his own growing bulge. He knew they would have to stop; that they couldn't do this in the office where it would be just a matter of time before they got caught, but it felt so good he didn't want to let go. It was finally Lucas who pulled away. His eyes were dark and his hair was tousled to Jack's surprise, as this could only have been his doing. He pulled his fingers away from the soft curls that twined so eagerly around them and took a deep breath, still looking into Lucas's dark brown eyes as he rested his forehead against the younger man's. They both chuckled softly.

Just at that moment, there was another knock on the door. Jack turned a little and dropped into his chair, then quickly turned and tucked his legs under his desk as Gertje walked in with a tray. Lucas tried to look careless as he picked up a piece of paper next to him.

"I figured since you two men don't know how to take care of yourselves, I would have to do it for you, so I brought coffee, tea and cake. Makes working all the more pleasant, don't you think?"

"Thank you," both men answered simultaneously. They had the hardest time not breaking out in laughter until she placed the tray on the small side table and left. As soon as she was gone they let it out.

"We are playing with fire, man," Lucas started, his hand in front of his mouth. "You're all flushed and your lips…" He bent down and loosely placed a kiss on Jack's lips, "…look recently kissed too."

"Well, it's not like you could stand up and turn around without looking…" Jack gazed at Lucas's crotch area, "…like you were standing at attention."

Lucas's face turned a little more serious as he placed his hand on Jack's. "So why don't I get us a hotel room on Friday? You think you can get away from the Secret Service?"

Jack stopped laughing too. "Yeah, I'm sure I can. It's not like I'm the President. I can go to the bathroom without them checking the men's room first."

"Four more days," Lucas sighed.

"Yeah, ehm, Lucas…" How was he going to tell the young man?

"What? You want to back out of this?" Lucas asked a little apprehensively.

"No!" Jack was quick to answer. "No, it's not that, I… never mind. It'll all work itself out in the end."

Lucas got up and bent down to kiss Jack again. "Yeah, lover. I'm sure it will."

Jack was reluctant to let go of the beautiful Brit. "You have to go, right?"

"Yeah," Lucas answered, "since it's clear we're not going to get any work done here."

Jack watched him walk toward the small table, pick up the two cups, and walk back to bring Jack his coffee. He then drank the now lukewarm tea in one swig, put the cup down and winked as he turned around to grab the door handle. He playfully threw Jack a kiss before he walked out.

Four more days.

Chapter Nine

"**So** are you all packed to go?" Jack inquired over morning coffee in his kitchen.

Maria was reading the New York Times. "Mmh, most of it."

"When's the train leave?" Jack tried to ask casually, sipping from his mug of coffee, hoping he didn't sound too eager.

"Around eleven thirty. Driver's picking me up after he drops you off and picks up Lucy," Maria answered while flicking the pages.

"When will you be back then? Sunday, right?" Jack again tried to sound casual, more like he was going to miss her than like he wanted to be home… alone… and showered… when she came in.

"Sometime in the afternoon. I think the train arrives at the Midi around three-thirty. Driver will pick me up again."

Jack made a mental note of the arrival time and tried to look at her over the rim of his mug in such a way she wouldn't notice. Tonight he was meeting Lucas in some hotel room in Antwerp, and he felt a pang of guilt. What was he doing? Maria was the best wife a diplomat could have. Undemanding but independent, smart, beautiful, loyal. Loyal… not like him. He couldn't even contemplate what would happen if she found out. If she found out he was not working with Lucas this weekend, but screwing Lucas. How could he ever explain to her that Lucas did things to him that she had never been able to do, and he hadn't even slept with him?

"Hey sleepy head. Snap out of it. Jack?"

As he looked up Maria was standing in front of him. He had clearly been deep in thought. "Sorry."

Maria walked off towards the hallway and Jack could hear her mutter, "I swear sometimes that man is so far out of it…"

As he realized it was almost time to leave, he jumped up and followed her. "Maire!"

Catching up with her in the hallway, he gave her a hug from behind and a kiss on the neck. "Have a great time in Amsterdam."

She turned around and gave him a quick kiss on the lips. "Don't work too hard this weekend. I know you're both workaholics, but try to make sure you see a bed from time to time, okay?"

As he saw the genuine concern in her eyes, it hit him again. After this weekend, he would know if it was worthwhile to cheat on her.

It wasn't until she was out of the hallway and up to the bedroom that her words hit him. *Try to make sure you see a bed from time to time…*

ALL day long Jack had a hard time focusing. He had arranged with Lucas that the Brit would book the hotel rooms. One fancy hotel suite in Jack's name, where they could set up 'an office', and a smaller hotel room as Lucas's cover. Jack had been tempted to call Lucas all day, just to hear his voice, to see if he was excited, to check if they were still on. Then he got a text message, "Antwerp Hilton old city centre exec suite your name be there B4 6pm".

This was really going to happen.

THE knock on the door was so quiet, Lucas wasn't even sure it had happened, so he waited.

There it was again. A single, shy, almost hesitant knock.

Lucas was on the other side of the door waiting, so when he abruptly opened it, Jack's hand was still in midair. He looked more vulnerable, smaller than Lucas remembered him. There was very little evidence that this was a powerful, decisive man. Even the suit that always looked tailor made seemed to fit him less than perfectly. The porter had brought his bags up a few minutes earlier, and Lucas, posing as the perfect assistant, had told the man where he wanted them and tipped him generously.

They stood there for a moment, neither of them sure what to do next, until Lucas stepped aside to let Jack into the hotel room. He brushed his hand against Jack's when he passed, but the older man walked on towards the window without acknowledging the contact.

"I'm glad you found it. I was worried you might not…"

"Your directions were very good," Jack interrupted flatly.

"…come," Lucas concluded, lowering his head, his hand still on the open door.

"Maybe you should shut the door."

"Yeah, right," Lucas responded as if he was suddenly awakened to the fact that this was a pretty ridiculous situation. They had arranged to meet at this hotel to cheat on their partners. The least he could do was make sure no one could see them. After quietly closing the door, he walked over to the window and stood silently next to Jack.

The American looked sad and maybe a little afraid. Lucas knew that his calm exterior was just that, a front, to cover up his nervousness. Suddenly Jack turned around and faced him as though he had come to a decision.

Jack's eyes were moist as he reached to cup Lucas's head with his hand and kiss him hungrily. Lucas gladly accepted the kiss and responded by letting his tongue touch Jack's lips lightly, carefully asking for access. He could feel the American opening up for him, until he felt himself being pushed away, then pulled back again, this time held in a tight hug. They were both catching their breath, and Lucas didn't know what to say, all he could feel was Jack's heart trying to beat its way out of his chest.

"I didn't mean to push you away, I'm sorry," Jack let his forehead rest against Lucas's. "Why do I keep doing this? I just…" He sighed deeply, searching for the right words. "…It's not like I don't want to, Lucas…"

The young man felt his lover distance himself from him. "But you feel like you can't, and I should just leave you alone," Lucas ended Jack's sentence.

"Yes… NO!" Jack let himself drop to sit on the bed, his eyes closing briefly as he exhaled loudly. He gently took Lucas's hand. "Please, just sit down for a moment. I'll try to explain."

Lucas swallowed, but didn't move. "It's okay, Jack, I understand. You have your career to think of and your wife. I should never have thought that this... us... was possible."

The American pulled on his arm, so Lucas finally sat down next to him, hunched over, staring at the floor.

"It's not like that, Lucas, please... I don't know how to act in this situation." Jack's hand was resting on Lucas's knee. "Because I've never been in this situation before."

Lucas straightened his back and slowly turned towards Jack, his mouth slightly open in amazement as it dawned on him. "Are you saying..."

Jack nodded, an apologetic smile on his face.

"You've never had a male lover?"

"Well, thanks for getting that sorted out," Jack snorted, looking away from Lucas, his hand still on the young man's knee.

"Why didn't you tell me?" Lucas asked, putting his hand over Jack's.

"Well, it's not the type of thing you can casually add to a conversation, Lucas."

"So I'm the first man you've been attracted to?" Lucas wanted to understand this. He moved his hand to cup Jack's chin and lifted it to make the American look up.

"God, no," Jack sighed as he shook his head. "I've always known I was attracted to men, ever since I fell in love with my best friend in high school. But even then I knew not to pursue it."

"So you've always known, just never did anything about it?"

"Why is that so hard to believe? I grew up in this world, where everything is about how people perceive you, and the last thing they want in their world is a queer diplomat!" Jack was clearly getting worked up about it, so Lucas squeezed his hand for comfort.

"I grew up in this world too, Jack."

This seemed to calm Jack down. "I know. You were just a little more adventurous than me, that's all."

Lucas rubbed his thumb over the side of Jack's hand. "We can take it slow, no need to rush." He picked up the older man's hand, turned it over and kissed his palm. "Are you hungry?"

Jack shrugged, and then smiled. "I think I'm too nervous to eat," he admitted.

"Well, we'll have to do something about that then," Lucas answered as he got up from the bed and took Jack's hand. He moved away, coaxing Jack to his feet and walked over to the large floor-to-ceiling windows. After he opened them, he walked outside onto the terrace.

"What are you doing?" Jack asked, reluctant to follow Lucas outside.

Lucas turned around and beckoned Jack. "Come here and I'll show you." He continued to walk backwards, making it impossible for Jack not to follow the enticing form. "This is the executive terrace. Private for five business suites, of which we occupy one. Now since it's the weekend, the other four are empty, and aren't booked until Monday."

Jack laughed and shook his head. This was his Lucas. He could see him charming the receptionist into giving him that information. "Exactly what sort of nonsense did you feed the hotel staff to assure us this much privacy?"

Lucas looked coy. "Not much. I just told the girl at the check in that my boss liked to go outside in the buff."

Jack threw his head back and chuckled. "You're crazy! For all we know that will ensure us an audience!"

Lucas laughed too. "She did seem thrilled you were a naturalist. No, seriously, they hear 'boss' and 'business man' and they think 'portly', 'middle aged' and 'saggy', so I think they will give it a miss."

They stood on the edge of the terrace, and it seemed natural for Jack to take a step closer to Lucas, putting his arms around his waist and his chin on his shoulder "It's nice out here. Very peaceful, you wouldn't know you were in the city center."

"Well, we are about five floors up and the square is car free, so that helps," Lucas answered, turning a little to look at Jack.

Jack pointed at the highest point in their vista, "That's a church?"

"The Cathedral of Our Lady," Lucas corrected. "Should have had two towers, but the second one was cut short because they ran out of money."

"You're quite the tour guide." Jack rested his cheek against Lucas's hair.

Lucas matched Jack's soft tone of voice. "It's not my first time in Antwerp, and I like to read up on the cities I go to. It's in all the tourist guides." He could feel Jack tighten his hold and they stood rocking back and forth for a while. "This is nice, but let's go back in, okay?"

Lucas led Jack back to their room, never letting go of his hand. Once inside he turned to close the drapes and felt Jack enfold him in his arms again. Lucas started fiddling with his tie in an attempt to get rid of some clothes. They were both accustomed to dressing professionally, but Lucas was starting to feel constricted in his shirt-tie-jacket attire. He felt Jack's breath on his neck, which was a very sensual feeling, but they needed to get a little more comfortable. Jack detected Lucas's fidgeting and loosened his grip, giving the other man the freedom to turn around. Lucas took Jack's face in his hands and looked into the grey-blue eyes. There was certainly some confusion in there and a touch of fear. "Tell me you're sure of this. Tell me you want this as much as I do." Lucas thought Jack needed to hear himself say it as much as Lucas needed to hear it and he wanted to be sure he wasn't pushing Jack to do something he didn't really want.

Jack nodded.

"I want to hear it from you, Jack. I want to hear you say what you want."

"I want you. All of you," Jack whispered.

Lucas slowly let his lips touch Jack's and allowed his hands to slip from his cheeks to his jaw, down his neck to the top of his shirt. He gently tugged the knot of the American's tie open. His movements were slow and deliberate, as if he was expecting Jack to lose his nerve and push him away again. Instead the American returned the gesture, slowly pulling the two ends of Lucas's black silk tie apart until they came away from each other. Lucas felt Jack smiling into the kiss they still hadn't broken, as four hands were fighting for maneuvering room in the small space.

"Maybe we should do this one at a time," Jack suggested, their lips only just touching.

"Or we could stop kissing?" Lucas offered.

"Hell, no!" Jack rebutted a little more loudly, as he pushed his body closer to Lucas's again and covered his mouth with a flurry of little kisses.

Lucas was smiling under his lover's bombardment and trying to get out of his jacket at the same time. He attempted to throw it onto one of the chairs but missed.

Jack chuckled as he saw the jacket fly across the room from the corner of his eye. He didn't care where their clothes ended up and sort of liked the idea they would be together in a heap. As Lucas was pushing his jacket off his shoulders, Jack let go of the young man's face one hand at a time to shrug off the garment.

When Lucas started unbuttoning Jack's shirt, the American wanted to help with that, too.

"Please let me do it?" Lucas asked, their faces still close together. "I want to peel the layers off slowly. Is that okay with you?"

Jack nodded and unbuttoned his shirtsleeves instead, letting Lucas take care of the other buttons. Somewhere in the back of his mind, he felt his patience being tested, but he saw the almost childlike innocence with which the young man was exploring his body and didn't want to break the spell. Lucas had, after all, asked nicely, and for some reason, this made Jack feel it was okay to surrender completely to Lucas's lead.

The Brit wrapped his arm around Jack's chest underneath the shirt and let his mouth trail down to his neck and collarbone.

"God, you taste heavenly," Lucas said to no one in particular as he continued licking a trail to Jack's nipple.

"I want to feel your skin, too," Jack answered, trying not to put too much urgency in his tone. He wrapped his arms around Lucas's lean frame and gently pulled the shirt up, releasing it from his trousers and giving him free access to Lucas's back. He could feel the tight muscles rippling under his hands every time Lucas shifted a little. He had been semi hard ever since they started kissing, but Lucas's hot mouth on his nipples and the soft skin underneath his hands had the blood rushing to his groin.

As if he was reading the older man's mind, Lucas raised himself upright again and rasped, "I've been teasing you, haven't I?"

"No," Jack answered, feeling like he needed to clear his throat too. Lucas stepped back a bit as he opened the top button of his shirt and quickly lifted it over his head, pulling at the sleeves when he couldn't get his hands free right away, only to reattach himself to Jack's mouth immediately after discarding the garment.

They struggled with each other's belts, until they realized the humor of the situation. Grinning, they moved apart momentarily, kicking off their shoes and getting rid of their trousers. Jack couldn't help but notice that Lucas was as hard as he was underneath his boxers.

As Jack was toeing off his socks, Lucas tackled him, throwing them down on the bed with a surprising force. He was pinned down underneath the young man, their fingers entwined, hands raised above their heads and his mouth invaded by Lucas's tongue. Jack didn't know whether to surrender completely or fight the young man a bit. As he tried to move his arms around, Lucas shifted his body to get better leverage and created some much needed friction for their still clothed cocks. His grip on Jack's hands was unnecessarily tight, and he was breathing heavily as he came up for air in between kisses. Jack could feel Lucas's heartbeat through his chest. When Jack tried to move again, Lucas halted and raised himself a bit. "Are you okay? Do you want me to stop?"

Jack smiled up at the glorious sight of Lucas leaning over him, his dark curls hanging down around his beautiful face and his eyes dark with lust. "No, I don't ever want you to stop. I've been waiting for this for thirty years."

"Ooooh," Lucas answered looking pained, "I wasn't even born thirty years ago."

"Don't remind me," Jack sighed, smiling.

Lucas looked Jack in the eyes and started moving his groin slowly back and forth. "Is this what you want?"

Jack could only nod. The friction between their hard cocks and the thin layers of fabric separating them made it difficult for him to think straight. Lucas's movements were slow and deliberate. He still held Jack's hands in his own and kept looking at his lover.

"Open your eyes, Jack, I want to see those beautiful eyes of yours turn liquid."

Jack hadn't even realized he had closed them, but when he looked up, his sight was blurry, out of focus. He felt the tension mount in his belly as Lucas kept up his steady grinding and he knew he was going to come, like a teenager, without even really being touched.

"Luke, I…. I'm…"

"Just let it happen, Jack, just let it," Lucas whispered. "I'll catch you."

Jack struggled to keep his eyes open as Lucas had requested. He knew he was going to come, maybe one more push… Then he heard a low groan and only barely recognized his own voice as he saw a broad smile break on his lover's face.

Lucas leaned down and Jack only just registered their foreheads touching through the haze of his bliss. "You're beautiful when you come, Jack." He was breathing hard. The release of tension was immense and slowly Jack started to understand what had just happened. "You're still…"

Lucas kissed his temple. "It's okay, we have time."

"I want to touch you," Jack replied, feeling courageous.

Lucas smiled broadly and moved his left hand along with Jack's right down between their two bodies. As Jack slid his hand underneath Lucas's boxers, the Brit stroked Jack's arm gently. Jack tenderly enveloped Lucas's bone hard member, and he felt the young man shudder at the touch.

"God, yes, Jack, your hand feels good."

It felt strange to hold another man's cock in his hand, but at the same time, it also felt right. Jack started stroking gently but firmly and heard Lucas moan with every move he made. He knew the young man was close. "Come for me, Luke," he whispered, urging the young man to relinquish control.

Jack felt Lucas thrust desperately, the young man's back arched under his fingertips and with a long drawn out shudder, he finally came. Jack became aware of the warm sticky liquid on his hand even as he heard Lucas sob out his cry of release. "So long, oh God, I've wanted that for so long, Jack." The voice trailed into silence as the slim body relaxed in Jack's arms, still trembling in the aftermath.

Jack floated off to sleep, still entangled with Lucas as he heard the young man murmur "… and we only just got started…"

Chapter Ten

LUCAS woke up when he felt something stir underneath him. He didn't want to get up just yet, but when he remembered what had happened, his eyes flew open immediately. He was in a hotel suite with Jack, and they only had about thirty-six hours together, so he wasn't going to waste them sleeping.

There was almost no light coming through the curtains now, but his eyes adjusted to the darkness and he could see Jack's face turned toward him, his eyes open.

"Hey there." Jack's voice sounded calm. "What time is it?"

Lucas crawled over his lover's body to the nightstand and picked up his watch. "Ten fifteen."

"Good," Jack chuckled. "For a moment there I thought we had slept the night away." He sat up and reached over to touch the young Brit. "Come here, I don't want to let you go before Sunday afternoon."

Lucas took his hand and dragged him to his feet. "In that case, you're going to have to take a shower with me then."

Jack pulled Lucas close and kissed him as he stood up, but Lucas played hard to get and made his getaway to the bathroom. He was a little surprised when Jack didn't immediately follow.

In fact, he was nicely lathered up by the time he heard Jack enter. He could hear the rustle of Jack's boxers falling to the floor and then there was silence. He was sure the American was watching him, and he took his time touching himself, letting his hands glide over his shoulders, then his belly and thighs. The idea that someone was enjoying the show made him slowly grow hard. As he started to gently stroke his cock, he heard Jack behind him and felt strong arms wrap around his stomach.

"Oooh, slippery!" Jack quipped as he ran his hands approvingly over Lucas's body.

"Jeez, what took you so long?" Lucas sighed, "I thought you didn't want to let me go?"

Jack laughed as he squeezed Lucas and kissed his neck. "I ordered some food. Have to keep our energy up, because I have the feeling you have quite some strenuous things in store for me."

Lucas turned around and hugged Jack back. "You bet I do, old man." He cupped Jack's head and kissed him passionately, letting his arousal touch the other man's thigh. "Seems you liked what you saw too." He pulled Jack underneath the streaming hot water and placed his hand on Jack's chest, stroking it down the slick skin slowly, while he admired his lover's body. "Can't say I mind what I see, either."

Jack smiled, shy all of a sudden as he pulled the younger man close again.

"Don't tell me she's never told you how beautiful you are, Jack?"

The American wiped the wet strands of hair out of Lucas's face. "Let's not… talk about that, okay?"

Lucas leaned in to kiss Jack's neck. "Well, you are beautiful, you know. You look so good in your smart business suit that all I could think of when I first saw you was how fast I could get you out of it."

Again Jack smiled timidly.

Lucas gently moved forward until Jack was against the wall of the shower. "Not too cold?"

The hot water filled the bathroom with steam, so Jack shook his head. "We don't have a lot of time. They're going to be here with dinner soon."

Lucas shushed him with a kiss, and Jack let himself be silenced. To hell with room service. They were the guests, and if that meant the staff had to leave dinner at the door, then so be it. Decision made, Jack kissed his lover back with total abandon.

He didn't know what he wanted to touch first. Lucas's skin felt smooth and soft underneath his hands, and the fact they were both soaking wet, standing underneath the fancy rain shower made it a curiously erotic sensation. Lucas tasted like soap and he would have looked like a little boy with his wet curls clinging to his smiling face, if it hadn't been for what he was doing to his lover with his hands and mouth.

Lucas's tongue trailed down Jack's neck and shoulder, over his collarbone to his nipple. He only licked the bud slightly, sending shivers down Jack's spine, then swiftly moved down to Jack's belly button.

The young Brit looked up at Jack defiantly as he knelt down in front of his lover, legs spread wide. Lucas touched himself, slowly stroking his erect cock. Jack saw everything as if it was playing in slow motion. Lucas was looking up at him, his eyes almost black with want, when he opened his mouth and teasingly slowly enveloped his lover's bone hard erection with his lips. Jack took a sharp breath in, trying not to come right that instant. As he watched his cock move slowly in and out of Lucas's mouth, he needed all his self-control not to thrust forward, but it was to no avail as he felt his belly grow tight.

"Luke, I'm...." Jack squeezed out before he came down Lucas's throat with a loud moan. He stood against the wall, Lucas's hand on his hip, when he felt his legs give out and he let himself drop to the floor, panting.

Lucas leaned in to kiss him, still touching himself. Jack could taste the slightly tangy, salty taste in Lucas's mouth that could only have come from his release.

"I want you as well," Jack told his young lover after Lucas broke the kiss to let him breathe. "I want you in my mouth."

Lucas looked at him as if he was trying to gauge the honesty of that statement and then slowly raised himself until he was standing in front of Jack. He placed his hand on the wall over Jack's head and leaned his hips forward so Jack was close enough to take him in his mouth.

Their positions now reversed, Jack could see this wasn't a bad vista, either. Hot water still streamed out of the showerhead, keeping them both warm against the cold tiles. Lucas placed his hand against Jack's cheek, and the young man's thumb stroked his bottom lip. As Jack sucked in the offered digit, he wrapped his hand around Lucas's cock and heard the young man gasp as he coordinated the stroking and touching.

He wanted to really taste Lucas, though, and slowly brought his stroking hand and his mouth together. As he gently took the head between his lips, he saw Lucas's muscles strain to keep from moving forward toward the hot mouth. His eyes closed and his head tilted back, Lucas was clearly close. Jack let his tongue skim the smooth surface of the head and explored the slit, making Lucas gasp again. He looked up and saw Lucas staring at him with glazed eyes. He felt Lucas move slowly in and out of his mouth, clearly holding himself back with all his might. Then suddenly, he felt the younger man's hand on his hair, roughly guiding him.

"Jack-g-uh!" Lucas cried out as Jack took almost the entire length in his mouth. He could taste the tangy-saltiness of Lucas, realizing they didn't taste exactly the same and swallowed everything the young man surrendered.

Lucas started to sway, and Jack grabbed his young lover to keep him from falling over. The young Brit collapsed on Jack's lap.

"I'm sorry," Lucas chuckled, his head on Jack's shoulder.

"No, you're not," Jack answered in the way that had become habit between them.

"Yes, I am." Lucas smiled a little lazily. "I should have given you a little more notice before…"

"Before you came? I could tell you were close, Luke. You are beautiful when you come too."

Lucas looked at him coyly. "Well, I didn't need much." He passionately kissed his American lover. "You have a really nice mouth."

They both looked up as they heard a knock on the door and the call "Room service". Jack looked at Lucas. "I better go get that." Lucas nodded and got up, pulling Jack to his feet. The American stepped out of the shower and gave his lover a quick kiss, "You stay here. Both of us hanging around here naked might look a little suspicious."

Lucas turned off the shower as he watched Jack wrap a towel around his hips and walk out of the bathroom still dripping wet.

LUCAS tried hard not to giggle. Jack had just poured soy sauce on his chest where the sternum dipped a little, and it tickled.

"I told you it was the perfect place for that, now here, taste this."

Jack expertly grabbed a bit of salmon sashimi with his chopsticks and dipped it into the puddle of soy sauce before he fed it to Lucas. "Now stop moving about or we'll have to have these sheets changed before we can sleep in them tonight!"

Lucas couldn't help but laugh at the seriousness of Jack's face. "Who says we'll get to sleep?"

The American took a piece of sushi and clearly took his time coating it with the sauce before putting it in his mouth. "Promises, promises," he answered, poking Lucas with his chopsticks. "You want some more?"

Lucas nodded. They were both on the bed, their hair still a little wet and towels wrapped around their hips. The towels didn't do much for decorum, but they would at least keep their minds on dinner for the time being.

Jack reached over Lucas's supine body to the food trolley next to the bed. He carefully chose a nice sushi roll and placed it in the centre of the soy puddle on Lucas's chest, letting it soak up the sauce. He looked at his young lover while he moved the rice and fish roll around a bit and held it over Lucas's mouth.

"Just take it between your teeth."

Lucas opened his mouth slowly and grabbed the offered food, smiling around it.

Jack leaned in and bit off a piece while kissing Lucas on the lips. He heard Lucas moan while they both swallowed the shared food. Jack let his finger run through what was left of the soy sauce and felt Lucas's muscles react to his touch. When he looked up he simply said, "There."

Lucas looked down and saw the word 'MINE' written on his stomach. He pulled Jack into another kiss, making the American lie next to him and then rolling both of them over until he was on top of him. "Not yet. I'm not yours until I've felt you inside of me."

"Do you want that? Do you want me inside of you?" Jack whispered.

"God, yes! If you want that, too, I mean, I don't want you to do anything you don't want!"

Jack silenced the young man with a passionate kiss, trying to convey that he wanted it too.

Lucas spread his legs so he was straddling Jack and moved back and forth like he had done just a few hours ago, the first time he had made Jack come.

Jack felt himself slowly grow hard again; knowing this time the fairly quick succession of their lovemaking would let him last a lot longer. It didn't diminish the passion he felt for Lucas, though, the feeling that he wanted to crawl underneath his lover's skin and melt into him. He fumbled to untie the towel around Lucas's waist and felt a pang of disappointment when the young man got up and moved to his suitcase on the other side of the room.

Jack scooted up until he was half sitting, but his face had obviously been easy to read, because Lucas smiled and explained, "We need a few supplies."

The young Brit returned with a handful of condoms and a small bottle of lube. He crawled back to his earlier position and took Jack's face in his hands. "Don't worry, I'll guide you through it," he murmured before kissing him again.

Jack let his hands wander over Lucas's back and cupped his ass, pulling him in closer.

"Do you want to prepare me?" Lucas asked wantonly, his eyes dark.

Jack nodded. "If you show me how."

"It's been a while, so I'll need some time," Lucas moaned against Jack's mouth. He moved a little higher, offering his neck for Jack to kiss as he grabbed the lube. "It's a muscle so you'll need to gradually tease it while I try to relax. Plenty of lube and one finger at a time." He grabbed Jack's hand, "Come here," and squirted a generous dollop of gel on his fingers.

Lucas moved a little higher up Jack's body and wrapped his arms around his lover's neck. They were deliciously close together, Lucas's weeping cock between their bellies, when Jack moved his hand around Lucas, trying not to get the lube all over. Considering he had never done this before, his aim was pretty good, but Lucas disentangled one of his arms to guide him, "There." He had his hand over Jack's and let his head fall back when Jack breached the entrance with the tip of his finger.

Lucas moaned, his mouth open and his head back. "A little more…"

Jack could feel the ring of muscle pushing tightly around his finger, but slowly felt it loosen as he carefully let his slick finger glide in and out.

Lucas's movements created some much needed friction for both of them, and Jack sensed his lover becoming more impatient.

"Add another finger, Jack," Lucas whispered in his ear.

Jack realized he loved looking at Lucas's face when he was like this, shutting out the world, totally oblivious to anything else but his own body and that of his lover. As he inserted another finger, he felt the ring of tightness again, but this time it yielded even more quickly than the first time. Lucas was breathing heavily now, telling Jack to go deeper.

"One more finger. Oh God, I can't wait much longer, Jack. I want you deep inside me. Fuck, Jack!"

With three fingers inside Lucas, Jack could feel him opening up to him. He was still going to be tight, but Jack was starting to become impatient too, his breathing speeding up in anticipation of feeling Lucas's heat around him.

Jack was surprised when Lucas moved away from him. The young man looked at Jack with dark, lustful eyes as he grabbed a condom. Reacting to the confusion in Jack's eyes, the Brit leaned in to kiss him. "I'm ready for you and I can't wait any longer," he explained. He ripped the foil packet open with his teeth and expertly rolled the condom on Jack's rock hard erection. With a few strokes he coated it with lube and then moved closer again. "God, Jack, I can't wait. Are you okay with this?"

Jack's anticipation was at such a pitch that he could only nod. Lucas understood and made it easy for Jack. He placed a hand on Jack's shoulder for support and raised himself a little, so he could slowly impale himself on Jack's slick cock.

Seeing himself disappear into the young man's body was an incredibly erotic sight, made even more delicious by the heat and tightness of Lucas's body around him.

He watched Lucas's face as the other man waited a bit, his eyes closed, his mouth open, adjusting to the feeling.

Jack reached for Lucas's nipple which was just out of reach of his tongue as the Brit started slowly moving up and down.

Opening his eyes slightly, Lucas smiled. "You look so serious, but you feel so good, Jack... so good... I can't begin to..." The young man gently placed his hand on Jack's face, tenderly stroking his cheek and lips as he kept moving.

Jack saw with wonder how Lucas was slowly coming undone around him. He felt so gloriously tight, and Jack started to realize what he had missed all those years. How he had deluded himself that making love to a man wouldn't be so very different from making love to a woman. Only Jack had never felt for any woman what he was feeling for the young man in his arms now.

Lucas shifted his movements until the hard cock was hitting all the right spots. He took Jack's face between his hands and kissed him. "Oh God, Jack, I'm so close... please tell me you'll come with me.... please!' he pleaded, his mouth against Jack's.

Jack could only nod. The sensation that he was giving his young lover this kind of pleasure sent his blood racing towards his groin. As much as he could from his position, he thrust upwards, feeling the waves of ecstasy wash over him. His head was light and his eyes swam as he came deep inside Lucas's body. He kept thrusting, riding out his intense orgasm, wanting the feeling to last forever. Lucas stroked himself between their bellies until Jack felt him tighten around him, clearly abandoning all control. Lucas's movements were uncoordinated and erratic as he pressed himself against Jack, shaking and barely breathing, letting ecstasy wash through him.

They stayed connected like that, holding on to each other for a long time as they slowly came back down to earth. After a while, Jack noticed that Lucas was shaking in his arms, so he reached for one of the abandoned towels and folded it around the young man's shoulders. "Better?"

Lucas nodded, his eyes a little hazy. "I was cold, but I didn't want to let go. I want to keep you inside of me, Jack."

"We're going to have to move sometime."

"I know." Lucas kissed him gently. "I know."

Jack cradled Lucas in his arms, slipping out of him as he laid him down on his back. He discarded the condom and got up, feeling a little unsteady on his feet. He retrieved a warm, damp washcloth from the bathroom and returned to sit down on the bed. As he gently cleaned off Lucas's belly he could still see the word 'MINE', now quite smudged, and Jack smiled. Lucas was his as much as he was Lucas's, and he wasn't looking forward to Sunday.

Chapter Eleven

A warm hand on his back awakened Jack and something even warmer was stroking his side. He was on his stomach on the bed and as he peered through his barely opened eyelids, he saw the space next to him was empty. As he turned his face on the pillow, he could still smell Lucas on the bedding. In fact, he was sure the whole room still smelled of sex. The memories of the night before made his groin stir and he finally opened his eyes completely. He found himself staring into the gorgeous chocolate brown eyes that had become delightfully familiar.

"Hey, sleepy head," Lucas said, his face tender and caring. "Rise and shine, I got us some breakfast."

As Lucas tried to get up from the side of the bed, Jack grabbed his hand. "Don't go." He rolled over onto his back, making a space for Lucas and saw the young man pull a large cup of hot liquid away just in time to avoid a spill.

"Hey, I thought, 'wake him up with fresh coffee and pastry', but all he wants is my body."

Jack's stomach growled and he lazily stroked his belly as he stretched his back. "I guess I could use some breakfast."

Lucas placed one of the paper bags he was holding on Jack's stomach and walked over to the large doors that led to the terrace. Balancing the coffee and the other bag of pastries, he opened the floor-to-ceiling window and walked out, letting the sunshine stream into the room. Jack could feel that the pastries in the bag were still warm and smelled the sweetness of cinnamon and honey. He got up quickly and slipped into a pair of jeans, following his young lover onto the terrace. Lucas sat on one of the benches eating.

"Come over here. I have sweet rolls, cinnamon, raisin…"

"You went out for those?" Jack walked over to Lucas and kissed the top of his head.

"Well, it's not like I could call room service, and I was starving. Besides there's a bakery right across from the hotel." Lucas leaned his head back to kiss Jack on the mouth.

"You taste like almonds."

Lucas held up the bun he was eating. "You want some? It's called 'Frangipane' and it's very sweet, but very good."

Jack took a bite of the offered food and wrinkled his nose at the sweetness before moving around Lucas and settling down on the terrace floor in front of him cross-legged. He took the cup of coffee and drank a large gulp, then picked out a croissant and took a bite of that.

"So what do you want to do this morning?" Lucas asked, his eyes squinting against the bright sunlight.

Jack looked up at the sky. "I think we missed out on 'this morning', but why don't we take a walk around town this afternoon? You know this place, right? So show me all the non-tourist bits."

Lucas smiled. "I don't suppose you'll hold my hand when we walk around?"

Jack raised one eyebrow. "What are you? A little girl?"

Lucas stuck his tongue out at Jack, feeling very juvenile, but it made them both laugh. "Well, it will be the first non-professional thing we do together, and we will be out in the open, among the people."

"Yeah," Jack mused. "We might bump into an American or two, who might recognize me or a Brit who might recognize you. Don't get me wrong, Lucas, but I can't exactly explain why we're this intimate with each other, can I?" He hoped Lucas wouldn't take it the wrong way, but he needed to be honest with his lover.

"I know," Lucas answered softly. "I know I can't touch you in public, but I still want to go out with you today."

Jack gave him a lopsided look. "What are you suggesting?" He saw mischief creep into the young man's face.

"I'm asking you out on a date," Lucas answered smugly, "We've never actually done that. So maybe we should start at the beginning. I'll take you out to dinner, my treat, so don't expect anything fancy."

Jack looked at him, trying to work out if he was serious. "Fine, but let's not make it too late tonight."

Lucas chuckled. "Oh, don't worry! If I have to keep my hands off you all day, it will be a quick dinner!"

THEY both walked out of the five star hotel dressed in jeans, shirts, baseball caps, and sunglasses. The weather was sunny and warm enough to wander around the city in shirt sleeves.

Lucas assured Jack that they had everything they could possibly want within walking distance of the hotel, so they made their way across the square to the fashion district and ended up stealing kisses and touches in the dressing rooms of Dries Van Noten's boutique, while picking out designer business suits for one another. They arranged for their suits to be delivered to their home addresses and continued on, strolling into used bookshops and eclectic music stores.

In one of the bookstores, Jack and Lucas were discussing buying an old book on the history of Antwerp when Jack heard a vaguely familiar voice behind him, "George, I told you it was him!" and then felt a hand on his arm. "Mr. Ambassador, so nice of you to come to our fair city. You should have called us, so we could have extended a proper welcome, invite you to our home!"

Jack turned around and smiled shyly, extending his hand. "Reverend and Mrs. Wallace. Nice to see you again!" He could see Mrs. Wallace eyeing Lucas, clearly expecting to be introduced. Jack hesitated for only a moment before he recovered. "May I introduce Mr. Carlton, representative of the British Embassy?"

Mrs. Wallace shook Lucas's hand with much fervor, her eyes wide. "Nice to meet you, sir." Still shaking Lucas's hand she turned to Jack again. "Fraternizing with the Brits, I'm sure you have lots of important things to talk about?"

She was clearly fishing. Lucas was the first to answer. "Yes, ma'am, but all classified, I'm afraid."

Luckily for them, Reverend Wallace was less enthusiastic and soon pulled his wife aside. "Mr. Ambassador, we'll leave you in peace now, I'm sure you are a very busy man!" and then to his wife, "Let's go, Clarice, can't you see these men have important business to discuss?"

Both men watched the older couple leave the bookstore. Lucas heard Jack sigh as soon as they closed the door behind them and he put his hand on his lover's. "That was close."

"I don't believe you. Classified! You made us sound like spies," Jack answered, almost visibly shaking.

Lucas chuckled. "Well, we couldn't very well tell her the truth!"

Jack looked around to make sure no one was watching them, but the store was empty. He wrapped his arm around Lucas and pulled him close. "I'm sorry, I just got nervous."

Lucas pulled back a bit. "They can't tell just by looking at us, you know."

Jack closed his eyes, sighed, and smiled. "Yeah, I know. Let's go."

OVER by the 'Grote Markt' in front of the City Hall, there was a stage set up, and a large crowd was watching an unknown music group. The cafés around the market were packed, so they bought drinks at one of the stalls and moved into the crowd. The Caribbean music was colorful and people were singing along. Lucas spotted a slightly less crowded space near one of the small potted trees at the side of the square and grabbed Jack's hand to lead him through the crowd. Jack felt as if all eyes were trained on them, but when he looked around, he realized people weren't really paying attention.

As they claimed the open space, Jack was also surprised to see a lot of people with their arms around each other and not just straight couples. He had seen men strolling hand in hand around the streets earlier, too. Moving a little closer to Lucas, who stood in front of him watching the music group, he snaked his arms around his lover's waist and hooked his thumb over the band of the young man's jeans. Lucas smiled and looked over his shoulder. There were two men standing a little bit away from them and they were not hiding that they were a couple, even kissing briefly at the end of a particularly romantic song.

"They are very liberal here, aren't they?" Jack whispered in Lucas's ear.

"Oh, I don't know about that. The sun is shining, happy music playing," Lucas answered with a broad smile. He moved a little closer, making Jack flinch. "Don't worry," Lucas whispered, "I'd love to kiss you right now, but I know we can't."

Jack smiled shyly, recovering his composure. "Well, even if I wasn't married, I couldn't see myself doing this with you in the States either."

Lucas returned to his place in front of Jack again and grabbed his hand to wrap it around his waist. "This is nice too, and nobody can see that," he whispered matter-of-factly.

Jack let himself relax. The crowd was packed together so his closeness to Lucas didn't look suspicious. Most people were looking at the stage anyway, and this way he could feel Lucas's delicious body close to his, smell the conditioner he used, and the Grey Flannel aftershave he had put on just before they left the hotel room.

"Why don't we grab an early dinner and then go back to the room, okay?" Lucas suggested, leaning back a little and looking over his shoulder.

Jack was beginning to think the Brit could read his mind.

THE small restaurant Lucas had chosen was in one of the side streets around the cathedral. Smells of garlic and coriander came from the kitchen and there was an outside terrace, surrounded by some potted shrubs. There was only one small table left in the corner, forcing the two men to share a rather narrow bench, something they assured the waitress they did not mind at all.

After they ordered falafel and pita dishes, the waitress brought a tray full of small cups of different sauces.

"Ooh, garlic sauce!" Lucas beamed, but then his face changed. "Okay, how about either we both eat it or we don't eat it at all."

Jack dipped his finger in and licked it. "I guess that's settled."

At that moment, two men with their arms around each other walked passed the terrace. As soon as they were out of earshot, Jack whispered, "This is the first country where it's so apparent how they are very tolerant here."

Lucas laughed, "We're just in the right part of the right city for this. I wouldn't generalize about the whole country though, besides I think you're just open to it now." He gave Jack a measured look. "You sound just like Lucy; she keeps seeing pregnant women everywhere."

Jack waited for the waitress to put their orders down and leave before continuing. "Have you two talked about having kids?"

Lucas shook his head. "Not really. Her father would probably nail her to the stake if she got pregnant before we got married. He barely talks to her now because we live together 'in sin'."

Jack chuckled. "Maria and I did the same in Denmark for almost three years. Her father wasn't happy either."

"So how come you and Maria don't have any kids?" Lucas knew this was a very personal question, so he added, "You don't have to answer."

Jack smiled, "Maria told me even before we were married that she felt there were too many kids without parents in this world, so we agreed that if we were ever posted to a third world country, we would adopt an orphan there. She wanted a true global family, you know, a kid from Guatemala, one from Ethiopia and one from Vietnam."

"And you?" Lucas asked. "Didn't you want a child of your own?"

"I've never felt the need to pass on my genetic traits." Jack looked away from Lucas at the people passing on the street. "I just wish we hadn't waited this long. Maria never felt the time was right, and we always ended up being posted to Europe, never to a third world country, either. Sometimes I think she's just fine with the way things are right now."

Lucas put his hand on Jack's. "You have time, maybe you should talk to her about it?"

"Let's not talk about Maria, okay? I'm here with you, not her."

They finished dinner, paid and tipped the waitress, and made their way back to the hotel in silence.

JACK walked into the suite and moved straight through to the executive terrace. He suddenly felt guilty about his betrayal, guilty about enjoying this time with Lucas, enjoying it so much that he was considering chucking it all in, anything to give his relationship with the young man a chance. Could he leave Maria? She was an amazing woman, but the things he felt for Lucas were so much more powerful than what he had ever felt for his wife.

He was leaning on the railing looking down over the square, when he heard Lucas's hesitant voice. "Jack? Are you okay? I'm sorry... I shouldn't have brought the subject up, I... I wasn't thinking. Could you just step away from the edge please?"

Jack took a step back, but didn't turn around. He heard Lucas move closer and stop next to him.

"Did you think I was going to jump?" Jack asked without looking at his lover.

"I don't know. Just... after we talked, you seemed so distant and..."

Jack could hear the restrained emotion in Lucas's voice. "What do you want from me, Lucas?"

"That's a very open question, Jack. What do I want from you?"

Jack felt Lucas's beautiful eyes burn into him and looked down at his feet. "Why are we here? I mean, was our life so bad that we had to run away from our women for a few nights of passion in a fancy hotel in another city? I like my life, Lucas. I like my job and all the sacrifices were worth it as far as I'm concerned."

"Was it worth living a lie for?" Lucas asked honestly.

Jack took his time thinking about his answer. "I'm not living a lie."

"What am I, then? A bloody experiment?"

Jack could see Lucas from the corner of his eye, but he didn't dare look aside.

"Am I just an eager young upstart you can use to see if these feelings you had for your high school friend were real or not?"

Jack finally turned towards Lucas as Lucas moved towards the hotel room. "Lucas!" he called after the other man.

"Forget it. There's an unused hotel room downstairs."

Jack caught up with him at the terrace window and grabbed his hand. As Lucas tried to pull away, Jack pleaded, "Lucas, please, I'm sorry." Jack pulled him closer and wrapped his arms around the Brit. "Lucas, I'm sorry if I made you feel like that. No one has the right to do that to you."

They stood by the terrace door, Jack's arms around Lucas, his chin on the young man's shoulder. Lucas stayed with his back to his lover, unsure of whether he trusted him enough to believe him.

Jack kissed the back of Lucas's neck. "I've never felt for anyone what I feel for you, Luke."

"I know," Lucas answered, his voice heavy with emotion. "I know what you mean. All the way over here yesterday, I was thinking of what kind of a job I could do where it didn't matter if I was married or not. If I were gay or not. I kept thinking if I could find a way to persuade you to look for another job, too." Lucas inhaled deeply. "It's silly, I know, not to mention naïve, but…" He placed his hands over Jack's and stroked them gently.

Jack moved them both forward until they were inside of the room and kissed Lucas's neck until he felt his lover relax in his arms. They made love on the neatly made bed until the sheets and pillows were strewn all around the room, taking their time to explore each other's bodies, bringing each other to the edge and then cooling down again, slowly touching and licking, nuzzling and kissing only to strike up the flame again, until finally Lucas came hard between their bellies and all over his lover's hand while Jack released his seed, buried deep inside of him. A long time passed before either could move to go clean up.

"**I** don't see why not."

Lucas was washing Jack's hair in the large bathtub next to the walk-in shower of the top executive suite. Jack's back and head rested on Lucas's chest and Jack was trying to tickle the Brit's knees on either side of him. He was beginning to think that this was one of the few places where his young lover wasn't ticklish.

"Well, only if you want to. I mean, I like seeing you turn to jelly and I like the feeling when I'm inside of you, but seeing you go all incoherent makes me wonder what it's like. Would you?"

Lucas poured a cup of water over Jack's head. "Well, it is amazing to feel you inside me, but I don't mind returning the favor, in fact it's nice to turn the tables from time to time." Lucas smiled mischievously.

"Your arse is mine, Mr. Ambassador."

Jack chuckled and playfully flicked some water in Lucas's face, but the butterflies had already started fluttering in his belly.

LUCY and Maria were served Sunday lunch in the dining car of the Thalys train between Amsterdam and Brussels. They had spent their two days in Amsterdam shopping between museum visits and were now on their way home.

"I'm only sorry it's over this fast. I had fun, Maria, thanks for taking me. I did miss Lucas of course, but I'll see him again this afternoon." Lucy was clearly still enjoying her train journey, but then her face turned a little sad. "If he's not still working, that is."

Maria couldn't help but think that it was strange this was the young woman's first train journey, just like her trip to Belgium had been her first time outside of the United States.

"I hate to burst your bubble, Lucy, but having him working at all hours almost seven days a week is what life with a diplomat is going to be like from now on."

"Is that what it's like for you and Jack? I mean, I've seen you two together, you love each other. He's considerate and caring and…" Lucy gave Maria a desperate look.

"The only time I have Jack for myself is when I kidnap him to some Caribbean island for a week, and even then he brings papers to read and I have to pry him away from CNN. It's been almost three years since our last vacation, Lucy. My last two attempts were shot down by a fire in a nightclub where three Americans were killed and the order to move to Belgium." She put her hand on Lucy's to show support. "I've always known Jack was married to his work. You learn to make your own life and to enjoy the moments you have with him, even if those moments are at banquets or receptions. There's a lot of good work you can do, honey, you just have to find your niche and build yourself a reputation. Believe me, I'm realistic enough to know I could never do the work I do if I wasn't the

Ambassador's wife. Lucas's job will bring you some really nice benefits; just don't expect a romantic marriage."

Lucy sighed, clearly not comforted by Maria's words. "I probably sound like a whiny girl, but I at least expected him to WANT to spend some of his time with me. I feel like such an... an ornament!"

"Listen, why don't you tag along with me? I can take you to the charity work I do and you can see if you'd like to do something like that too. Then I'll throw a little hint in Jack's direction about you feeling a bit neglected by Lucas. He'll probably mention it to Lucas and as a side benefit, it might make him feel guilty enough to take me on a vacation. How does that sound?"

Lucy's face lit up and Maria nodded gracefully, happy with the way this was turning out.

Chapter Twelve

LUCAS woke up alone. What he really wanted was to sleep a little more, since neither he nor Jack had wanted to spend their last night together asleep, but suddenly the uneasy feeling crept up on him that maybe Jack had already left. He jumped out of bed and grabbed his watch off the nightstand. Quarter to eleven. They had agreed to leave around twelve so Jack should still be here. He grabbed the sheet off the bed and wrapped it around himself, then dashed out on to the terrace. No Jack. Bathroom?

Lucas stopped in his tracks at the door of the bathroom as he caught sight of Jack standing in front of the large mirror. The man was wearing only boxers and leaning forward, shaving carefully.

"You look like one of those Greek statues," Jack remarked, eyeing Lucas.

Discarding the sheet, Lucas moved to wrap his arms around Jack. He put his chin on Jack's shoulder and looked at their reflections in the mirror. "I wish we could just stay here. Never go back to the real world."

Jack put his hands over Lucas's and leaned into the touch. "You know we can't, Luke."

"I know." Lucas sighed, squeezing Jack tight. "Just don't want to let go right now."

Jack lifted his arm and twisted around so he could cup Lucas's head and kiss him passionately. "We'll be all right, Luke," he promised unwisely. "We'll find a way to make it work."

As they got their things together to leave the hotel room, Lucas felt the tension mounting. They hadn't really talked about the future and even though he was sure this felt good to Jack, too, he was also pretty sure the American wasn't going to leave his wife for him. Was he a fool to think they could actually have a future together? Could he be content to be just a lover, the man on the side? Even though they had only spent two nights together, Lucas knew this wasn't just a fling for him; he knew that what he felt for Jack was not like anything he had felt for his previous boyfriends. This was love, at least for him.

Jack had gone down to check out already and as Lucas scanned the room one more time before he left, his eye fell on some condoms that were left on the nightstand. He quickly walked back in and stuffed them in the pocket of his jacket, next to his wallet.

THEY drove back to Brussels together almost in silence, both realizing they had some choices to make, but both afraid to discuss them. Jack dropped Lucas off at his apartment in the European District and drove on to his house in Tervuren. He sat in the driveway for more than an hour, going over the events of the weekend, before he felt he could enter the house.

"LUCAS?"

Lucas heard Lucy call him from the hallway while he was making tea in the small kitchen. "I'm here!" he called back, taking a deep breath. The weekend was definitely over. He heard Lucy drop her bags and then the staccato sound of her fashionable heels on the old wooden floors.

"I can't believe you're actually home!" she squeaked.

He tried not to tense up as she threw her arms around him and kissed him on his cheek. Yup, she was definitely back.

"Hey, Lucy girl," Lucas smiled at her, trying to look happy she was back. "How was Amsterdam? You want a cup of tea?"

She shook her head. "Amsterdam was amazing! All the old buildings and the canals and all those quaint little cafés. It's so different from Brussels too; it's hard to imagine it's only three hours away by train. The train was nice as well, very luxurious."

He let her rave on about how amazing everything had been and how Maria had shown her so many things, like the Van Gogh Museum and the Rijksmuseum. Lucas felt his mind drift off, thinking about how wonderful his weekend had been and how he could never tell her about it.

"And we walked into this coffee shop and they were smoking pot, right in front of us, well in front of everyone really. After sitting there for a while, I swear the air was so thick, we were both high by the time we walked out."

"They're more tolerant of soft drugs in The Netherlands," Lucas mentioned absent-mindedly to show he was listening.

"I know but this was just…oh well. How was your weekend?"

"Fine," Lucas answered trying to sound bored.

She moved closer again, seductively wrapping her arms around his neck. "Poor baby, you look really tired. I hope he didn't work you too hard, honey?"

"Yeah, well, you know how it goes." Lucas tried hard not to lie to her outright. He felt like telling her the truth though. *Actually, Lucy, he did work me hard. Right into the mattress. We fucked in the bathroom and on the sofa in front of the open window. He made me scream his name and I get hard just thinking about him.* But there was no way he could hurt her like that.

She leaned in to kiss him, but he turned his head, so her lips ended up over his temple. "Why don't you take your cup of tea, pop a movie in the DVD and settle on the couch. I'll get the laundry together and we can order pizza or something tonight, okay?"

She was sweet really, he knew that and she loved him, so he smiled at her and kissed her on the forehead. "Thanks, Lucy. That sounds great, but I'll help with the laundry if you like."

"Don't be silly. You work a lot harder than me. Just relax and I'll take care of everything." She rubbed her hand over his chest and then moved to the hallway where their weekend bags were sitting.

Five minutes after Lucas started watching the movie he had chosen, he was sound asleep on the couch.

LUCY smiled as she heard his familiar slow, shallow breathing and closed the curtain of the sitting room window to darken it. Maybe she could do this. She liked taking care of Lucas, and if Maria could do it, so could she. The Christensens were definitely a good example. She was going to take Maria up on her offer and do some charity work while she was studying. That way she wouldn't feel so lonely sitting at home waiting for Lucas to come back and she would meet lots of new people, get to know this country a bit more. If nothing else, it would look good on her résumé and it would help her become more comfortable around people she didn't know. She admired Maria and her way of always looking beautiful and confident in every conceivable situation. Nothing could faze that woman.

As she was sorting the laundry she noticed three buttons missing on one of Lucas's fine shirts. They usually came with one extra button, but three missing buttons was a bit much. She made a mental note to check the other shirts to see whether there were any loose threads on those, too. It was probably a manufacturing flaw.

After turning on the washing machine, she started unpacking their toiletries, putting their toothbrushes together again in the little green cup on the rack over the backroom sink and placing his razor and shaving cream behind the mirror. Neither of them had taken a lot of stuff on their weekend outing, but she checked all the side pockets of their bags anyway.

MARIA walked in, closely followed by the driver who was wheeling in her suitcase.

"Will that be all, Ma'am?"

"Yes, thank you, Paul." She tipped the man and then walked over to Jack who was sitting at the kitchen counter reading the Sunday Times.

"Hey, stranger." She put her arm around Jack's shoulder and as he looked up, she quickly kissed him on the mouth. "Did you miss me?"

"Naah," Jack answered, her hand still on his cheek as he demonstratively returned to reading his newspaper.

"Oh well, I guess you don't want your present then, either." She walked away in the general direction of her suitcase and threw him a teasing look as she picked up her bags and walked towards the hallway.

Jack felt guilty all over again. He had been screwing around behind her back while she was away for two nights and she even bought him a present. For a moment, he wished he could turn back the time, but then he thought of Lucas and the feelings the young Brit conjured up in him. He let his face rest on his palms, remembering how he and Lucas had made love last night. It hadn't been just sex anymore. It was much more beautiful than just indulging their lust for each other; they had taken plenty of time discovering each other's bodies. He could still feel the beautifully toned chest and shoulders under his hands, the dark nipples hardening as he thumbed them. He could still taste Lucas's skin. How could he even contemplate giving all that up? How could he turn away from the one person who had made him feel alive for the first time in... for the first time ever?

"You work too hard, Jack."

Jack jumped as Maria's voice in his ear shook him out of his reverie. He hadn't noticed her returning to the room.

SHE had noticed how tired he looked when she walked in. It looked like he had barely slept since Friday and she made a mental note to pamper him tonight, since tomorrow was the start of what no doubt was going to be another busy working week. She knew her husband was a workaholic and he was even worse when she wasn't around. It was endearing, she supposed, how Jack would always bury himself in work. He really needed a hobby.

After she had come down the stairs again, the present she had bought him under her arm, she had decided to order some food to be brought in. Then she would challenge him to a game of Scrabble tonight, and try to get his mind off work.

She had slipped into jeans and a T-shirt upstairs and was barefoot, so Jack didn't hear her come in. His face was in his hands. Beating him at their favorite word game would be a cinch!

"You work too hard, Jack."

Jack looked up at Maria. "Hey."

After gathering his thoughts momentarily, he looked behind her back at the tubular package she was holding. "Can I see it?"

"Uh huh." She shook her head, turning it away from him.

"You're a tease, Maria Francesca!" He used her full name when teasing her, knowing full well it worked every time.

She pursed her lips, "Yes, I am." She held out the poster tube, just beyond his reach. "You know you like it."

Jack waited for a moment, then lunged forward and grabbed the tube before Maria could pull it away. "Gotcha!"

He shook it teasingly before opening it and rolling out two posters. As he let them fall open on the counter he hummed appreciatively, "Dali and Miró."

She came in closer. "I know how much you like the Dali, but I think that drab office of yours needs some upbeat art, so perhaps the Miró's a bit more appropriate."

He looked at her affectionately, "I think the office can take the Dali, too."

She walked around the counter and smiled. "Great! I'll have them framed and brought over to the Embassy, then."

Jack returned to his newspaper. "Thanks, Maria."

She realized he must be very tired, giving up on teasing her so quickly. She looked at him sitting there, a little worried he wasn't sleeping enough, but knowing things would work themselves out. And if they didn't, she was sure Jack would make them turn his way, even though his fatigue was probably caused by a crisis of conscience right now. Maria was smart enough to see that persuading the Belgians to add troops to the post-war clean-up effort went against everything Jack believed in. They had talked about this sort of situation arising before Jack decided to take on the commission and she felt sure Jack would find a way to live with himself while managing to do his job.

She gathered the newspapers and magazines that always seemed to be strewn around any place in the house where Jack chose to start reading and planned out their meal. She would call the small restaurant where they often had dinner and ask for a menu for two to go. One of the drivers could go and pick it up and then they could have a quiet night together.

"EXPLAIN this to me, Lucas!"

Lucas was rudely awakened by Lucy slapping her hand down on the coffee table. She stood in front of him, her arms defiantly crossed and a storm brewing behind her eyes. Tentatively he let his gaze wander to what exactly she had thrown on the table and felt himself wake up fully when he realized she had found the condoms.

"I didn't think we needed those, Lucy," he tried.

She shrugged, then sighed, "I can't believe you. Do you really think I'm stupid? I turn my back for two nights. Just two nights and you go and screw someone else behind my back."

Lucas could tell she was seething. He couldn't believe she found them. They were in his jacket pocket. What was she doing going through his jacket pockets?

"Who is she, Lucas? Do I know her?"

No, but you know him. "Lucy, it's not what it seems...." His voice trailed off as he watched her turn around and head off into the kitchen.

He closed his eyes. If he was completely honest with himself, he wanted her to know, but then she'd ask who it was and the last thing he wanted was for her to find out it was Jack. He couldn't let her find out it was Jack.

Lucas got up and slowly walked into the kitchen, where an unopened pizza box was sitting on the table.

"You ordered pizza," he stated rather sheepishly.

"Don't change the subject." She was looking at the floor, her arms still crossed in front of her. Lucas could feel her eyes on him, her gaze sharp enough to pierce his skin. "I followed you half way across the world, left behind everything I knew to come to this... this... impossible country. And now I find out I can't even trust you enough to leave you to your own devices for two fucking days. You said you had to work, you were going to spend the weekend working with Jack and...."

She was breathing heavily as she stopped mid-sentence and Lucas could see her mind working. He tried to look neutral, tried not to show his fear, but he just knew she was putting two and two together. And no matter what, that couldn't happen; she couldn't find out about Jack. He was going to have to lie outright to her.

"Please tell me it's not... Oh Lucas, please tell me you didn't... you and him... you corrupted him? He's a married man, Lucas, and you seduced him, didn't you?" Her rage turned into something else. Something he couldn't quite put his finger on. Was it pity? Disgust?

"No," he answered. "It's not what you think. Don't be so stupid, Lucy."

"I thought it was over, Lucas. I thought you weren't going to fall for men anymore. But you... I saw you with Jack and I saw the way you looked at him. I couldn't believe it... didn't want to believe it, because you were with me, and the boys... the men were all in your past. You told me it was all in your past!"

"Luce, please, you have to believe me. Jack has nothing to do with this." His voice was quiet, strained in an effort to keep himself calm.

"Well, you would cover up for him, wouldn't you? Your precious American Ambassador. I wonder what his perfect wife would think about this. I wonder what would happen if I told Maria what her husband had been up to all weekend."

Lucas regained his composure. If she thought she was going to blackmail him, she had another thing coming. "I don't believe you, Lucy. I must congratulate you on your imagination though. You find some condoms and you immediately assume I'm screwing Jack. Do you know how ridiculous that sounds? You might as well jump to the conclusion that I'm screwing his perfect wife. That's just as likely, Lucy!"

Lucas looked at her, hoping he would see doubt in her face. His breathing steadied as he saw her calm down.

"I was looking for change, for the pizza guy," she said. "He couldn't change a fifty Euro bill... and there they were, Lucas, right next to your wallet. Why would you have them in your pocket? Why would you buy condoms if you didn't intend to use them?"

He put his hand on her arm, but she pulled away.

"It was late and I was tired. I missed you, and, ok, I admit it, I went cruising. But nothing happened, Lucy, I chickened out." He hated lying, but then again, he had been lying for a long time. Not as blatantly as this, but still...

"But you wanted a man again," she sighed and closed her eyes for a moment. "Why, Lucas? Why was I not good enough for you any more? Why now?"

She brushed passed Lucas on her way out of the kitchen. He could hear her opening drawers and doors in their bedroom, so he followed her.

"Lucy? What are you doing?"

She closed the bag she was stuffing and tried to get past Lucas, but he blocked her way. "If you believe for one second I'm sharing a bed with you ever again. Now please step aside."

"Luce…"

"You're… you're disgusting, my father was right all along. Just stay away from me, you make me sick!"

Lucas took a step back, letting her pass.

"I'll collect the rest of my things tomorrow when you're at work."

"Where are you going, Lucy?" Lucas asked, surprisingly calm.

Lucy narrowed her eyes as she looked at him. "As if you care."

He heard the front door slam shut and let himself drop to the bed. He ran his hands through his hair and recalled each word she had said. He knew she wasn't coming back. She looked timid, but he knew she was one determined woman, something she had proven at the beginning of their relationship by accompanying him here.

So much bad could come from this, but he was really only afraid of one thing. That Lucy would call her new friend Maria.

He had to get in touch with Jack, at least give him some advance warning.

Chapter Thirteen

"SHE knows, Jack."

Shit.

Jack heard Lucas sigh on the other end of the telephone line.

"Are you okay?" Jack didn't know how to react. "Is she still there?"

"She just left, doors slamming and everything. You can imagine, she was pretty pissed off."

"How…?" Jack was testing the water, to see how Lucas was really feeling about this.

"She found the condoms. I didn't tell her anything, Jack… but she came up with your name pretty quickly and I'm afraid she'll tell Maria." Lucas sounded calm but also uneasy, a little scared and worried, nothing like the confident young man Jack had always seen.

Now it was Jack's turn to sigh. "How exactly did my name come up? I mean, she was guessing, right?" He remembered Lucas's remark that people couldn't tell they were together just from looking at them. Maybe Lucy was smarter than he gave her credit for.

"She knows me, Jack. She knew I'd had male lovers before she came along. I didn't get the chance to ask for details, because I denied it."

"Good," Jack was quick to answer. Too quick. He frowned, mentally kicking himself. "I didn't mean that. I mean…maybe she believed you and she won't say anything to Maria."

Lucas stayed surprisingly calm, clearly recovering his usual form. "Yeah, that's what I thought. I just wanted you to be prepared in case she does go crying on your wife's shoulder." And then after a bit of silence, "I'm sorry, Jack."

This was a complication Jack didn't care for, but he couldn't say that. He spoke again. "Don't be. Who knows? Lucy might be back tomorrow, once she's calmed down and realizes just how irresistible you are."

"That's not funny, Jack."

"Well, she might. You said you thought she believed you, so there's hope."

"Hope for what, Jack? You sound like you actually want me to continue this charade with Lucy. Besides, I know her, she doesn't back out of a decision. In fact, that's what I liked about her. She's gone, Jack, I just... I just wanted you to know. Be prepared."

If Lucy was really determined to leave Lucas, the chance that she would tell Maria was considerable and that worried Jack. That stupid little girl could ruin not only his marriage, but also his career. As soon as the thought crossed his mind, he knew it was unfair to blame Lucy for his decisions; but he had to do something. He wasn't the type of man to sit and wait.

"Listen, I think I can get away, why don't I drop by your apartment tonight? We need to talk and that's easier done face to face."

"No," Lucas answered decidedly. "I don't know where Lucy went. Just in case she does call Maria for some reason, it will look suspicious if you suddenly have something urgent to attend to after my girlfriend leaves me. I'm fine, really. We'll talk tomorrow, okay?"

Jack heard the click on the other side of the line and put the phone down. He was sitting in his home office, where he had retreated after hearing Lucas's voice. Lucy leaving complicated things considerably. Rumors spread quickly through the diplomatic community. They would have to be even more careful than before.

He rested his face in his hands.

As he saw it, there were a couple of things Lucy could do and he didn't like either of them. The most likely course of action was for her to call Maria and ask her for advice. The women had become close friends, so that would be a logical step. He knew women, there would be tears and eventually Lucy would let spill that she suspected Lucas was having an affair and that the other woman was actually a man. Maria's man.

The other thing Lucy could do was expose them.

Starting a rumor was easy. It would just take one well-placed comment to certain people that she had left Lucas because he was more than chummy with the U.S. Ambassador. Jack knew denying the rumor would only make it worse, and he would need Maria by his side to show people it was all a hoax. Knowing Maria, he would have to convince her it was all a lie or she might not be prepared to show her support.

Jack realized he didn't know how his wife would react, though. Maria wasn't the emotional kind, but she might feel hurt, and she could be fairly ruthless, so revenge would be sweet, at least for her.

Damn. Was it all worth it? He loved his job; he wasn't prepared to lose it over a fling. What did he feel for Lucas? Did he love him? Or was it just lust? Comparing what he felt for Lucas to what he felt for Maria was like comparing apples and oranges. It was love in both cases, but for Lucas, it was all consuming, passionate and mind-boggling, while his love for Maria was comfortable, reliable and calculated. Which type of love would still be there in ten years' time? Did he see himself still loving Lucas then? Would their love survive two wasted careers? What if this caused his professional downfall? Would he hold it against Lucas?

Jack scratched his head with both hands, trying to get his mind in order. Lucas didn't want to see him. Maybe it was for the best. Maybe they should lay low for a while. It would certainly help him to get his mind in order.

THE rest of the week was spent at the usual frenzied pace, running from one meeting to the next, showing his face at various trade conferences, International Schools, and in the committee that was preparing the gay marriage bill. Jack was glad he had so much to occupy his mind. Usually he didn't go to these meetings alone; there was always someone from his Embassy staff accompanying him, if not to brief him on the way, then to introduce him to their negotiating partners.

Nights were another thing, though. Even though he was trying hard not to think about Lucas, he found himself avoiding Maria. They had never had the most prolific sex life, but now he was making excuses not to be in the bedroom with her when she was going to bed. If he couldn't avoid her, he pretended to be asleep. He kept telling himself to just get it over with and screw her again, dispel any doubts she might have. As it was now, if she knew or even suspected something, this avoidance would make him look even more guilty.

Only he couldn't. He would sometimes look at her when she had her back to him, in moments when he knew she wouldn't notice but no matter how hard he tried, he couldn't conjure up any feelings of lust. When he was alone, it was easy, his mind would naturally drift to Lucas and he would feel himself grow hard. He just had to picture Lucas's lust soaked eyes and how dark they would grow when gazing into his and he would have a hard time not touching himself.

By Thursday, he couldn't hold back anymore. They hadn't spoken since Sunday night and Jack hated leaving things hanging, so he picked up the phone to call. In the middle of dialing Lucas's work number, he stopped. They couldn't talk about this on the phone; this was about them, their relationship. This was about the decision whether what they had was worth being called a relationship or whether it was just a good fuck. Instead of calling, Jack decided that he would pay Lucas a visit that evening after work.

It took him some persuasion to make Mark, his ever conscientious Secret Service man, understand that Jack could drive home without surveillance and that there was no need to call the men at the house to give them an ETA. He couldn't go into details, of course, but finally agreed that he would call in to say he was okay.

He had dropped Lucas off on Sunday, but hadn't actually been inside the apartment. He found his way there and ran up the three flights of stairs, pausing in front of the door, more than slightly out of breath. As he reached for the doorbell, he could see the names on the sticker above it: 'Lucas Carlton – ~~Lucy Marsh~~' – and smiled. That answered his first question.

He wasn't sure how Lucas was going to react, though. What if Lucas was angry with him? Jack had left him to his own devices for four days and anything might have happened, including Lucas deciding it just wasn't worth it.

Jack turned around, chickening out, scared of what was behind the door. He paced the small hallway trying to make up his mind and had his back to the door when it opened.

"Will you stop wearing out the tiles and come inside?" Lucas was keeping his voice down and Jack thought he looked amazing in his faded red T-shirt and camel cargo pants.

Jack tried to read his face, to see if he was in a bad mood or if he was mad at him, but Lucas's eyes were warm and inviting and a small smile was playing on his lips.

"Come in before the neighbors start talking. It's bad enough that they keep asking me where Lucy is." Lucas reached out and grabbed his arm, pulling him inside and closing the door behind him.

"Why are you here?" Lucas asked, his voice soft, free from any hint of accusation.

"How did you know I was out there in the hall?" Jack asked, eyeing Lucas suspiciously.

The young Brit smiled, alternately looking at Jack and checking out a spot on the floor behind him. "The door has one of those..." he waved his finger at the door, "spy holes? And I heard footsteps, so..."

"We need to talk, Luke."

"Yeah, I guess we do."

"Has Lucy really gone?"

"She's gone."

Lucas looked Jack straight in the eye.

"Did she say anything about telling Maria?"

"I don't think so."

They stood there, looking at one another, both of them wondering how the other was feeling, searching for a clue in one another's eyes, but it was Jack who made the first move, suddenly stepping towards Lucas, seizing the young man's head in his hands and kissing him passionately.

Lucas gasped with surprise even as he eagerly answered the kiss, opening his mouth to invite Jack in, hungrily sucking and biting the American's lips.

It felt wonderful to have his lover's arms wrapped around him and Jack turned with Lucas in his arms and pushed him against the door, kissing him with even more determination now he had a firm surface to press against. He needed to come up for air, but he didn't want to lose the contact that sent shivers of desire running through his body, so he let his mouth trail along the young man's jaw and neck.

Lucas tried to get Jack out of his coat, smiling at the hunger in Jack's seduction.

After shedding the jacket, Jack ripped his tie off, letting it land wherever gravity took it, and placed his hands against the door on either side of Lucas's head. He pushed against Lucas, grinding into him with his whole body until the Brit moaned against his mouth. They had only been apart for four days, but it already felt like coming home after years apart. How he could ever have imagined giving this up was beyond him.

Lucas pulled Jack's shirt up, running soft firm hands over Jack's skin. Jack squeezed his hand between their already close bodies, popping the button on his trousers. As Lucas's hands trailed down his back to cup his ass underneath his clothes, he knew exactly what he wanted.

Jack raised his head slightly.

"I want..."

He nipped at Lucas's bottom lip,

"To feel you…"

He pulled the swollen lip with his teeth making Lucas moan.

"Inside me."

Jack's voice was husky and as he pushed away from his young lover, he saw Lucas's smile, those swollen lips and delicious dark eyes and he knew he would get what he wanted.

"It's about time," Lucas answered quietly, squeezing Jack's cheeks to pull his crotch closer.

"Bedroom?"

Lucas shook his head slowly. "That's not a good room." He pushed himself away from the door, driving Jack backwards, and turned away to escape Jack's groping hands.

"Where are you going?" Jack asked, not letting him get away that easily, "Don't go."

Lucas kissed him again and moaned as he pulled away "So needy… hold that thought."

He disappeared into the bedroom and returned almost immediately. "Now I'm all yours, for as long as you want me."

"What," Jack murmured, but was cut off when Lucas attacked his mouth again. He was guided towards the couch and realized what Lucas's little excursion to the bedroom had been about when he heard the crisp sound of a condom wrapper. They tripped over each other and the furniture, almost falling on the way there, because they were trying to get each other out of their clothes without stopping the touching and kissing.

Lucas pushed Jack down onto the couch and stripped him of his trousers and boxers all in one go. As Lucas raised himself again, he let his cargo pants drop, revealing himself to Jack in all his glory. The American couldn't stop himself from leaning forward to capture Lucas's proud erection in his mouth, but Lucas stopped him, dropping to his knees. "Don't," he said softly. "There's only one place I want to come tonight and that's deep inside of you." He kissed Jack tenderly, "Let me take my time and do this properly." Lucas took Jack by the shoulders and gently pushed him back against the cushions. "Just lie back and relax, because you'll be seeing stars by the time I'm finished with you."

Both men caught their breath, looking in each other's eyes as Lucas gripped the back of Jack's knees and pulled him into a slump on the couch. The American panted with anticipation, squeezing his eyes shut for a moment, afraid that looking at Lucas's hungry eyes and wicked smile would make him come right there and then. He had just managed to get control of himself when he felt the heat of his lover's body over his, their leaking cocks rubbing up against one another.

"I need you to relax, Jack," Lucas whispered in his ear. "Breathe through your mouth. Close your eyes. Just let the sensations take you wherever they will. Don't think, just feel. I won't hurt you, I promise."

Jack could only nod as Lucas moved back and squeezed the lube over his fingers. He wanted this so much, he felt like he was going to burst. Lucas had told him to close his eyes, but he wanted to see this. He remembered Lucas's face of utter bliss the first time he had prepared him and he wanted the full sensation.

Jack gasped when his lover took his cock in his mouth, slicking it up with his saliva. He widened his eyes and hoped Lucas would understand this was not helping him to last. Speaking at this time was not an option either, as Lucas released Jack's cock and let a cold slick finger circle his puckered hole.

He reached out his hand, but Lucas pushed it away.

"Don't tease, Luke, please, I need you…"

Lucas eased his finger into the unbreached muscle, stopping at the first knuckle. He was taking his time, not to tease, but to allow Jack to adjust as he slowly opened the ring of muscle and pushed his finger deeper.

"Relax, Jack, you're very tight."

Jack's blurred vision clearly registered the Brit's appreciative smile and he opened his mouth wider, as he felt another finger join the first. It burned a little, but since Lucas was not moving his fingers now, Jack willed himself to relax even more.

"Deeper," he panted, looking straight at Lucas.

The young man chuckled, "If you can still talk, I'm clearly not trying hard enough." He scissored his fingers a little and brushed past a smooth patch inside of Jack, making the American cry out and clamp down his muscles. Lucas leaned forward, not moving his fingers. "Easy, relax, I won't do it again."

"No!" Jack sighed. "Don't… do it again." He was seeing stars already and Lucas wasn't even inside of him yet. At least not how he wanted him inside. He bit his lower lip and welcomed the chill of the lube Lucas added along with a third finger.

"God, Luke, I can't wait… anymore."

"You're almost ready, love," Lucas whispered a little breathlessly. He tried not to brush over Jack's prostate again, fearing it might really send the American over this time, but he felt Jack relax so he slowly removed his fingers. He fiddled under the pillow to find the condom he had slipped under there and quickly took off the wrapper. He was still hard and aching for stimulation, stroking himself a few times before rolling on the condom.

"God, you look hot touching yourself."

Jack watched him hungrily, impatiently, so Lucas smiled. "I want to be nice and hard for you, love." He squeezed a generous dollop of gel into his hand and lubed up his erection, pouting his lips at Jack teasingly before leaning over and kissing him hungrily.

"Are you ready?"

Jack nodded, opening his mouth again slightly. He grabbed the back of the couch to brace himself as he felt the tip of Lucas's cock breach his hole. The burn increased and he tried not to resist it, as Lucas slid into him ever so slowly.

Lucas was breathing heavily on Jack's neck, trying to hold himself back. "Fuck, Jack, you're so tight." What he really needed was to thrust inside his lover, but he knew that would hurt Jack and that was the last thing Lucas wanted, so he waited, one hand on the back of the couch next to Jack's head and the other gently stroking his lover's chest.

"Tell me when you're ready," Lucas asked softly.

"Go!" Jack answered, his voice strained. "Just... move gently."

Lucas did just that. He rocked back and forth slowly, watching his lover's reaction and taking his cues from the involuntary moaning that came from deep inside Jack.

The American was growing accustomed to being filled and as Lucas leaned in to kiss him, Jack spurred his lover on. "Harder, Luke, please. I want more."

This was all the encouragement Lucas needed and as Jack lifted his knees instinctively, changing the angle of the thrusts, the pitch of his moans changed. Lucas pulled out almost all the way every time, only to plunge back deeply, creating slapping skin-to-skin noises. They were both breathing heavily, close to climaxing.

"Come... with me... Luke," Jack cried out, arching his back away from the couch, his eyes open wide.

Lucas found his lover's gaze and saw the ecstasy flood Jack's face as he felt his own groin tighten, signaling the point of no return. As Lucas rode out his orgasm, he continued to thrust deep inside Jack, until he felt his lover tighten around him and hot sticky fluid sprayed between their bellies. When he finally collapsed onto Jack's limp body, he felt how the man still shuddered in reaction to his climax. He also realized their fingers had somehow become entwined and their lips were almost touching, just like the first time he had made Jack come in their Antwerp hotel room. As he remembered, Lucas let his lips ghost over Jack's cheek and tasted the salt of tears. He untangled one of his hands and wiped the wetness away. "Are you okay?"

Jack took his time answering, languidly opening his eyes. "I love you, Lucas. Why wouldn't I be okay?"

AFTER getting cleaned up, both men ended up on the couch again, unable to get enough of touching each other and slowly letting reality creep back in.

Jack had taken a moment to call Mark as he had promised in return for this private time away from everything. He was told that Mark had covered for him with Maria, giving her the message Jack was in a meeting that was expected to last a good few hours.

"So you trust Mark to keep our secret?" Lucas asked, a little uneasy.

"Mark doesn't know the finer details. I just told him I needed some time away and I couldn't tell him where I would be."

"Yeah, but your Secret Service guys are pretty thorough. He probably followed you here, just to make sure you're okay, and who says he's not sitting in his car outside of this apartment block waiting until you come out?"

"You're being paranoid, Luke," Jack answered softly, but deep inside he knew his lover might well be right. Mark probably knew something was up. Jack and Lucas could only hope that Mark was also good at keeping the information to himself.

Lucas lay on his side, his back against the couch and Jack in his arms, spooning him. They were still naked, but the sultry city heat was only just dissipating so they were warm enough just staying close together.

Jack tilted his head back a little. "We need to talk, Lucas. We need to face reality."

He heard his young lover sigh and felt the Brit's warm lips on the back of his shoulder. "I know. It's just... I like our own little reality here and if we talk, we let the whole bad world into it."

Jack smiled. "I know. We can still have this, Lucas, our own little reality, just for you and me." He put his hands over Lucas's and pulled the young man's arms tighter around his body. "But I think we both need to know where we stand."

Jack felt Lucas nod and kiss his neck again. "I love you, too, Jack."

The American sighed. "I need time to tell Maria, Luke. I can't just spring this on her. She has as much invested in my career as I do and if this all blows up in my face, she needs alternatives as well. I owe her that much."

"I don't want you to give up your career, Jack. I know how much this means to you! We can wait it out, see where this gets us."

Jack turned onto his back, wanting to see his lover's expression. "You mean keep hiding, keep sneaking around like this?"

Lucas leaned forward until his forehead touched Jack's. "If we come out, we won't have careers, Jack. Neither of us. I don't know about you, but I don't know what I would do if I wasn't in this line of work."

Jack brushed a curl away from Lucas's brow and placed a kiss on the young man's forehead. "I don't intend to keep this charade up forever, Luke. I want you to know that."

"I know." Lucas smiled at Jack. "Now you'd better get dressed and go home."

"Sick of me already, hey?" Jack teased.

"Yeah, old man. Go back to your wife. Before she catches on."

Just for a moment, Jack wondered if there was any truth in the statement, but Lucas couldn't hold the serious look for long and burst out laughing. Then his face turned serious again, but this time it was a softer look. "We'll be all right, Jack. Something will turn up, some opportunity that will put us somewhere away from the public eye, where it's okay if you don't have the perfect wife."

Jack nodded, knowing full well they were deluding themselves. At least now they had a little more time.

And Lucas had said he loved him.

Chapter Fourteen

AT the height of the European resistance against the war, Lucas was in Jack's office preparing for their Paris meeting with the German, Belgian and French ministers. They had just finished a conference call with the American Ambassadors to France and Germany and they agreed they were ready for the tough negotiations.

Lucas gathered their papers as Jack packed his briefcase full of 'homework'.

"So how late did you tell Maria we would be working tonight?" Lucas asked, not entirely without an ulterior motive.

"Eight-ish," Jack answered, a smile curling his lips.

"That gives us…" Lucas checked his watch, "about two hours."

"Yeah," Jack answered, eyeing his lover's lean frame. "Two hours."

Both men were startled out of their reverie when a Secret Service man burst into the office.

"Mr. Ambassador? The Embassy is in lock-down," the man glanced at Lucas. "Mr. Carlton? I'm afraid we can't let you leave either, you'd best call anyone who needs to know. We might be here for a while."

"What happened, Mark?" Jack asked, genuinely concerned.

"Bomb threat, sir. The tunnels have been cleared for about a kilometer on either side of the suspect vehicle. No traffic is allowed in a two kilometer radius."

"They've blocked all the roads, too?"

"Yes, sir. Could I ask you and Mr. Carlton to remain in your office for the time being? It would make the head count easier, sir. And please stay away from the windows."

Jack looked over at Lucas and sighed. "Very well, there isn't much else we can do anyway, I suppose? How close is this car?"

"You can probably see it from here, sir, at the exit of the tunnel."

It was the first time Lucas could recall hearing a less than professional tone in the Secret Service man's voice. Clearly the threat was a serious one.

"I'll leave you now, sir. I have the rest of the floor to cover as well. If there is anything you need, you know where to find me." With that, the Secret Service man left the office.

Jack and Lucas looked at each other from across the room, unsure of what to do next. Lucas walked over to the window to look at the car.

"Lucas! Mark said stay away from the windows. If that thing detonates, there won't be a pane of glass left whole in the building."

The tension in the room was palpable and Lucas laughed nervously as he walked away from the windows and over to Jack. "I must say you sure pick your Secret Service men. So what do I need to do around here to be manhandled by Mark?"

Jack was a little startled by Lucas's question, but quickly recovered and grabbed the young Brit by the wrist, spinning him around instantly. While Lucas was getting over his surprise, Jack used his body to push him face first into the intricately carved door.

Lucas realized he couldn't move, not even when Jack freed one of his hands so he could lock the door. "Hey, some self defense training they give you ambassadors!"

"Well, you wanted to be manhandled," Jack whispered in his ear. "I just don't think Mark should have the pleasure."

"Oooh, Jack," Lucas teased in a high-pitched voice, a little unsure of what was happening as he was still rather tightly pushed against the door, but willing to go along. This was quite a difference from Jack's usual gentle and more passive nature, but Lucas's body was reacting to his situation.

Suddenly Lucas felt his jacket being pulled off his shoulders to just above his elbows, making it even harder for him to move his arms. Jack pulled him away from the door with one hand on his neck and another holding his hands pinned to his back, marching him over to the desk.

Jack was rough with him and Lucas could feel the blood rushing to his cock as he was pushed against the front of the desk. Jack let go of his neck to push some of the paraphernalia on the top of the desk aside, sending papers twirling down the sides. Lucas also caught Jack placing the standard 'family photo' face down before returning the hand to his neck to push him down.

They were both breathing audibly now as Jack pulled Lucas's hips away from the edge of the desk and fumbled in one trouser pocket, then the next. Lucas knew what Jack was looking for and decided to be helpful. "Briefcase, calculator pocket," he mumbled.

"Stay put," Jack ordered, his voice a little rough, as he went to get Lucas's briefcase.

Lucas was not about to budge. He even kept his hands behind his back.

In no time, Jack was behind Lucas again. He placed the condom and lube right in front of Lucas's face as he unbuttoned the young man's trousers and tugged them down, not bothering to pull any further when they caught on Lucas's spread legs.

The Brit could feel Jack's hard-on grinding against his arse as the packet of lube was opened. He was going to get fucked, hard, over the Ambassador's solid oak desk, while a madman was trying to blow up a car outside. Welcome to the Diplomatic Service!

Lucas inhaled sharply when the cold lube was smeared against his guardian muscle. Almost immediately a finger entered. "Go on, I can take another one, Jack," Lucas moaned, breathing through his open mouth in an effort to stay as relaxed as possible. "God, I want you inside me, Jack."

Suddenly, a knock at the door. Then another, more urgent than the first. "Mr. Ambassador?"

Mark's voice. He was attempting to open the door.

Lucas closed his eyes and pursed his lips. Thank God Jack had the foresight to lock it.

The knocking stopped. They could hear the muffled voices behind the door. "Did they leave?" "No sir, I was at my desk the whole time.

They're probably totally focused on their discussions as usual. I swear that man goes completely deaf when he's working."

Lucas was afraid Jack was going to stop, but then he felt the fingers scissoring inside him and he opened his mouth again to breathe.

Jack leaned over to whisper in his ear. "If you want me to stop, I will."

"Hell no!" Lucas answered, probably a bit too loudly. Realizing this he whispered, "I'm ready Jack, I can take it."

Jack unzipped his pants and took the condom and what remained of the lube package from the desk. Then right after he shoved Lucas's boxers under his buttocks, Jack entered him in one hard stroke.

They were both breathing hard; Lucas trying to accommodate the sharp burning feeling and Jack trying not to move to give his lover time to adjust.

Then the phone rang.

"Fuck," Jack muttered.

"Hell yes!" was all Lucas managed to say. The burning feeling was subsiding and Lucas wanted Jack to start moving. Arching his back a bit, he pushed his buttocks back suggestively.

Jack got the message and started thrusting. "Ignore... it."

"I... was... going... to." Lucas answered, his voice a little strained. Jack was dishing out some hard thrusts and, Jeez, it was good. He could barely move underneath Jack and the edge of the desk dug into his hipbones, but he didn't care.

Jack let go of one of his wrists and Lucas managed to free his hand and grab the desk, knocking over a container of pencils and nearly sending the lamp crashing to the floor.

The phone was still ringing and they heard Mark's voice shouting once again on the other side of the door.

"Wait just a minute... I'm coming!" Jack answered, his voice tense.

Lucas knew he wasn't going to last long. Jack was hitting all the right spots and his own bone hard cock was caught between his belly and the smoothly varnished desktop. His aching length was receiving ample friction, but it was only going to be a matter of time before the Secret Service agent would manage to open the door.

A ring of the phone, an incessant knock on the door, a thrust from Jack's cock hitting his prostate, while the American was still holding one of his hands behind his back. Lucas was so close.

"Come for me, Lucas, come, baby," Jack moaned in his ear.

"God, yes!"

Jack's movements became more urgent and less coordinated at the same time Lucas felt his belly grow tight. When he felt Jack's release accompanied by a low groan, it pushed him over the edge too, and he climaxed, stifling a cry as his legs gave way. Jack's breath was warm against his neck and the American's weight felt good against his back.

As he grew limp underneath Jack, he pulled his arm from between them and realized his shoulders were going to be sore in the morning. A small price to pay for so much pleasure.

The phone stopped ringing.

"Thank God for that," Jack murmured as he pushed himself up.

The American walked around to the other side of the desk, still not altogether steady on his feet and popped a box of tissues on the table in front of Lucas. "We have to look presentable when they burst in here," he stated apologetically, still a little breathless as he dropped into his chair.

Lucas smiled up at Jack and hoped his shirt had been more or less out of the way of his release. As he pushed himself away from the surface of the desk, he could tell from Jack's face his hopes were in vain.

"It's a good thing you do your own laundry now, Luke," Jack chuckled as Lucas started wiping himself with a tissue.

The desk hadn't entirely escaped unscathed either, and Jack gave it a wipe while Lucas tucked his shirt into his pants.

"So how do we look?" Lucas asked as he adjusted his tie.

Jack got up from the desk and grabbed Lucas so he could give him a passionate kiss. "Totally fuckable." He smiled as he let go and walked over to the door. "I'm going to let Mark in, okay?"

Mark was right there when Jack opened the door.

"Everything okay?" Jack asked in his most professional voice.

Mark's face showed he was a little unsure of exactly how to answer that question. "DOVO has sent a message to tell us the bomb was defused, sir. The lock-down is called off...with your permission, of course, sir."

Both men watched Mark look around the room suspiciously.

"Will that be all, Mark?" Jack asked one hand still on the door.

"Yes, sir," Mark said reluctantly, but he didn't move from his spot.

Lucas could tell the Secret Service man didn't entirely trust the situation, so he tossed him a question.

"Are we allowed to leave the office now?"

"Yes, sir."

"Very well. Thank you for taking charge and staying on top of the situation. Wonderful job!" Jack stated, closing the door in Mark's face.

Lucas moved behind him and tucked the back of Jack's shirt in. "I'm glad you didn't turn around."

Jack turned and smiled at Lucas. "I thought he was never going to leave."

"He was only doing his job," Lucas teased.

"I bet he's wondering why it's me that gets to fuck you over a desk and not him," Jack shot back.

"Oh gosh, I hope not!" Lucas answered. "Do you think he...knows?"

Jack's face turned serious now too. "I can only hope his imagination doesn't stretch that far."

"Well, they might have heard the moaning."

Jack looked slightly worried. "I think we can trust Mark and Mrs. Claessens to keep that to themselves."

Lucas pursed his lips. "I think your secretary is on our side, but I'm not so sure about Mark. Of course I don't know him the way you do."

Jack quickly kissed his lover. "Don't worry so much." He traced the lines on Lucas's forehead. "You're cuter when you smile."

Chapter Fifteen

ON an occasion where several U.S. Ambassadors would be meeting together, the host Embassy would usually provide them with accommodation. However, this time the Paris Embassy was undergoing extensive renovations, so the guests were kindly offered hotel rooms.

As Jack and Lucas compared keycards on the way to their respective rooms, they realized they were not only located on the same floor, but also seemed to be in adjoining rooms. As they entered their suites, it got even better when they noticed the connecting door.

"This can only be Gertje's doing, right?" Lucas asked.

"Well, I don't see the embassy personnel here coming up with the idea to let the Ambassador and the U.K. representative practically share a room. I'm sure she called the hotel in her perfect French as soon as she found out where they were going to put us, just to relay 'her' Ambassador's precise needs. Too bad we'll hardly be here." Jack obviously regretted that this was going to be a working weekend.

Lucas noticed Jack looked tired and worn out. After he hung up his spare suit and shirts, he walked over to Jack's room in time to catch him popping two little white pills in his mouth and swallowing them dry.

"You should really drink something with those, Jack," he offered as he walked over to the mini bar and grabbed a bottle of Evian. "You're not feeling well?"

Jack shrugged. "Just tired, I guess. Might be coming down with a cold or something. I have the mother of all headaches."

Lucas moved a little closer and wrapped his arms around his lover. "You could call and ask them to start the informal talks tomorrow morning?"

"Naah, the sooner we get our cards on the table, the easier it will be to talk to the powers-that-be tomorrow afternoon. These talks always take longer than you think and if they do go smoothly, well, we can sleep in tomorrow." Jack gave his young lover a teasing look, but it didn't keep Lucas's worries at bay. There was definitely something wrong and this was certainly not the weekend to get sick.

Within minutes, they were in their work suits and out the door to a car waiting to take them to the U.S. Embassy.

As Jack had predicted, the talks were difficult. Each Ambassador had his own reasons for preferring one tactic over the other to persuade their respective governments to change their minds. At one point, Lucas suggested that maybe they should try talking to their own host countries separately, but this was met by a very clear 'you are too young and inexperienced to understand this' look from four of the people around the table.

When Lucas looked at Jack for support, he saw the American clearly struggling. He was sweaty and pale and his eyes were red and dull.

At one a.m., it was decided that they should all get some rest and resume their talks at nine in the morning. As Jack got up from his chair, Lucas noticed him swaying a bit and he grabbed his arm to keep him steady.

"You okay?" he whispered, a concerned look on his face.

Jack quickly recovered and pulled his arm free as soon as he noticed some of the other ambassadors looking their way. "I'm fine," he croaked, his voice a little thick and unsteady.

Lucas worried all the way back to the hotel and then some more as they walked into Jack's room and the American wouldn't let him stay.

"Go to your own room, Lucas. It's a short night and I'll only keep you awake."

Lucas didn't know how he was going to persuade Jack to let him stay. "I want to take care of you, Jack. Please don't push me away? I'm worried, you're obviously sick."

Lucas's plea was met by a stern gaze from Jack. "Lucas, I'm fine, I just need to sleep, because I feel like my brain is fighting its way out of my skull right now."

Lucas sighed and admitted defeat, but he was not about to give up completely.

He got into his own bed and lay there listening to the sounds in the next room.

Some time later he woke up hearing a low thump and a muffled curse. Lucas didn't want to get up right away but when he heard Jack cough and then the sound of glass breaking, he decided he'd better have a look. He knew better than to turn on any lights, fearing this would aggravate Jack's headache, but he made his way over to the bathroom where he could just discern the American leaning against the side of the door.

"Don't come any closer. There's glass everywhere." Jack's voice sounded low and hoarse.

Lucas stopped in his tracks, realizing he was barefoot. "Is it okay if I turn on some lights then?

A grunt was all he got for an answer, but he backed up anyway and turned on the light in his own room, hoping that it would provide enough visibility without making Jack's headache any worse. He also slipped his shoes on so that he wouldn't cut his feet.

When he looked up he saw Jack still leaning against the doorpost, his eyes pinched shut and his face turned away. He heard the glass shards crackle underneath his shoes as he walked over them.

"Stay there, Jack, I'll get you your shoes."

The American pushed him away. "Just go, Lucas. Just…" he was making pushing gestures with his hands, "…leave me alone."

Lucas, not easily put off, made his voice calm and soothing. "Just let me get you to bed in one piece. I'll clean up the glass and then let you sleep. What were you doing here anyway?"

Jack, his eyes still closed, gave an aggravated sigh. "Getting a fucking drink of water, what does it look like?" He flinched as the loudness of his own voice echoed in the small bathroom.

"Fine, I'll get you a drink of water, but just let me help you get to…"

"Just get the fuck out of here; you're not my fucking wife. I don't need a fucking baby sitter!"

Lucas inhaled deeply, trying to keep his own emotions under control as he moved across the dimly lit room to where Jack's shoes were. Even though he didn't exactly like being compared to Maria, he tried to stay calm, figuring he would be pissed off as well if he were this sick. When he returned to Jack, he cleared his throat before he spoke, so his voice would sound soft but firm. "Listen. Your shoes are right in front of you. I'm sure you are not stubborn enough to walk barefoot across broken glass."

He moved to his own room to get a clean glass and some water and when he got back Jack was sitting on the bed, his head in his hands, but wearing his shoes.

Lucas handed the older man the glass. "Drink up and I'll fill it up again for later."

Jack drank the water greedily, some of it running down the side of his jaw, but he refused to give the glass back.

Lucas frowned at how Jack was acting. "Well, if you want to be an idiot and hurt yourself again when you wake up thirsty in an hour's time, fine, see if I care!"

With that Lucas stormed out of the room, back to his own.

The next morning the connecting door was locked. Lucas slumped back down on his bed and sighed. This was the 'in sickness and in health' bit of the relationship, wasn't it? Maybe this was it with them, maybe this was Jack telling him that he was just a good shag and when shagging was out of the question, that he wasn't needed. Lucas was still worried about the American though, so he got up and knocked on the connecting door.

"Jack? Jack, please let me in?" He sighed when he didn't get an answer. "At least tell me you're awake and you're okay?"

Still no answer.

He thought about forcing open the door, but then realized he was probably overreacting. Jack was most likely already at breakfast downstairs.

He didn't see his lover again until he arrived in the lobby to wait for the driver. Jack looked like he hadn't slept at all and he was suppressing a cough.

"You okay?" Lucas hesitantly offered.

"Yeah, I'll live," Jack stated blankly. The car ride was spent in uncomfortable silence, Lucas wondering what was going on in Jack's head. Was Jack just sick and tired or was he tired of him? Was this affair they were having becoming too much? He decided to leave it be, knowing full well they could only discuss it in the privacy of their room.

The talks with the other ambassadors seemed a little easier this morning, with most of them having had a relatively good night's rest, so they were soon thoroughly prepared for the meeting with the leaders of the countries that resisted joining the Americans and Brits in their 'Alliance'. Lucas was impressed with Jack's resilience. He knew exactly how little the man had slept, how sick he was, but the American was focused and to the point.

As usual the talks weren't conducted with the countries' leaders but with their 'lesser' representatives, the deputy foreign ministers and later the foreign ministers themselves, but progress was non-existent. It kept boiling down to the same thing. America was too pushy, had acted irrationally during the invasion and was now asking for help in restoring peace to a country they had plummeted into turmoil. The representatives of Belgium, France and Germany were not prepared to send troops into a country where the chance of casualties was high to help solve a problem that was, in their eyes, caused by the arrogance of America assuming a role as the police force of the world.

Lucas was already good enough at reading Jack's body language to know that he agreed with that viewpoint and that this was making Jack's job all the more difficult. He also noticed Jack was starting to have problems focusing, but knew better than to intervene. The American's eyes became more bloodshot by the minute and he looked pale and sweaty once more as things finally began to wrap up.

The Belgian Prime Minister, German Bundeskanzler and French President were brought in at the last minute to finalize the talks.

Jack, having the seats of the European Union and NATO in 'his' country, was given the last word on behalf of the ambassadors. His voice was strained and thick, but like the consummate professional he was, he also sounded in control and calm and Lucas wondered if he was the only one who realized just how sick Jack was. The American talked about the necessity of showing a united front, of how these three countries not only weakened the stance of the western nations against the Islamic fundamentalism that was taking over the world, but also weakened the European Union.

It was no use, as was expected.

As Jack got up from the table to shake hands with his counterparts, Lucas could see him flinch but quickly recover. It wasn't until the political leaders had left the room, and it was just the six U.S. Ambassadors and U.K. Foreign Officials again that Jack literally collapsed. Lucas was on the other side of the conference table when he saw the American turn grey. The Ambassador to Germany was quick enough with a chair to prevent him from falling down after Jack knocked against him. "Well, it seems they left just in time," the portly American chuckled. "Christensen here doesn't seem to take defeat very easily," he added to their host.

Lucas was quick to come around the table and squat down in front of Jack, studying his pale face. "Can't you see he's sick? Call a doctor, please." The Ambassador to France raised an eyebrow and called over one of his assistants.

Jack raised his hand. "No, no doctor."

Lucas put his hands on his lover's knees. "Jack, please, you're clearly sick, you need…"

Jack shook his head. "I have a cold, maybe the flu, nothing worse than that. Let's go back to the hotel so I can sleep."

A tall young man with a heavy French accent leaned over the two of them. "Your car will be here shortly, sirs."

Lucas noticed the raised eyebrows and unsure looks in the other men's eyes as he helped Jack up from his chair and put his arm around his shoulder.

ONCE inside the hotel room, Lucas helped Jack out of his suit jacket. As he put his hand on his lover's back he realized Jack's shirt was soaking wet. "Jack, you're burning up, let me help you."

Jack was too exhausted to struggle and let Lucas pull his shirt off him. Lucas pushed the American into the bathroom and wet a washcloth to wipe across his face, shoulders and chest, before pulling him back into the dimly lit hotel room.

"Here, sit down," he whispered and returned a little later with dry boxers and a fresh T-shirt. Before he helped Jack change he offered him a glass of cool water.

"You're not allergic to aspirin, are you?"

Jack didn't reply immediately.

"Love, it's important. It'll help the fever go down and maybe ease the headache too, so you can sleep."

Jack shook his head and smiled faintly. "Aspirin's fine. Thanks."

Lucas handed him two tablets. "Now take these and drink the whole glass. You need to drink, Jack, because judging from your shirt, you've lost a lot more fluids than that glass already."

Jack did as he was told and after handing his empty glass back, wanted to lie down.

Lucas could see from Jack's face that his whole body ached, so he helped him to settle on the bed. As Jack's body touched the fresh sheets, Lucas saw him shiver. He quickly stripped to his boxers and T-shirt as well.

"God, I'm cold," Jack groaned.

"I know, love, hold on, I'm right here." Lucas wrapped the blanket around Jack and got into bed with him, wrapping himself around Jack as well. Slowly the shivering and chattering teeth subsided and Jack's breathing calmed down.

The next morning Lucas woke to the soft sound of a travel alarm. He was on his side, Jack asleep in his arms. The damp washcloth he had moistened over and over again to put on Jack's neck until the painkillers started their work was now discarded on the floor. He smiled at the congested snoring sounds coming from his lover. At least they had gotten a few hours of sleep and Jack didn't feel anywhere near as warm as he had during the night.

Lucas quickly slipped out of the bed and made his way to his own bathroom.

When he got out of the shower, he wrapped a towel around his hips and returned to Jack's room, finding the bed empty.

"Jack? You better?" he asked, still keeping his voice down.

Jack was getting out of the shower as well and Lucas couldn't help dwelling on his lover's lean, muscled body, but his eyes stopped at Jack's dark rimmed eyes.

"Yeah, better. Not great yet." Jack coughed loudly, holding on to the sink.

"Maybe you should call a doctor when you get back home though," Lucas suggested.

Jack shrugged and smiled faintly. "I'll be fine. I feel much better than last night, thanks to you."

Lucas moved closer and put his arm around Jack, but the American pulled away.

After seeing Lucas's confused face, he explained, "Don't want to make you sick as well."

"You slept in my arms, Jack. If you could infect me, I'm sure the damage is done already." Lucas sighed and let his gaze drop to the floor. "Or is it just an excuse? If you want to end this, just tell me. I can take a lot of crap, Jack, but in a relationship... a real relationship, I want honesty. I didn't break up with Lucy to land myself in another delusional liaison."

"It wasn't an excuse, Lucas. I'm sorry I pushed you away. Come here." Jack extended his arm and motioned to Lucas to come closer. "The honesty bit is hard. I told you I needed time to tell Maria."

Lucas moved closer, facing the mirror and let Jack wrap his arms around him. "This isn't about Maria, Jack, it's about us." Lucas's face relaxed a bit as he took in the sight of them, semi-naked, hugging in front of the mirror. "You really look like shit, Jack."

"Yeah, I guess I do, but I feel better than yesterday. Not great yet, but getting there." He coughed to stress the point.

Lucas smiled defiantly back at him in the mirror. "Too bad... I would have enjoyed fucking you in front of this mirror."

Jack smiled too. "Believe me, it's not as much fun as you might think."

Lucas turned around with a teasing look on his face. "You mean, you and... Maria... in front of the mirror?"

Jack nodded shyly, rolling his eyes.

Lucas chuckled. "I always figured she would be a bit of a kinky woman. Now why don't I order us some room service so we can have breakfast here before we go home, lover boy?" He kissed Jack's forehead and gave him a tight hug before leaving the bathroom.

Jack looked at the dark circles around his eyes. Why did he tell Lucas about what he and his wife had done in front of the mirror? And even more strangely, there wasn't any jealousy in Lucas's eyes when they talked about Maria. Did Lucas know she was no competition?

He sighed. His only consolation was that he looked marginally better than he felt.

Chapter Sixteen

LIFE returned to normal after the Paris meeting and Lucas and Jack settled into a routine. They would meet at Jack's office at least once a week to discuss all kind of work related business and managed to keep their passion for after hours, when they would make love at Lucas's apartment before Jack went home to Maria.

Jack hadn't told Maria anything yet, though, and Lucas didn't push the issue. Their professional lives were going well and they were fairly secure in their feelings for each other.

THE American National Security Advisor was scheduled to spend exactly twenty-two hours on Belgian soil to address the European Union, so Maria had been kept busy organizing the social part of the visit. A buffet lunch would be held at the embassy after an official welcome at the airport, requiring Maria to spend several hours a day at the Embassy.

Gertje walked into Jack's office with the security details of the visit for him to sign.

"I'll be glad when this whole visit thing is over," she sighed.

Jack chuckled "So Maria will be out of your hair?"

"What would make you say such a thing?" she asked, feigning innocence.

"You and Maria just rub each other the wrong way. No need to hide it," Jack answered her amusedly.

"Well I don't *have* to like her; I'm not married to her," she teased, "but I won't deny it'll be nice, for both of us, when all this is over again."

She was sorting the papers, which were strewn haphazardly across Jack's desk as usual. "Your calendar is clear for the rest of the day. Would it be okay if I leave a little early tonight? My husband has a doctor's appointment and he wanted me to be there. Annemarie will be here to fill in for me if you need anything."

Jack looked up from what he was signing. "Yeah, sure. In fact I may leave early as well. I don't get the chance very often."

As he returned his gaze to his papers, she smiled at him in a motherly fashion. She knew he wasn't going home to his wife, but since it was none of her business, she knew better than to tell him she knew. She only wished she could be at the office to cover for him like she had done so many times before.

"Well, would you like to go over your calendar for tomorrow now or shall we do it in the morning?" she asked after he gave her the signed papers back.

"Tomorrow's fine, Gertje. Go on and say hi to Eddy for me." He shot her a toothy smile and she gave him an appreciative look back as she left his office and closed the door behind her.

She worried about him. Maria wasn't stupid, and all this sneaking around was bound to come to his wife's attention sooner or later.

JACK had called Lucas to arrange to meet a little earlier, but he was still the first one to arrive. Luckily he had his own key to Lucas's apartment now.

Lucas burst through the door just a few minutes later and they barely made it to the bedroom as Lucas hastily pulled his clothes off while hungrily attacking Jack's mouth. When he realized Jack was less eager, he stopped.

"What's wrong?"

Jack gave him an amused smile. "I was going to say we have all the time in the world tonight. Maria won't be home until around midnight, so we can take it slow."

"Are you telling me I'm wearing you out, old man?" Lucas answered teasingly.

"No, I'm telling you we have time for dinner together, maybe watch a movie…"

Lucas threw Jack a mock disappointed look.

"But since you're practically naked already…" Jack looked teasingly at Lucas, knowing the careful scrutiny would make his young lover nervous, before launching himself at Lucas, wrapping his arms around him and cupping the Brit's ass with his hands, pulling him closer to his growing bulge. "You can have your way with me first."

Lucas didn't waste any time as he grabbed on to Jack, wrapping his legs around the American's hips. The two of them fell onto the bed and they both laughed as the basic Ikea creaked under the onslaught.

"For a moment there I thought we were going to end up on the floor," Lucas admitted.

"Well as long as we don't crash into the downstairs neighbor's room, I don't care where we land."

Jack gently brushed the curls away from Lucas's forehead and the young man stopped chuckling. "God, I love you."

Lucas smiled quietly as Jack shifted his weight so he was completely on top of him.

THE sound of a cell phone woke Lucas. He realized the warm body leaving his arms was Jack getting up to answer the phone, and it dawned on him they had fallen asleep, and that he had no idea what time it was.

They had made love slowly and easily, by now so used to the way their bodies reacted to each other that it was comforting, but by no means dull. Jack treated Lucas to a slow teasing blow job, right up to the point where Lucas thought he wouldn't be able to take any more, and then left him hanging, to crawl up next to him, asking to be fucked. Lucas could never resist Jack when he was that needy, because Jack never failed to give himself completely to the feeling of being possessed by his lover. And Lucas would do absolutely anything to make the American's body shake and shudder from the strength of the orgasm he gave him. They stayed close together afterwards, enjoying the feel of the shivers and the aftershocks, until their melted bodies succumbed to sleep.

Jack lay down beside Lucas again, shaking the young man out of his pleasant reverie.

"Will you marry me?"

Lucas wrinkled his forehead and smiled. "What *are* you talking about?"

Jack looked at Lucas with so much love in his eyes, he knew he could only nod, but he was curious to know what had prompted this sudden question.

"Gertje just called," Jack explained. "It's all over the news. They passed the law, Lucas. All they have to do is publish it and people of the same sex can get married in this country."

"Well, even so, I don't think you can marry me before you divorce Maria."

Jack leaned in to tenderly kiss his young lover. "I know, but... it just felt good to ask you, that's all."

"What time is it?" Lucas asked quietly, bringing them all the way back to earth.

"Time to leave, I'm afraid."

JACK arrived home just before eleven, hoping that would give him plenty of time to shower and crawl into bed, before Maria arrived home from her Women's Club visit to the Ghent Film festival. No such luck, though.

When he walked in he could see the light was on in the library and that could only mean that Maria had come home before him. For a moment he thought he could get away with quietly making his way upstairs, but realized it would only delay the inevitable, so he walked over to where Maria was sitting underneath a reading lamp with a book.

"You're home early." His voice sounded loud in the quiet room.

"And you're late, Mr. Ambassador."

Whenever she used that term, her voice was usually soft and teasing, but that wasn't the case now.

"Yeah, I got held up." He tried to stay vague.

"Meeting?" Maria asked, icy cold.

"Yes, something like that." Jack could sense he was treading on thin ice.

"According to your secretary, you left early today. You should really get your stories straight if you're going to lie to me, Jack." She looked up piercing him with her dark eyes.

"Actually Mrs. Claessens left before me so she wouldn't know, now would she?" Jack tried.

"It wasn't your little adoring fan I talked to, Jack, it was the young girl, Annemarie."

Jack wondered for a moment whether he should just tell her, but she looked angry and upset, and the only way they could have a decent conversation would be if she were calm and relaxed. He would just have to play it by ear.

"She's just a general secretary; she wouldn't know my calendar. You're making a mountain out of a molehill, Maire. I'm tired; I'm going to bed."

"Not so fast, buster. You really think you can keep your pathetic little secret from me, don't you? Don't be ridiculous."

Jack smiled, trying to defuse the situation. "What are you talking about?"

"I know about you and your... your pretty little boyfriend." She narrowed her eyes at him as she spat out that last word. "In fact, I've known for weeks."

Jack raised his eyebrows and gave her a 'what are you rambling about' look.

"I just couldn't believe you'd really be so stupid to jeopardize our lives this way."

Jack knew she wasn't kidding. They were going to play hardball and Maria always played to win, but he wasn't about to deny Lucas.

"I don't see that much has changed in our lives, Maria." He said reasonably. "You still go to your American Women's Club. You're still organizing the social events of the Embassy. You are still the Ambassador's wife."

He could tell she was regaining her cool.

"I've seen you look at other men, I've even wondered..."

"About what?"

"About where you're real interests lay. But I didn't care."

Now she was showing her real colors.

"Of course you didn't care. As long as you got what you wanted out of this relationship, right?"

Maria got up from her chair and leaned on the desk between them. "Because I never thought you'd be prepared to risk everything by screwing around behind my back, Jack. We are a good partnership, what the hell did you think you were doing?"

Jack sighed, trying to gather his thoughts, trying to gather his courage. What would happen if he just told her he loved Lucas? That he could no longer live without him and that they should quietly get a divorce, so she at least could save face?

He could tell she was softening a bit, cocking her head to one side like she always did when she was trying to get him to see things her way. "We've got all we want here, why are you risking it like this?"

He couldn't back down now. "Well maybe *you* have all you want..."

She shrugged and started to look defensive again. "Oh, so I'm not good enough any more? Is that it? After all I've done for your career!"

"Maria, you know it's not like that."

"That's all the thanks I get? My wonderful, dependable ambassador husband is screwing around behind my back, and of all the bloody people he could do it with, he chooses to shag a little rent boy from the British embassy."

"You don't know what you're talking about. He didn't need to persuade me." Jack tried to stay calm and pretend he didn't hear her take a stab at Lucas.

"I won't ask what he's got that I haven't since that's bloody obvious, but Christ, Jack - why now? Why him?" She was mellowing again, her tone less angry. Right now, he hated how well they knew each other. He hated the fact that he could read her like a thermometer and he knew that she could do the same with him.

"I wish I knew, Maire. I wish I knew why. It would make it easier to explain why I've kept those feelings at bay for so long, but now I can't anymore."

"No, you wouldn't know, would you?" Maria spat out, furious at hearing Jack use her nickname during an argument. "If you did, that would mean you were thinking for yourself instead of letting your fucking dick do it for you! YOU SCREW UP OUR LIVES, make me a laughing stock, AND YOU DON'T KNOW?" Maria launched herself at Jack and he grabbed her hands, preventing her from hitting him.

Jack closed his eyes, blindly fending her off, trying to keep himself from lashing out as she had done. He didn't want to lose control of himself.

"Maria, it's... I love him." There it was. Jack hadn't said Lucas's name, but he knew that she knew who he meant. He couldn't deny his love for Lucas, not to her. She deserved the truth from him.

Maria backed off, breathing hard, her hair unraveling from her always neatly tied up bun.

"Love? Don't talk to me about love. You just used me, and this is all the thanks I get?"

Jack inhaled deeply, trying to catch his breath as well. "I used you no more than you used me. My position got you exactly where you wanted to be, Maria."

"So what? In time, you'll find out that your little tramp is just using you too!"

Time to defend Lucas, since Lucas wasn't here to do it himself. "Why would he use me, eh? It's not like he can benefit from this getting out. It's not as if my contacts will help his career, not like they've helped yours, anyway."

"Don't be naïve, Jack. He probably collects Ambassadors like trophies, then moves on to another country, another prime piece of forbidden ass," she said with this superior, mocking look on her face that Jack had always loathed.

"He's not like that, Maire. You don't know him."

"Oh and you do, after a few weeks of letting your dick do the talking? Tell me another one..." She was seething.

Jack realized that if he didn't keep his cool now, they would both end up in the newspapers.

But Maria wasn't backing down yet. "I can't believe you would be this selfish! What has he done to you? If you'd thought of me even once, you wouldn't have done it at all. You're a fool, Jack."

Jack swallowed. "I did think of you. I wanted you to be able to walk away from this with your head held high."

Maria snorted. "Walk away? You can forget that! This stops here and now!"

"Says who?"

"Says me, as usual."

"You can no longer dictate my life the way you've been doing for the past fifteen years, Maria."

Maria threw him a disgusted look. "What?"

"You know what I mean." Jack wasn't about to back down now.

"You mean you're not going to stop this foolery? Oh, for god's sake, Jack, wake up!"

"I can't do it anymore. I can't keep up this charade any longer."

"My point exactly. Get rid of him."

"And what? Return to this lie of a marriage?"

"Jack, it's not a lie; we make a good team, everyone says so…" Maria was turning on the charm again and he so didn't want this.

"We've been more friends than lovers for years, Maire."

She shook her head. "And what's wrong with that? That's more than many couples have."

"I want more. I need more. Maria... I love him; I can't push that away."

"It's an affair, Jack, a stupid affair. It can only ruin us if we let it."

"I've felt more alive with him than I have in the past twenty years."

She laughed. "Oh for Christ's sake, listen to yourself. You sound like a cheap novel."

"Maria, you can move on from this. I'm sure you can have your own career. You have an excellent reputation in the foreign service."

"FUCK OFF, JACK! I don't want to move on, I want what I have here and now. Don't you think for one second I'm going to make this easy for you and your little tramp." She clenched her fists until her knuckles turned white. For a moment he thought she would try and hit him again. "Don't you realize what this will do to us?"

"Not if we handle it right, Maria. Lots of people get divorced."

"You will ruin everything we've worked for. All your successes will be forgotten."

Jack tried to appease her by smiling. "No, they won't, not…"

"All people will remember is the scandal of the Ambassador and his little British boyfriend."

"Not if we handle this carefully."

"Carefully? Not bloody likely, if you think he's getting off scot-free you have another thing coming."

"Leave him out of it, Maria!"

"I'll make sure the right people at the British Embassy hear about this."

"Maria, don't… don't drag his life through the mud as well."

"And I suppose Lucy knew about this?"

"You mean Lucy wasn't the one who told you?"

"No, it wasn't. Lucy disappeared without a word. But you have two people covering up for you, your 'secretary' and your Secret Service agent – only they should learn to get their stories straight."

"Why did you have to drag them into it?"

"Because they think I'm stupid. They think they can pull the wool over my eyes."

"Well, I can assure you, Gertje certainly doesn't think you're stupid."

"Oh, she can't see beyond her wonderful 'Mr. Ambassador'."

This wasn't going anywhere. "Maire, let's talk about this when we're both a little calmer, okay?"

"There's nothing to talk about. You tell lover boy it's over and we get back to work. Otherwise neither of you will be welcome in diplomatic circles ever again by the time I'm finished!"

"Be sensible, Maria. Get out of this gracefully or you won't have a reputation left either."

"Let me know whether you want your little tramp or me. Your reputation is my reputation, you stupid man, and now…" she looked down at her watch "I'm going to bed… alone. I'll see you at breakfast."

"Don't count on it," Jack couldn't help saying.

Chapter Seventeen

IT was way past midnight when Lucas was awakened by the doorbell. There wasn't a single person he could think of who would have the audacity to buzz him at this hour on a work day, unless the building was on fire or something equally dire. He scrounged around in the dark for a pair of trousers and slipped into them half way between the bedroom and the living room.

As he opened the door, he covered his eyes with his hand, shielding them from the glare of the hallway lights.

"Jack, what the…"

"I told her, Luke."

"Well, don't just stand there. Come in! Did she throw you out?" Lucas was rubbing the sleep out of his eyes, trying to make them focus. "You want some tea?"

Jack dropped to the couch and waited until Lucas came back with two steaming cups.

"She was home already when I got there. She said she knew… about us."

Lucas, now fully awake, tried to give his lover an understanding look as he sat down next to him on the couch. "Did Lucy tell her?" His voice was barely audible.

Jack leaned against Lucas, shaking his head as he rested it on the young man's shoulder. "I asked her for a divorce and she said no."

Lucas's heart leapt at hearing Jack's confession. He hated to see his lover this sad, but at the same moment, he was almost jumping for joy over the fact that Jack had so clearly chosen him.

He tried to keep his voice neutral when he spoke. "I'm sure she just needs time to think about it, Jack. Once the night has passed and she realizes she's truly lost you, she'll understand it's better to do this quietly and in some… mutually understanding kind of way. She won't choose to fight about it and make it a big public spectacle." He placed his hand gently on Jack's thigh as Jack curled against him, so he did what his heart urged him to do and wrapped his arms around his lover. They stayed like that for a while, not talking or even looking at each other, just staying close together. Lucas felt Jack relaxing in his arms and started to think he could get used to this. "You can stay here, Jack."

Jack looked up at him. "I need to sort this out, Lucas. I can't let her turn this into a sideshow. So we'll need to lay low for a while. Can we do that?"

Lucas's heart cringed at the intense sadness in Jack's eyes. "Haven't we been discreet all this time?"

Jack moved to kiss Lucas; his eyes closed and Lucas could almost see the tears building up behind his lover's eyelids. "Please give me time and space to solve this, baby?"

Lucas could only nod as Jack left him sitting on the couch. As he heard the front door close, he pulled his knees up and wrapped his arms around them, suddenly feeling the cold.

"THANKS for meeting me here."

A few days after the fight with Maria, Jack had called Sean and invited him for drinks after work. They went to a café in the inner City of Brussels, far enough away from the European district that they wouldn't bump into anyone from the other embassies.

They were both nursing their third beer and had been talking about the old times, when they were still anonymous junior staff members, being sent to whatever embassy needed their particular expertise.

Sean knew that even though he and Jack were old friends, these days time was too precious for both of them to waste it getting plastered in a bar.

"I can't believe you asked me here just to talk about the old days, so shoot; what is it you really wanted to talk about?

"Well, I need your expert advice on something, Sean," Jack sighed. "Something personal."

Sean chuckled and took a swig from the pint. "So you figured, let's ask the guy who's made a total disaster area of his own private life. You're the one who always used to give me advice, remember?"

Jack didn't smile. "I asked Maria for a divorce."

Sean looked up at Jack and the smile left his face as he saw his friend wasn't kidding. "Christ, Jack. I always figured you two were perfectly matched. What happened?"

Jack shrugged. "We were pretty good together, but far from perfect, Sean." He didn't know how much he could tell Sean. Would his old friend understand?

"Well, no marriage is perfect, mate, but you and Maria always made it look so effortless and she is a better diplomatic wife then all three of mine put together." Sean chuckled and then added, more seriously, "What went wrong?"

Jack sighed. He couldn't just blurt it out, no matter how close they were, not everything at once anyway. "I met someone else."

"Come on, Jack," Sean's smile returned. "Is it that redhead that works at reception? She must be quite something if you're willing to leave Mrs. Perfect for her."

"It's not her." Jack got out his wallet to pay for the beers. "Listen, Sean, I was wrong to come here. I'm sorry I wasted your time."

Sean grabbed Jack by the arm as he tried to get up. "I'm sorry. That wasn't very clever of me. Just sit down. You obviously want my advice, and I am clearly saying all the wrong things."

Jack let himself fall to the chair again. "Well, you are the master where foot in mouth insertion is concerned." A brief smile crossed his face.

"One of my many talents." Sean showed his most disarming smile. "So I gather she wasn't amused when you told her there was someone else?"

Jack shook his head, still staring at the table. "She won't give me a divorce."

"She can't stop you now, can she? I know she can't, my first wife tried. Just file for divorce, cite irreconcilable differences and that's it."

Jack looked up at the ceiling and sighed. "She'll drag us through the mud, hang us out to dry. The press will have a field day."

Sean looked directly at Jack, who was still avoiding his eyes. "Us? You and your girlfriend? She'd better get used to the scrutiny if she's going to fill Maria's shoes, Jack."

"Me and him, Sean." Jack looked at last, seeing Sean's face change from amusement to astonishment.

"You're pulling my leg, aren't you?" Sean's astonishment grew as Jack slowly shook his head, "You're serious? Jack! A man? Christ, you really know how to screw up a career, don't you? I mean, are you sure about this? Have you thought of the consequences?"

"Well, if I'd planned it, don't you think I would have done it slightly differently?"

"Yeah, but hell, mate, a bloke? I mean, you've never said anything..."

Jack shrugged. "It's not the kind of thing you just casually tell your best friend, now is it?" Jack grew a bit quieter, more pensive. "After all, I didn't want to lose you as a friend, Sean."

"Forget that, mate, as if it would bother me... but... you've been married for what? Fifteen years? You have the perfect diplomat's wife and a very senior position in the diplomatic service."

"Sounds perfect, doesn't it? Well, it isn't."

"Now all of a sudden you've decided you fancy blokes and you're going to throw away fifteen years of marriage *and* your career for some guy?"

Jack thought Sean's voice was a bit loud so he lowered his own, not wanting to draw attention to them. "It's not all of a sudden and it's not like I *decided* this. Look, Sean, forget it, all right."

"C'mon, you're kidding me, right? Who the hell is it anyway? One of your security guys, makes you feel safe in these nervous times or something?"

"No, it's not a security guy." *He probably thinks I fancy Mark,* Jack realized.

"Hey, maybe that's it? It's a symptom of stress. You're overworked; you need a break."

"Oh, I need a break all right. Forget it, Sean. Stress doesn't make you fancy guys. I've always..." He sighed. "I've always liked men, I just never... acted on it."

"And you choose now? Brilliant timing, mate. And who the fuck is it then? Anyone I know?"

"It doesn't matter who it is, Gallagher."

Sean narrowed his eyes and looked at his friend. "I think it does."

"Why?" Jack realized his voice was steadily increasing in volume and toned it down. "Just to satisfy your curiosity?"

"I know you too well. There's something more here; you're hiding something."

Jack sighed and shook his head. He couldn't very well tell Sean it was Lucas. Sean was Lucas's boss and would probably fire him over this. Perhaps he wouldn't, but he couldn't just come out with it, not without discussing it with Lucas first.

Sean narrowed his eyes. "It's like when you knew that Shannon was seeing that journalist. You tried to tell me, to warn me. Prepare me for the fallout. You've got the same look on your face now."

"Well, I'm sorry, Sean. I can't... Just trust me on this one, okay?"

"Why do I have feeling of déjà vu here, like I'm missing an important point again? At least, I know it's not my bloody wife you're fucking around with."

"That's the Gallagher I know. Brilliant strategist, but always in the dark when it comes to feelings."

"Okay, you've told Maria about this guy, so I guess you're really serious?" Sean looked at his friend sympathetically.

Jack wished he could trust him with it, could trust him with the knowledge he was in love with his liaison.

"Yeah. I guess I am... serious. Didn't tell her, though. She found out."

"And now she's well pissed off?"

"As you can imagine... you know her, Sean."

"Jeez mate, you've sure made a pig's ear of this one. What the hell is Washington going to say?"

"Well, I can certainly kiss this job goodbye. Last time he ever picks a Democrat, I suppose. We're all a bit too liberal for his taste anyway and here I am making that abundantly clear to him." Jack shrugged.

As Jack looked up he saw Sean's eyes glisten with mischief. "Although I suppose once the job goes...well, Maria isn't going to hang around, is she? I presume you're going to resign? Rather than let them push you..."

Jack looked at Sean, his face serious. "So you think she'd leave if I quit this job? Well, I'm not a quitter, Sean! I got where I am by sticking to my guns." Jack sighed as he said the words.

"Well, look at it objectively, mate. Maria's a great diplomat's wife, that's for sure, but if you're no longer a diplomat, and you're telling me things aren't so great between you anyway, what's she going to stay for?"

"Somehow I don't think she cares how badly we're doing, Sean. She's holding on to her lifestyle. She says this is what she's been working for all her life and she's not about to let me take that away from her."

"I know it's not your style, mate, but there's quitting and there's being thrown out in a blaze of publicity – which would you rather have?"

"I could definitely do without the publicity. But Maria's threatening to make it a media circus anyway."

"Listen to me. If you are really serious about this... whoever, you'll leave now while you're at the top. If you quit first, then the papers aren't going to be so excited about it all. Get a job back in Washington, something that's not so exciting; she's not going to be so keen to hang around then, is she?"

"I can't just walk out in the middle of all this mess, Sean. I have loose ends to tie up. After that... I don't know, sometimes I think I want to see this through and then sometimes I think I can't do this to him."

"What do you mean, do this to him? What are you worrying about *him* for? You're the one losing the job, the career, the partner..."

"It's not just me, Sean." Jack looked up at the ceiling and murmured to himself, "jeez, three marriages..." and then directly at Sean, "There's two of us in this relationship!"

"You're not telling me this bloke is married with some kind of high profile career too?"

"I'm not telling you anything more, Gallagher!"

"No, you're not... and that's what's worrying me. So what are you going to do? And what can I do?"

"I'll have to get back to you on that one, Sean."

"Because you don't know, or because you're not telling?"

"I have to try and sort it out with Maria first, then if I really can't make her change her mind..."

"She's one hell of a determined woman, Jack. Reminds me of our dear old Maggie, the lady's not for turning and all that."

"I might need your support in the talks with the Belgians."

"Well, I'm sure Lucas will help you there. He's quite the up and coming star at our Embassy, you know. If only he had a wife like Maria..."

Jack tried to keep a straight face. The last thing he wanted was Sean picking up on his reaction to that last statement. "Listen, I better go home before Maria has the locks changed."

"Thatcher would have done it the moment you left!"

"Well, technically I haven't left yet."

Jack got up and threw ten Euros in Sean's direction.

"Ten bloody Euros? Fine, I won't take it personally. I guess I always knew I was a cheap date."

Jack couldn't help but smile. Sean was a good friend. He just hoped it would stay that way.

ALL week long, Lucas arrived early for work. He'd been having trouble sleeping. He missed Jack and found that burying himself in work was preferable to lying there mulling over their relationship. It didn't ease the ache, but at least it occupied his mind.

Jack had told Lucas he loved him and proved it numerous times, but now Maria knew and the doubts crept in after Jack had asked him to lay low. So this was what it was like sleeping with a married man.

Lucas finished a lengthy report on his liaison duties and the Anglo-American alliance concerning the war and realized he had time for a cup of tea before presenting the paper to Sean. The drinks counter was behind all the secretaries and above it was a TV screen that was usually muted but invariably tuned to show the BBC World broadcast. Lucas's eye was drawn to the CNN logo and the news ticker. Although the crawling words were just moving out of sight, he read 'KIDNAPPED IN BRUSSELS'

Lucas stared at the TV wondering how long it would take for the item to roll across the screen again, but when it didn't re-appear within a few seconds, he turned to one on the secretaries.

"Who has the remote? Can you turn up the volume, please?"

One of the young girls dipped into her drawer and produced the remote control. "We can't turn it up too loudly, and it should really be tuned to BBC World."

She pointed the controls and clicked one of the buttons making the busy CNN screen disappear and the much calmer background of the BBC World News desk come into view.

"No!" Lucas snapped at the girl. "There was something on the news ticker I wanted to know more about, change the channel back!"

She raised her eyebrow at him, clearly not impressed, but turned the TV back to CNN anyway. The volume was up now and the reports were all about car bombings in Iraq and suicide bombings on buses in Israel. Lucas watched the news ticker intently, waiting for the Brussels item. Lucas was unsure why reading those words had made him so anxious and he tried to tell himself it was probably nothing, but something in the back of his mind reminded him that Mark had told him there was a reason for all the security around the American Embassy. He just wanted to be sure, he wanted to be able to go back to his office with his cup of tea and laugh about it, maybe later tell Jack on the phone what had happened.

There it was on the screen, while the news anchor was still talking about all the extra money the U.S. President was asking Congress to support his war effort:

- U.S. AMBASSADOR KIDNAPPED IN BRUSSELS –

Lucas gasped audibly. *Oh my God! Jack.* Then he turned to the young girl and ripped the remote out of her hand.

"Mr. Carlton, really!"

He felt his stomach turn and all the blood drained from his face as he flicked the channels in a desperate attempt to get more information. The Flemish Belgian TV was showing repeats of the nightly news, but nothing more. The Walloon Belgian channels were not showing any news at all. No news either on the Dutch channels, so he went back to BBC World, not even aware he was muttering "fuck, fuck, fuck" each time he pressed the button without finding anything.

"...just minutes ago. Eyewitnesses report two or three shots being fired. The Ambassador was accompanied by his driver and a Secret Service man. We will be updating this story in the course of the morning as more information becomes available."

Lucas was stunned, unable to think clearly. Jack had been kidnapped. Who? Why?

What if the shots fired had been aimed at him?

Call the U.S. Embassy.

Lucas turned around and grabbed a phone, dialing Gertje's number from memory.

"United States Embassy, how may I help you?" This wasn't Gertje, this was the front desk.

"You're not Gertje, eh... Mrs. Claessens."

The friendly voice returned. "No, sir. All calls are directed to the front desk. Who may I say is calling?"

Lucas knew he had to try. He took a deep breath, trying to control himself. "My name is Lucas Carlton. I am the British Liaison Officer for your Embassy. I would like to speak to Jack's... Mr. Christensen's secretary, Gertje Claessens."

"I'm sorry, sir, but I can't redirect you. Can I take a message?"

It was like talking to a bloody answering machine. "No, you can't take a message. Forget it!"

He dropped the phone on the desk, making the secretary closest to him jump as he stormed off in the direction of Sean's corner office.

He threw open the door and marched into the room without knocking. Sean took one look at his liaison officer's tense features and realized that something was very wrong.

"They won't talk to me at the U.S. Embassy and the news isn't telling us anything more, either," Lucas blurted out without preamble.

Sean gave the young man a stern look and then nodded at the men around the table. "We can resume this tomorrow after your report is finished. Thank you, gentlemen."

Lucas froze as he realized he had burst into Sean's office in the middle of a meeting.

As the men left the office Sean turned to Lucas. "Close the door, and you better have a damn good explanation for disturbing this meeting!"

Lucas inhaled deeply and licked his lips before answering. "Someone has kidnapped Jack."

Chapter Eighteen

"MARK?"

"Mark, are you okay?"

"Mark, wake up."

Jack sat close to his bodyguard on the dirty floor of what looked like a garage. He was sore from being roughly shoved down after Mark had fallen against him, unable to defend himself, with his hands tied behind his back. He moved his shoulders a bit and then his hands, to promote circulation, but they were constantly tingling from lack of blood supply. He had some trouble breathing, but he didn't think it was a major problem. As long as he didn't inhale too deeply, he was fine.

Mark was another matter, though. The Secret Service man had managed to get his hands untied and when the two masked men noticed, one of them pointed his gun. Jack was in the line of fire and Mark did what he was trained to do: he jumped in front of Jack. Reflex made the younger assailant fire and Mark had taken the bullet for his Ambassador. Jack could only hope that Mark's Kevlar vest had taken most of the impact, but he was sure he had seen some blood splatter across the agent's perfectly white shirt.

Also… Mark wasn't moving, but Jack hoped he was still alive. He couldn't hear Mark's breathing and that worried him, because it was nearly quiet enough to hear his own heartbeat. Jack tried to move so he could place his ear against Mark's chest and sighed in relief. He could hear a faint heartbeat and quick shallow breathing. Mark was alive.

As Jack lifted his head from Mark's chest, the wounded man stirred and opened his dark eyes. The agent looked disoriented and frightened and his breathing, now clearly audible, was still very fast and shallow.

Jack knew if he stayed calm it would be easier to settle Mark. He had, after all, been trained how to react in situations like this. "Easy, Mark. You're hurt, but you're going to be fine. Try to calm down and breathe easy."

Mark swallowed and his face contorted in pain. "Can't…"

"Okay, look into my eyes and breathe with me. You can do this."

"What?" Mark was trying his best to slow down his breathing, but he was shivering violently.

Jack tried to keep his voice level, but it wasn't an easy feat. "We were cornered at a stoplight; two guys jumped into the car and held us at gunpoint. They shot into the air a few times, and then made the driver speed away. They got rid of him when he didn't want to do what they wanted." He paused, wondering how much he should tell his bodyguard. "I think you were shot, Mark. They tied my hands so I can't check. Can you move at all?"

Mark shook his head, his breathing a little less desperate, but still shallow. "No…"

LUCAS and Sean watched the BBC World News, which was not very forthcoming with information.

Sean had been put on hold at the American Embassy after he had blown his lid and pulled rank on the young receptionist. Finally, Someone else came on the line.

"Stacey Tanner, Junior Protocol Officer. Can I help you, sir?"

Sean smiled nervously. "Stacey love, what's going on?"

"Mr. Gallagher, hello. I'm afraid we don't know much more than they are saying on the news, sir. Two armed men got into Mr. Christensen's car. Mark Jones was with him. The driver was thrown out of the car and left by the side of the road. He's in hospital, but he's fine. No statements have been made, no responsibility claimed, and no ransom demands either. We are in lock-down and trying to bring as many Embassy personnel as we can to the Embassy." Her voice sounded nervous, but Sean could tell she was trained for this.

"Maria?"

"We're keeping her inside the home and have dispatched extra security personnel over there."

Sean sighed. "She knows what's happened?"

"She has been fully briefed, sir."

"Fine," Sean answered in as professional a manner as he could muster. "Can I have your direct line, please?"

"Reception now has my orders to redirect you to me immediately, sir."

"Thanks, Stacey."

Sean put down the phone and turned to Lucas. "Now tell me exactly just how close you and Jack are."

"**I** know I've been hit, sir. I'm sorry."

Jack sighed. He was afraid of this. He was going to have to keep Mark calm, but alert. "I think in these circumstances you'd better call me Jack. And stop apologizing. You saved my life."

"All part of the job, sir..." Mark gritted his teeth, clearly biting away the pain. "Jack."

Jack tried to remember his terrorism training. "We should look at our assets here. Your hands are untied."

"I can't move, Jack," Mark cut in. "I can't move anything."

"*THE Belgian driver of the Ambassador was found by the side of the road and taken to a hospital. He was well enough to be questioned by the police, but they are keeping a tight lid on any and all information in light of the investigation.*

Jack Christensen is an experienced U.S. Ambassador with earlier postings in Europe and South America as well as the Middle East. He was accompanied by a Secret Service man who remains unnamed, but is said to be a well trained, experienced member of the service."

"They're not saying anything!" Lucas burst out.

"Calm down, Carlton." Sean had never seen the young man this frightened. Lucas was always confident and in control, but the way Lucas behaved now suggested very personal investment in the well-being of a certain American Ambassador. Sean was starting to realize why Jack hadn't been able to tell him who the man was that was making him think about leaving his wife.

"Lucas. I know about you and Jack," Sean started tentatively.

The young man turned his eyes from the TV screen towards his superior. For an instant, Lucas looked trapped and then regained his composure. "I… I don't know what you're talking about. Jack and I have been working together closely, so yes, I'm worried about him. We've been spending a lot of time together and of course we've become friends…"

"And then some, it seems. Lucas…" Sean sighed. How was he going to tell the young man Jack had all but confessed to this? Ah, to hell with it. "Jack told me."

Lucas slumped down on the chair, defeated.

"He didn't mention your name, Lucas. He was always discreet. He just told me he was thinking of leaving his wife for a man, and I think that man is you."

Lucas's head was in his hands now. Sean wondered if he was crying, but as the young man looked up an entirely different emotion was visible on his face. This was determination and resolve, the go-getter attitude for which Lucas was hired in the first place had replaced the scared look.

"So we just sit here and do nothing?"

"Well…" Sean was thinking quickly. "I have a friend in the Brussels Police Force I could call."

"So do it!" Lucas ordered, and then he remembered who he was talking to. "Please. Sir."

Sean picked up the phone and dialed. Lucas heard him talk to the man on the other side of the line, explaining the situation. After a few nods and 'I see's' he replaced the telephone.

"Mark was carrying a GPS homing beacon. If he and Jack are still together, then they should have them within the hour."

JACK was startled out of a fitful sleep by a loud rumble in the next room. He was hurting from his bruises and from falling asleep on a hard concrete floor with Mark's body resting against his. His bodyguard wasn't moving and the fear that the young man had died crept up on him again. How could he have fallen asleep?

A blinding light entered the otherwise pitch-dark room as a door gave way to the two men in combat gear who had broken its seal. Three more followed as Jack watched apprehensively. Either they were being rescued or they were going to be killed.

Jack's eyes were still adjusting to the light when a hooded man with an assault rifle crouched beside him and spoke in perfect English, but with a heavy French accent. "Mr. Ambassador? I am Sergeant Lefebvre, Belgian Military Police; we have come to rescue you. Are you hurt?"

Jack shook his head. "Take care of Mark first. He was shot, I don't know if he's still…"

"Do not worry, sir, we will take care of him." A young man in a jacket with fluorescent stripes reassured Jack while he examined Mark.

Jack was pulled from underneath Mark's limp body and a sharp pain pierced his side, stealing his breath.

LUCAS ran into the emergency room of the University Hospital and slapped his hand on the counter of the dispatch station. "Mr. Christensen" he barked. "I need to see Mr. Jack Christensen, U.S. Ambassador, he was brought in here a little while ago!"

The white-dressed women sitting behind the counter gave him an annoyed look.

"Mr. Carlton?"

Lucas turned sharply and saw a man dressed in a dark suit, hands folded in front of him and a discreet earpiece in his ear.

"Please follow me, sir."

Lucas was escorted through a maze of corridors and elevators to a locked door, which the security man opened with a key card. The large plaque on the door said 'Intensieve Zorgen'. Lucas's Dutch was good enough to understand that this meant 'Intensive Care', and it stopped him dead in his tracks. Jack was badly injured, otherwise he wouldn't be in the ICU. He had probably been shot. The thought turned Lucas's heart to ice.

"Mr. Carlton." The man held the door for him and continued calmly but with a certain insistence. "Please don't dawdle."

Lucas took a deep breath as he entered the ward. At least Jack was alive and they were going to let him see him. He was therefore rather disappointed when he was led into a small waiting room. "Could someone just tell me if he's okay?" he asked the man who had led him there.

"Someone will come to see you shortly, Mr. Carlton," he was told dispassionately as the man left him alone.

Lucas couldn't sit down. He tried to look through the gaps in the shutters that covered the windows, but found himself staring at a wall on the opposite side of the corridor. Nurses and doctors walked in and out of a room at one end of that corridor; some of them carrying equipment. Lucas couldn't read their faces and his fear grew with each passing second.

What if Jack was dead? The hospital sometimes left people in the ward so relatives could come and pay their last respects. He shook his head. No. That couldn't be.

"Lucas?"

He turned around and saw Maria standing near the entrance of the waiting room. She was wearing trousers and a sweater and her hair was untied. Her face looked worried and there were dark circles under her eyes.

"Maria… how is…"

"He's fine. A bit banged up, but nothing that won't heal," she answered quickly. Lucas could tell she was trying hard to sound unemotional and she wasn't looking at him.

"Can I see him?" Lucas tried, his voice soft.

"No," she stated firmly, "I don't think that's a good idea, Lucas. It's enough that you know he's all right." She started to turn around, so Lucas took a few steps towards her and grabbed her arm.

She pulled away and gave him a hostile look. "You have no claim on him."

Lucas tried to keep his emotions in check. "Don't you think that's for him to decide?"

"He has decided," Maria snapped. She then clearly regained her composure and narrowed her eyes. "Do you know what happens to discredited U.S. diplomats, Lucas?"

"Jack didn't do anything wrong, Maria. He fell in love, that's all." Lucas was trying to keep his breathing calm, but not succeeding very well.

"In this administration, that's plenty, young man," she continued, her tone condescending. "They won't fire him, you know. He knows too much about the inner workings of U.S. diplomacy. They will bury him under a mountain of paperwork in Washington, make him write reports on proposed foreign policy, make him use his extensive foreign experience in some dead end office job where they can keep an eye on him. That will be his future. And why? Because of an indiscretion with a junior British diplomat. He will hate you for it, because you will have ruined everything he ever wanted for a career. Everything he's ever wanted will be out of his reach. You only get one chance at this, Lucas. I'd like to see how far that 'love' will carry you then." Her eyes were wide and dark and staring intently at Lucas. Then she seemed to calm down again. "He knows that now."

Lucas's chest tightened. She was right. The American President and his party were trying to get a ban on same sex marriages written into the constitution. They would never let a gay man keep such a publicly visible position. An Ambassador was a country's calling card and had to display everything that was good about a nation. Maria was right. Lucas's love was going to cost Jack everything he'd ever worked for.

"At least let me say goodbye to him," Lucas asked, fighting his tears.

Maria looked straight at him and inhaled deeply. "Fine. Follow me."

Lucas was amazed that she was going to let him in to see his lover and he steadied himself as he followed her down the corridor. He had to be strong for Jack.

She nodded towards the door and let Lucas enter by himself.

Jack was on the bed in a white hospital gown with the hospital's logo on it. He smiled at Lucas when he saw him enter. "Hey there. You're a sight for sore eyes."

Lucas felt the tears well up again, but took a deep breath. The last thing he wanted to do was cry like a girl. "Hey."

He took Jack's out-stretched hand and squeezed it.

"You okay?" Jack asked softly.

Lucas felt a single tear roll down his cheek and wiped it away. "What are you asking me for? You're the one in the hospital bed."

Jack tried to chuckle, but this clearly hurt too much. "Just a bit banged up, that's all."

"Yeah, Maria told me," Lucas answered.

"You saw Maria?"

Lucas nodded. "So how badly banged up are you?"

Jack smiled. "Two cracked ribs, a few bruised ones, a broken collarbone and a bruised jaw. Oh yeah, and a concussion from when they knocked me down. The drugs they gave me take the edge off. Mark's worse, though. He took a bullet for me. They tell me he's alive, but they're still working on him."

Lucas sat down next to the bed and raised Jack's hand to his lips to kiss it. "I'm so glad you're okay." He inhaled a few times trying to keep himself from becoming too emotional.

Jack shushed him. "It's okay, Luke. Everything will work out." He opened his hand to touch Lucas's cheek and they sat there for a while enjoying their hands entwined until Lucas noticed Jack had fallen asleep.

He kissed his lover's hand one more time and gently placed it on the bedcovers. "Never forget that I love you, Jack," he whispered to his sleeping lover before he walked out of the room.

Impasse

FUNCTIONS: the necessary evil of his public office.

To Jack, Christmas always felt like such a fake affair at the Embassy. It was one of those things you should celebrate with your family, yet he was supposed to show up at a reception Maria organized for all the Americans who wouldn't be able to celebrate with their loved ones. How ironic, Jack thought, that he had lost almost everyone he loved these past months. First Lucas had left. The last Jack had seen of the young man was in hospital. No goodbye, nothing. Sean told him that Lucas had been granted educational leave and had left to finish his Master's degree at Stanford University. Then Jack got a phone call from one of his brothers to tell him that their parents had been killed in a car accident in Namibia. Their bodies were flown to New York for burial and he had settled all their affairs, dividing their assets equally between himself and his two brothers. For a moment, he had thought of flying on to California to try to get in touch with Lucas, but he felt it would only make matters worse.

Maria was still there, of course, still the ever devoted wife. As if nothing had happened.

He still loved her dedication, the way she could totally set aside her own feelings when it came to doing what needed to be done. But he didn't love her any more, not as a wife at least. He had taken up residence in the guest room, not wanting to share a bed with her now, and she hadn't argued. The nights were long and lonely. He missed Lucas and he often woke up in the middle of the night realizing he had dreamt about his young lover. Ex-lover. There was no changing that now. Not now that he had chosen to continue his diplomatic career.

In a minute they would be going out to greet their guests, and he would no doubt be complimented on his lovely wife again. The charade continued.

"So are you ready?"

Maria looked lovely in her strapless night blue dress, her hair carefully sculpted and pinned back. Her make-up was flawless and she smiled at him warmly as she straightened the lapels of his jacket and wiped some imaginary specks off his shoulders.

"You look lovely, Maria."

"Thank you, so do you," she gracefully accepted the compliment as she took his hand and led him into the reception hall.

It was quite busy in there. Stacey had already done a great job welcoming their guests and he and Maria would soon be making their rounds, greeting Presbyterian ministers and businessmen. There would be eggnog and turkey sandwiches and a speech on the meaning of Christmas around the world.

Jack felt his eyes wander over to the entrance from time to time, secretly hoping that a beautiful young man with dark curls would walk in again.

But he knew it wouldn't happen.

Negotiations Resumed

Chapter Nineteen

"LUCAS, I need a big favor."

Liz leaned over his desk in her usual flirty-without-ulterior-motives sort of way.

"I really need this afternoon off, but since I'm the senior officer, I've been stuck with the assignment from hell."

Lucas knew she was a bit of a drama queen, so he didn't take the 'assignment from hell' too seriously. "So you want me to take over from you, leaving you with a free afternoon to go shag that guy from the Italian delegation, right?"

"Lucas!" she rebutted, feigning insult. "We don't just shag. His wife is always in Italy, so he told me he's divorcing her."

"Yeah, that's what they all say, Liz, just to get you in the sack. But they never leave their wives, believe me, I know." He shook his head and conceded. "Fine! What's the job? You and Mister Italy go shag like bunnies; I'll stay here and work for a living."

"All I know is: former U.S. Ambassador who has a job interview here in the U.N. building. You are *not* to let him wander around alone. After the interview, you will be told whether or not you need to help him fill out his security requirements. So either you escort him outside or you help him get a security badge."

Liz was in turbo mode, clearly eager to leave as soon as possible, so Lucas didn't waste any words either. "Briefing folder?"

Liz produced a dark blue file from behind her back. "You will find your average, very stuffy, middle aged career diplomat at the front desk...." she checked her watch, "In about ten minutes."

Lucas knew it would probably take him at least fifteen minutes to walk to the front desk, so technically he was late already. Luckily he knew the inside of the U.N. building like the back of his hand and with a short run across the public arena, he could make it just in time.

On the final stretch, he opened the folder, so he would at least know who he was looking for. His heart stopped.

The head shot on the visitor's pass was a photo of Jack.

He stopped just around the corner from the courtesy desk and leaned against the cold stone wall. Could he face Jack? Could he actually walk up to him and pretend nothing had happened between them two and a half years ago? Maybe Jack wouldn't want to see him? He couldn't blame the man for feeling resentful, of course; Lucas hadn't even said goodbye after seeing Jack in the hospital.

Lucas often wondered if he had done the right thing. In retrospect, he felt he should have stuck around, waited for Jack to make up his mind and do what they had talked about. Now it seemed they both had different careers, but Lucas wondered what would happen if Jack saw him here. He felt torn in half. On the one hand, he wanted to call the PR office and try to get someone else to give Jack the tour; on the other hand, this was a chance for closure. To put a stop to the 'what-ifs' that had been running around his head ever since that night at the hospital. Besides, if Jack got the job, they'd bump into each other on a regular basis.

Lucas took a deep breath and slipped into his professional role. He could do this, be accommodating, pleasant and welcoming, no matter who was in front of him. He was a public relations officer for the United Nations for Christ's sake!

As he rounded the corner, Jack was right there. Lucas immediately recognized the light grey suit as being the one they had picked out together on their first weekend in Antwerp and he felt his throat go dry. It was like time had never passed, like he could still go over to him and see that spark in those beautiful blue eyes. Jack looked so handsome, a little thin maybe, but still…

"Jack?" Lucas cleared his throat, trying to sound professional, but failing miserably at ridding his voice of emotion.

Their eyes met across the courtesy desk and Jack's face went pale.

"Lucas." A weak smile appeared on Jack's face as their eyes met briefly. The American took a deep breath as he scanned around the hall.

"I didn't know... you work here?" Jack asked rather hesitantly.

Lucas nodded, "I'm in Public Relations now, and I'll be showing you around this afternoon. If that's okay with you, of course?"

Both men stared at each other for a few moments, until Lucas regained his composure and gestured to Jack to step through the metal detector. He then handed Jack a visitor's pass.

"You need to..." he gestured to his own jacket lapel, since he felt uneasy making any kind of move in Jack's direction, "pin it on. Has to be visible at all times. If you're hired, I'll get you a personnel badge later."

Jack nodded and clipped the badge onto his jacket.

"So when's your interview?" Lucas asked as they proceeded to walk across the hall towards the elevators.

"At four," Jack answered blankly, looking around and taking in the majestic view.

"You're early." Lucas was amused by that, since this was so different from the always busy and therefore, always late Jack that he remembered.

WALKING through this grand building next to Lucas, Jack realized he hadn't really been all that nervous for this interview. Getting the job here would make life considerably easier, but it wasn't an absolute necessity, and besides, he would probably be found to be overqualified again. Now all of a sudden, his suit was uncomfortable and he felt sweaty and warm. Did he want a job in a place where he would no doubt bump into his ex-lover on a regular basis? Even though Lucas clearly didn't want him any more, Jack's feelings for the young man hadn't changed. He didn't know if he wanted to hear why Lucas had left, but then again it might help him close that chapter of his life for good.

Jack looked sideways and saw Lucas was still smiling at the last comment he had made. Something about him being early.

"Well, I was promised a tour," Jack answered abruptly.

"You're in luck then. Since I started here as a tour guide, I know the place inside and out." Lucas started to feel a little more at ease with the idea of having a full hour to talk to Jack. Maybe it was good to clear the air, put their relationship to rest once and for all.

"So how's Maria?" he asked tentatively.

Jack looked up, but not directly at Lucas. "She's fine… I hear. She's working in the Sudan, for UNICEF."

Lucas stopped and turned towards Jack, feeling his heart jump.

Noticing the Brit was no longer beside him, Jack stopped and turned. "We're divorced, Lucas."

Jack's voice sounded unemotional, but it still made Lucas breathe heavier. Now they really needed to talk. If Jack was divorced, perhaps their relationship might have actually meant something.

"Jack…" Lucas stared at the floor, afraid to look the American in the eye. "We need to talk about… a few things." He looked up. "Why don't we go to the PR lounge and grab some coffee. We can talk in relative privacy there."

LUCAS was grateful the small lounge was practically deserted when they stepped in.

"I didn't know about you and Maria, Jack. I'm sorry."

"No, you're not," Jack was quick to rebut, smiling at Lucas. He was starting to relax around Lucas again, falling back into their old repartee.

"Okay, maybe I'm not," Lucas answered, clearly remembering how Jack would always pick out the times when he didn't really mean it. "What happened?"

Jack chuckled. "You happened, silly."

Lucas felt tears well up in his eyes as the power of Jack's statement sunk in. *Stop acting like a girl, Luke.* He shook his head. "Then I'm truly sorry. Sorry for leaving like that, sorry for not having the patience to stick around, sorry for being too scared to stand up to Maria, and sorry for putting our careers before everything else!"

He felt Jack's hand cover his and then the American spoke softly.

"Not a day has gone by that I didn't think about you, Luke. After the hospital, when Sean told me you had left, I didn't understand, but when Maria acted so smug about you leaving to save my career, I knew she had something to do with you... not saying goodbye. I just didn't know how much of it was her blackmail and how much was your decision."

Jack picked up Lucas's hand and kissed it tenderly, sending shivers through the young man's body. "I'm not making any assumptions here. I'm sure there's someone else in your life by now, so just tell me and I'll leave you alone."

Lucas needed to be honest with Jack; he just didn't know how. "Well, there is and there isn't. It's a little difficult to explain." He waited for a moment, trying to decide how much he was going to tell him. "Why don't I give you the tour, and I'll drop you off where you need to be for your interview. Afterwards, come and meet me at the second floor of the DC-2 building and I'll try to explain." Lucas took a deep breath. "So what are you interviewing for? Secretary-General?"

Jack snorted. "No thanks; no more high profile jobs for me. I'm happy to stay in the shadows. They apparently need a Senior Interpreter who is fluent in three official U.N. languages and has experience with international politics."

Lucas smiled. "Sounds like you. English, Spanish and French right? Be sure to mention Danish, Swedish, Norwegian and a little Dutch. They may not be official languages around here, but the delegates of those countries may need you for those, too. I don't see why they wouldn't give you the job, Jack; you're perfect."

Jack smiled shyly. "Well, we'll see what they say, okay?"

THE interview went well, and they were clearly impressed that a man of Jack's experience was willing to take a simple interpreter's job.

He had been open and honest with them, explaining his interest in going back to college part-time, while trying to rebuild his life after his divorce and seeking out a job away from public scrutiny.

The men doing the hiring knew they'd be foolish to let this one slip by and hired him on the spot.

ON the way to the place where Lucas asked to meet, Jack started wondering what Lucas was going to show him. The Brit had been fairly

vague when he answered the questions about his private life and that made
Jack curious. Of course he knew he couldn't lay claim to Lucas. It wasn't
like his marriage had been the only hurdle they had needed to conquer, but
his interest was sparked nonetheless.

The elevator to the second floor gave way to a small waiting area
and lots of corridors, so Jack decided to wait right there. He relaxed a bit
now that he knew he had the job and he would be coming here on a
regular basis. It did mean he had to sort things out with Lucas, though, and
that meant figuring out his own feelings. As he thought about what had
happened between that ill-fated night in the hospital and today, he realized
he had unconsciously made up his mind a long time ago. The end of his
diplomatic career and his divorce had all led him to this one moment, but
he knew not to get his hopes up too much.

It was actually a bit more than ten minutes later that Lucas
emerged from the elevator, clearly in a hurry. "Sorry I'm late." He smiled,
a little flushed and out of breath as if he had been running "So did you get
the job?"

Jack looked at the excited face of his former lover and wondered if
he should tease him a little. He decided against it.

"Yeah."

"I knew it! They would have been fools not to hire you!" Lucas
grabbed Jack's arms, squeezed them and then let go. He leaned in a little
closer and whispered, "I want to hug you, but no matter how open minded
they are here, we'd better not."

"I'll take a rain check." Jack smiled, grateful for Lucas's self-
restraint, since he wasn't entirely sure about his own. "So why did you
bring me here?"

Lucas's beaming smile lost some wattage as he nervously asked
Jack to follow him.

Chapter Twenty

THEY walked into a corridor adorned by children's drawings and before it really started to sink in with Jack he heard a shrill voice coming from in front of them. "Daddy, daddy, daddy."

He saw Lucas bend down to pick up a beautiful little girl running over to him, her arms stretched out. She had a wide smile that made her gorgeous brown eyes go all tiny, and her face was encircled by the most amazing flurry of dark brown curls. There was no mistaking her for anyone other than Lucas's daughter.

"So did you have fun today?" Lucas asked the little girl. She nodded, making the curls dance around her face and then planted a loud and very deliberate kiss on Lucas's lips.

"I want you to meet someone, honey, is that okay?"

She looked over her father's shoulder at Jack and hid her face in the crook of his neck.

Lucas turned around with her in his arms and smiled at Jack a little apologetically. "I'm sorry, she's only two." He wiped the curls away from her cheek, exposing a sulky face. "Honey, this is a very special friend of mine, someone who's very important to me. Say hi to Jack." And then to Jack, "Jack, this is AnnElise."

When the little girl turned into Lucas's embrace again, Jack caught his desperate look and tried to convey understanding with his own.

"She'll come around, Jack; she just needs a little time, because she's not really used to strangers."

Jack smiled again, trying to process all the information he had just received. He had so many questions for Lucas, but he knew a lot of them could not be asked with AnnElise present. He would have to be patient.

Lucas seemed to be able to read his mind. "Jack, I want to explain this to you in more detail, but I'll understand if you don't...." He was clearly unsure of how to proceed. "What I would really love is to take you out to dinner, but why don't you come home with me. She'll be down for the night by 7:30 and then I'll fix you dinner."

Trying to keep the atmosphere light, Jack was quick to answer. "Oh, you cook too now?"

Lucas smiled, looking relieved. "Sort of, yeah, well, I have stuff in the house to cook with and sometimes it's even edible."

"Why don't I see what I can whip up for us in your kitchen, while you take care of AnnElise and then we can talk after she goes to bed, okay?"

Lucas nodded and Jack saw the young man's eyes flood with tears. He looked around to see if anyone was watching, but no one was paying any attention to them, so he placed his hand on the back of Lucas's neck, just above AnnElise's arm and pulled him in for a quick kiss. "It's okay, Lucas, we have a lot to talk about."

JACK was in the tiny kitchen of Lucas's one bedroom apartment, opening cabinets and drawers, trying to decide what to make them for dinner. He smiled at the fact that it was actually a fairly functional kitchen, with lots of utensils, most of them fairly new, but used. Lucas apparently did some actual cooking from time to time.

When they walked in, he had scanned the living room and found no evidence of anyone else living there. It was a little disorganized, with lots of toys lying around. There were a few pictures stuck to the fridge, mostly of AnnElise, some of them also of Lucas, but no mother. He was fairly certain Lucas lived alone with his daughter.

He could hear them in the bathroom, chatting away. AnnElise used mostly single words, but she was clearly very good at making sure she was understood.

A few moments later, she burst into the kitchen, dressed only in a diaper and laughing loudly, closely followed by Lucas chasing her with a towel. "Come here, you little monster, we need to dry those curls of yours some more." When she spotted Jack in 'her' kitchen she froze, eyeing him suspiciously.

This gave Lucas the chance to grab her and lift her up. "Are you ready for a sandwich?"

"Yes, Daddy!"

"Can Jack make you a sandwich?"

She looked at Jack and clearly decided to give him a chance when a smile broke on her face.

"What do you want on your sandwich, honey?" Jack asked, keeping his distance, but liking the fact the little girl was warming up to him.

"Baby meat, p'ease," she answered decidedly.

"Baby meat?" Jack asked Lucas questioningly.

"Baloney," Lucas mouthed, making both men snigger.

Jack made her a sandwich with the sliced pink meat and sat down next to Lucas, who held AnnElise on his lap as she ate her sandwich with much gusto. He was amused to see her trying to share her crusts with Lucas and felt himself warm to this picture of domestic happiness. Was it too soon to hope that maybe he could be part of this one day? He knew he still loved Lucas. He'd never doubted that, but seeing the man again made it all the more clear to him. Could he hope for Lucas to love him back? Would AnnElise accept him in her father's life?

He woke from his daydream when he heard Lucas tell AnnElise it was time for bed. "Will you give Jack a goodnight kiss?"

"'Ack?" She asked.

Lucas chuckled, "Yes, Jack."

She wiggled herself off Lucas's lap and walked over to the American. "Nigh' nigh' 'Ack" She stretched up, puckering her lips and Jack couldn't help but laugh. He received a big girl kiss on his lips.

"Night night, AnnElise."

WHEN Lucas came back to the kitchen about fifteen minutes later, Jack was dishing out the steaming Fettuccini Alfredo.

"Hope you're hungry? I haven't cooked for two in ages."

Lucas rubbed his thighs and sat down. "Starving, actually. This is a rare treat."

It felt weird, but a good kind of weird, to sit here in the small kitchen eating together. Their relationship had always been about stealing time together and spending it in hotel rooms or Jack coming over to Lucas's apartment for a quick shag after work. They had never been this... domestic.

Lucas found himself looking at Jack as the American explained about the interview he'd had that afternoon and why he wanted to work at the U.N. Jack tried to find the right words and succeeded as usual, but in his effort to do so, focusing on an invisible spot on the table, not on Lucas.

And Lucas found himself falling in love all over again. Could he hope the feelings Jack had for him back then were still there? Jack had come to his apartment with him, but perhaps he was just lonely, new to another different city and eager to connect with an old friend again. He didn't know whether he could stand being just an old friend to Jack. On the other hand, seeing his former lover with a two year old hadn't seemed to faze Jack either.

"This was really delicious." Lucas pushed his empty plate away and rubbed his stomach.

Jack smiled, clearing the last strands of pasta from his own plate as well. "It was nice to be able to cook for someone again."

So he was lonely.

Jack started clearing the table, but Lucas stopped him. "Hey, you cooked, you don't have to do the dishes too! We can just put them in the sink and I'll do them in the morning."

"Daddy!"

Lucas smiled apologetically. "She never wakes up again, usually."

Jack threw Lucas an understanding look. "You better go see to her."

Lucas cursed internally as he made his way to his daughter's bedside.

A few minutes later, Lucas returned to the kitchen to find Jack standing over the sink, washing dishes.

He walked over to him and couldn't resist putting his hand on Jack's back. "You really didn't have to, Jack."

"I don't mind. I can't let you do all of this alone, Luke."

As Jack turned his head to face him, Lucas could see the sadness in his eyes, so he moved behind him, wrapped his arms around Jack and put his chin on the American's shoulder.

"I missed you."

He could feel Jack swallow hard. "Me, too. God, Luke, me, too."

Lucas tried not to be disappointed as Jack continued washing the last pot. He grabbed the dishtowel off Jack's shoulder and quickly dried the dishes.

As he put the last pot in the cupboard, he saw Jack wiping the counters and stopped him.

"Enough, Jack." Lucas grabbed the older man's hand and pulled him out of the kitchen. "We need to talk, clear the air, seriously." He cocked his head when Jack wouldn't smile and quickly placed a kiss on his lips. "Come."

"Hey, I remember this couch," Jack remarked, trying to lighten the mood.

"Shipped over from Brussels courtesy of the British Foreign Service. Now sit!" Lucas commanded. He returned a few minutes later with two cups of tea and sat down next to Jack.

"I owe you an explanation for AnnElise."

"No, you don't." Jack rolled his eyes. "Not that I don't want to know. I just don't want you to feel you 'owe me' anything. She's lovely and no one would ever mistake her for anything else but your daughter." Jack took Lucas's hand in his and squeezed it.

"She's Lucy's," Lucas stated, looking at their hands.

"And where is Lucy now?" Jack asked carefully.

"I actually haven't seen her since she left me in Brussels. I didn't even know she was pregnant then."

Jack looked confused. "So how?"

Lucas sighed. "I left Brussels after our... you know. You know when I left." He smiled at Jack. "I needed to get away, get my priorities straight. So I went back to Stanford, figured if I buried myself in books it would clear my head and I might end up with the Master's degree I needed so much."

Jack shifted in his seat and turned a bit more towards Lucas, never letting go of his hand.

"I knew it was futile to try and get in touch with her. It wasn't like I wanted her back and I knew she didn't want me, so... One morning, I got a phone call from her sister. I mean the woman could never stand me when I was still seeing Lucy and now she's calling me?"

Lucas looked up at the ceiling and inhaled deeply. "She told me to come to the University Hospital if I wanted to see my daughter before she was handed over for adoption."

Jack raised his eyebrows. "Wow, what a way to tell a guy."

Lucas snorted. "Well, I told you she didn't like me."

"If she didn't like you, she would have stayed quiet about the whole thing." Jack looked as if he was trying to understand the situation. "Sounds more like she wanted to hurt you."

"I suppose. Anyway, you can imagine it was a bit of a shock, but I went over there; what else could I do? The nurse showed her to me and I knew right then that I had to fight for her. *She* was going to give my daughter away! I talked to a doctor and an adoption counselor there and they told me she had put 'father unknown' on the birth certificate."

It didn't escape Jack that Lucas had called Lucy by her name only once this evening.

"So it took two paternity tests and a judge, but two weeks later I was shopping for baby stuff like a mad man."

"And you never looked back after that, hey?" Jack asked, compassion in his eyes.

"Man, it was tough!" Lucas chuckled at the memory. "I can tell you. The sleepless nights pacing the bedroom, trying to get her to settle down? I often wondered where I had left my brain when I signed her papers."

"And now?" Jack tried to look into Lucas's face, but the young man was staring at the floor.

As Lucas looked up, Jack saw that his eyes glistened with tears. "She's so much a part of me, Jack, a part of my life. All the sacrifices, they're nothing compared to the love I get from her. She loves me, Jack, even when she's cross with me for not allowing her to do certain things, even when I tell her no and she throws a tantrum. In the end, she always comes back to me and puts her little arms around my neck and I just melt."

"Well, I can certainly see she would have that potential, yes," Jack acknowledged. He wanted to take Lucas in his arms, but was afraid to. They weren't exactly sitting close together, so he tried a different approach. "This couch certainly brings back memories."

Lucas chuckled. "Yeah, it does. That's why I couldn't leave it behind in Brussels. I sold all the other furniture to my replacement, but I couldn't imagine anyone else... sitting on this."

They were both thinking of the past, smiles on their faces, when a shrill cry pierced the silence.

"Was that?" Jack asked.

Lucas nodded and got up. "I don't know what's wrong with her tonight."

Jack got up as well. "Listen, I better leave."

Chapter Twenty-One

"**No!**" Lucas sighed, "I mean, I'll be right back, I'm sure she's fine and I... I want to say goodbye to you properly."

Jack couldn't resist the young man's pleading face and sat down again. As Lucas left to go into the bedroom he could hear his soothing voice speaking to AnnElise. He couldn't make out what Lucas was saying, but the intonation was sweet and loving. After a little while, his voice went silent and Jack wondered what was going on. He got up again, slowly tiptoeing over to the half opened bedroom door. When he looked inside, he could see Lucas standing over the baby bed. AnnElise's bedside lamp twirling slowly, painting elephants and mice and giraffes on the ceiling and all over her father and Jack could clearly see Lucas's smile.

He quietly moved over to stand behind Lucas, careful not to startle him. He could feel the heat radiating off the Brit's body and tried not to touch him, but when Lucas leaned ever so slightly toward him, Jack moved close enough to let his chest touch Lucas's back.

"She's beautiful, isn't she?"

Jack moved even closer, peering over Lucas's shoulder at a peacefully sleeping AnnElise, his hands still clasped behind his back.

"Mmmh, she is," Jack kissed Lucas's shoulder and his neck, "just like her father."

Lucas let his head fall back. He reached up to place his hand on the nape of Jack's neck and the American wrapped his arms tightly around Lucas's body. Lucas twisted his head and offered his lips, so Jack did what he had wanted to do since laying eyes on the Brit a few hours earlier and for every hour since they'd been apart: taste his lips, mouth, tongue.

Lucas spun in Jack's arms and deepened the kiss. The last two and a half years simply disappeared as Lucas moaned into the passionate kiss, opening up completely for Jack.

They managed to stop kissing when AnnElise stirred, but they were still in each other's arms as they both peered into the crib. AnnElise moved restlessly, but remained asleep.

Lucas chuckled.

"What?" Jack asked quietly.

"I feel a recurring theme in our relationship coming up."

Jack gave him a questioning look.

"You're staying over, aren't you?" Lucas asked brazenly.

Jack nodded. "I'd like to."

Lucas kissed him quickly, then took his hand and switched off the bedside lamp. "Come on."

He led Jack out of the bedroom and back to the couch. "I'm sorry but I'm not ready for a two year old watching us while we're making out."

The American smiled. "Well, this couch does hold some very fond memories."

The couch had soft cushions and a deep seat that easily accommodated both Jack and Lucas lying close together and they took their time getting reacquainted, touching and occasionally kissing. After all their hurried, passionate lovemaking of the past, it was as if they had all the time in the world now.

"So how did you manage to divorce Maria?" Lucas asked, his hand slowly caressing Jack's back. "She made it pretty clear to me she would never let you go."

Jack kissed Lucas's forehead. "Yeah, I'm sorry about that." He rolled his eyes. "I had to resort to some fairly drastic measures."

"Oh?" Lucas asked, slightly amused at Jack's frown.

"It's a long story. "

Lucas checked his watch. "We have about six hours until AnnElise will be screaming for my attention. Until then, I'm all ears."

Jack chuckled. "Okay."

"**WHAT** are you doing, Christensen?"

Gallagher was clearly furious, but Jack couldn't care less. They were on a short break from yet another meeting with the Belgian Prime Minister and Defense Secretary, trying to persuade them to see the joint American-British standpoint that NATO needed to send a large amount of peace keeping troops to help the war effort and that the Belgians were not helping at showing a united front.

Jack was tired, still not fully recovered from the busted ribs and bruised jaw he had received in the kidnapping attempt, and he was fighting for something he didn't believe in.

"Do you think we should send hundreds of young men and women into battle for this?" Jack narrowed his eyes at his friend.

"My point is, it doesn't matter what we think, Jack. Our job is to stand by the choices our countries make and to support them." Sean turned around, his hands raised in defeat. "Why am I explaining this to you?" He looked at the American and whispered, "This is treason, Jack! Those guys that manhandled you fucked with your head, didn't they?"

Jack sighed and took a sip of his cup of coffee. "This is the decision of a few ego-trippers, Gallagher, and you know it. It's my President's economic reasons and your Prime Minister's brown-nosing. Christ, Gallagher, the guy is so far up my president's ass that he has a say in what he has for breakfast."

Gallagher snorted and shook his head. "There are ways of doing this, Jack, and this is not the diplomatic way. They'll have your head on a plate for this, and mine too, if I'm not careful."

The Belgian Prime Minister and his tubby Defense Minister returned to the table, and Jack and Sean sat down as well.

Jack cleared his throat. "Sir, can we talk off the record for a moment?"

Sean shot him a deadly glance.

The PM nodded to the secretaries to leave the room, and Jack got up again. He walked over to the door to close it after them and then paced towards the window.

"I realize my Secretary of State was instructed to threaten you with sanctions if you didn't help us persuade the French and Germans to close the ranks. I was asked to tell you as well, that the American Military would stop using your Antwerp port and that there would be trade sanctions. As a last resort, I was to threaten the extrication of the NATO headquarters."

Jack looked at Sean who was sitting upright in his chair, staring at the tabletop.

"I can tell you now that the threats are all bullshit."

He saw the two ministers look at him, then at Sean, then back at him.

"If your people don't support this, neither should you. You're a small country, but an important one, because you don't let the big guys stare you down. I'm not saying you can stop this war, or that you can actually accomplish something by not joining NATO's peace keeping force, but I'm telling you to follow your heart, something I should have done a long time ago."

Jack nodded at the two stunned politicians and walked out.

"YOU actually said that?" Lucas asked, his eyebrows climbing towards his hairline.

"Yeah," Jack answered shyly. "I was sick and tired of hiding, of lying to everyone." He kissed Lucas tenderly. "I knew Maria would never grant me a divorce unless I was everything she didn't want me to be."

Lucas looked him in the eye seriously. "Sean was right. What you did was treason, Jack!"

"I know, but you know what? It felt damn good. It was like the world dropped off my shoulders. I walked out of that building, and there was oxygen in the air. I could breathe at last. The Prime Minister knew better than to blab about what I had said, so nobody outside that room ever knew. They figured I had suffered a nervous breakdown, and I went along with it. I even saw a shrink. Had her write me up as vulnerable and a bit of a loose cannon. They gave me six months of 'vacation'."

"And Maria?"

Lucas still had deep lines on his forehead and Jack let his fingers gently ghost over his lover's furrowed brow as he brushed aside the loose curls.

"She understood that if I was willing to blow my career over this that I was serious. We had a really long talk. Both did some crying. Talked some more."

Lucas's worried smile made him continue.

"We shared a lot in fifteen years of marriage, Lucas. She's a wonderful woman; I'll always think that. She deserved an explanation."

"What was there to explain?" Lucas wondered a little sternly.

Jack rested his forehead against the young Brit's. "I told her I loved her. Like a sister, or a friend. I told her I loved you in a way that was so different that I had got to the point where I couldn't hide it anymore."

"But I was gone. I wasn't there anymore, and you didn't know where I was."

Jack smiled at the way Lucas was trying to look at him without breaking contact.

"You sound like Maria."

Lucas poked him in the ribs.

"Owww." Jack put his hand on the spot Lucas had prodded and feigned pain, pulling away as much as he could

"I'm sorry; your ribs still hurt?"

Jack pulled Lucas close, hoping this would wipe the worried look off his face. "No, silly. It's all healed. I meant what I told her, Luke. I knew I loved you more than I had ever loved anyone. The pain of losing you dulled a little over time, but when I saw you again today…"

"I didn't know if I could face you," Lucas admitted. "I saw your mug shot on the visitor's pass in my briefing folder and my heart stopped."

"Why?"

"I walked out on you, Jack! And even if you forgave me for that, there was AnnElise and…"

Jack silenced him with a kiss.

"AnnElise is perfect, Luke. Seeing you with her, the way you care for her and love her… it made me fall in love with you all over again. "

He looked up at Lucas seriously. "I know this is all very sudden, but I hope I can continue to be part of your lives, Luke, yours and AnnElise's."

Lucas looked up at him. "Are you serious?"

Jack nodded. "If you'll have me."

Lucas cuddled even closer to Jack. "You'll be sick and tired of us soon enough, Jack. AnnElise is quite a handful, you know."

Jack just smiled.

THEY both woke up a few hours later hearing AnnElise talk to herself.

When Lucas realized they were still on the couch, limbs entangled, he apologized. "She does that all the time."

"She never cries?"

Lucas shook his head. "She did when she was a baby, but now she doesn't unless she's really hurt. She ran through the house the other day and ran into the side of the door. All she said was 'Lise bang' and then she continued running."

"She must feel really safe around you," Jack answered quietly.

"You think so?" Lucas asked, a little unsure.

Jack nodded. "So what are the plans for today?"

"Well, it's Saturday, so, we get up, have breakfast and around eleven, I drop AnnElise off at Liz's to play with Liz's boys, which she loves by the way, and then I do some grocery shopping and take a walk around. It's usually my time away from everything, but I'd love to share it with you!"

Lucas looked at Jack in such a way that Jack couldn't deny him anything. Not that he wanted to. "So when do you have to pick up AnnElise?"

"Around three. By that time Liz's had enough of the kids, believe me!"

"Nice of her to baby sit," Jack remarked.

"Well, single parents have to help each other out. You'll get to know her two boys soon enough, because we take turns."

Jack smiled at the idea that Lucas seemed to take for granted that he would be around from now on.

Chapter Twenty-Two

THE morning went by smoothly. AnnElise was still a little shy around Jack, but by the time they arrived at Liz's place, she insisted on saying goodbye to Jack as well as her dad before running off to the playroom.

Liz was her usual forward self when it came to the introductions. "So you're the Ambassador who's had a hold on Lucas's heart for the past three years."

Jack smiled a little shyly, but figured his best defense was an offence. "Well, I was the married one, he was the irresistible one."

He gave Lucas a sideways look and could tell Liz clearly liked what she saw. "Well, at least he has taste in men."

She turned to Lucas and kissed him on the cheek. "Go have fun. Leave her here as long as you need." She winked at Jack.

When they were outside again, Jack couldn't help himself. "She's quite something, isn't she? Exactly how much did you tell her about us?"

Lucas chuckled. "One very desperate night, we ended up in the emergency room with AnnElise. She had a high fever and I couldn't get her to calm down, so I called Liz, who had just been left by her boyfriend while pregnant with baby two. She poured her heart out while we were waiting in the emergency room and so did I. She pretty much knows everything, Jack."

Jack wasn't entirely sure how he felt about what Lucas had just told him.

"She's really great, and she only cares who a guy sleeps with if she has the smallest chance of it being her. So you're safe. In fact she probably set us up that day I gave you the tour. I'm sure she knew who you were from your bio, because I never mentioned your name."

IN the supermarket, Jack realized they must sound like an old married couple, discussing what they were going to have for dinner and for breakfast the next morning. They hadn't even discussed any kind of future together, but already shopped as if they lived in the same house. Normally this would have scared Jack, but oddly enough, it didn't now. They were going to try and build a life together, and all the discussions that could flow from that were reserved for later.

Now they were in the personal hygiene section and Lucas was waving around some 'personal lubrication'.

"Now there's a dead giveaway," Jack responded a little quietly.

Lucas's face turned serious. "Would you mind if the check out girl thought we were gay judging from our shopping basket?"

Jack took some time to reflect on that question, but eventually answered, "No, I guess not. It just takes some adjusting, I suppose. I have to start thinking of myself differently."

A shy smile broke on Lucas's face. "You are no different from when you were still married, Jack. Gay is not who you are or what you are. It doesn't define you."

Jack looked around and then put his arm around Lucas to pull him close and kiss his temple. "I know. It's just a little strange to be so open about it after denying it for most of my life."

Lucas chuckled. "You're nuts, but I love you for it. Now tell me, do we need to buy condoms too?"

Jack became a little shy again. "Well if I recall, the last person I had sex with was you, and I have been tested since then, so…"

Lucas grabbed him and kissed him full on the mouth. "Same here, believe it or not. So no condoms." He winked at Jack, who was looking at him a bit baffled.

"What? I'm a single father with a two year old. But you surprise me. I thought you would have cruised around a bit, you know, tested this newfound interest a little?"

Jack shook his head, his face soft. "I have to admit I thought about it, I just never… it wouldn't have been the same."

Lucas felt himself go all warm as Jack made that confession. "I think we need to get to a private room somewhere quickly, don't you think?"

Jack chuckled. "Yeah. Why don't I show you my apartment?"

They got a nice smile from the check out girl as she scanned the lube.

JACK'S apartment was the complete opposite of Lucas's, located in the nice part of Manhattan, practically in walking distance from the U.N. Buildings. It had a doorman and nicely maintained elevators and hallways.

Lucas let his eyes drink in the elegant, slightly overbearing opulence.

"I inherited this apartment from my parents. When they died, my brothers got a horse farm in Argentina, and I settled for this," he stated apologetically.

"I'm sorry about your parents," Lucas was quick to answer.

"Yeah, you could say it was a shitty couple of years." They set the groceries on the counter of the open kitchen and Jack took Lucas's hand. "Come on, I'll give you the grand tour."

The apartment was mostly empty, with white walls and very little furniture, just a comfortable leather couch in the living room and a huge painting on the wall. It was a colorful abstract, with barely legible words scribbled all over and pieces of printed paper glued into it and then painted over. Lucas moved a little closer to it, still not letting go of his lover's hand and then realized the signature on the painting was Jack's.

He gave the American an astonished look. "Jack, did you paint that?"

Jack raised his eyebrows, admitting it wordlessly.

"Oh my God, it's impressive!"

"But do you like it?" Jack asked, clearly more than a little unsure.

"Yeah, well, you have hidden talents, man. Like is not the word. I think it's amazing."

Jack chuckled at the dumbstruck look on Lucas's face. "I have about twenty canvasses in the studio, but this is my favorite. I always wanted to paint, just never had the time to before."

Lucas turned into Jack's arms and kissed him passionately. "As much as I want to stand here playing galleries, I have to pick up AnnElise in about two hours, so…"

Jack nodded. "I'll show you the bedroom."

Lucas dipped into one of the paper shopping bags before following him and triumphantly dug out the lube.

Jack chuckled. "God, you're such a romantic, aren't you?" he said as he pulled Lucas closer to him.

"No, I just don't want to hurt you, that's all." Lucas answered cheekily.

Lucas never got the chance to look around the bedroom before he felt Jack's hands all over him, stripping him of his clothes. "On second thought, I want you inside me, Jack, I missed this so much."

They continued, hungrily exploring each other's mouths, rubbing up against each other's naked skin.

Jack couldn't believe he was making love to Lucas, after he'd resigned himself to the thought that it would never happen again. He wanted to take it slow, afraid that his pent up lust wouldn't let him last long enough to actually make it inside of Lucas, but it felt so good to let his hands slide over the smooth, almost hairless skin. "Slow down," he pleaded breathlessly, dropping onto his back.

Lucas smiled and pulled Jack back on top of himself. "I don't want to take it slow. I want you now and we can do this slowly a hundred more times… later."

Jack smiled into the kiss, realizing Lucas felt the same urgency as he did. He felt his lover reach out for the lube and giggled as he got to it first.

"Quickly," Lucas panted. "Don't need much time, just a big… dollop." They both laughed at the situation and their own impatience, but were soon panting as Jack entered Lucas with first one, and then two fingers. It all felt very familiar and Lucas realized it was reassuring, knowing exactly what to expect. He knew he trusted Jack completely and that only made it better.

Lucas's dark, lustful eyes were slightly unfocused as he looked at Jack. He moaned as Jack took hold of his already hard erection. "Come inside me, Jack, I'm ready."

Lucas returned the gesture, lubing Jack up carefully. It felt strange to think there wasn't going to be any barrier between them now, no condom separating them.

As Lucas spread his legs wide, Jack positioned himself and slid slowly inside his young lover. "Are you okay?" he asked. It took all his self-restraint to hold still as Lucas's heat enveloped him and a low moan rose from Lucas's throat.

"Feels so good, Jack, please... start moving.... a little," Lucas pleaded before he wrapped his arms around Jack, pulling him into a hungry kiss. His hands travelled down to cup Jack's ass, urging him on with every thrust.

Lucas was tight and when he inserted a finger in Jack's passage, the American didn't manage more than a few thrusts before he came, shuddering, inside his lover.

It took Jack a few moments to realize Lucas hadn't come yet. Still gasping breath, he moved down his lover's body until he could take Lucas's rock hard cock in his mouth.

"Fuck!" Lucas cried out, tangling his hands into Jack's hair, guiding him. Jack knew Lucas was close, and he sucked hard, letting his tongue graze the entire length.

"Oh my God, Jack!" Lucas gasped as he tensed and then came into Jack's mouth with a long sigh.

Jack moved up, still kissing and licking, making Lucas twitch more than once, ending by languidly claiming Lucas's mouth. When they came up for air, Lucas laughed. "It's been ages since I've tasted myself in your mouth."

Jack pulled him closer and after some fiddling managed to get both of them under the covers of the bed they hadn't bothered to turn down. "You can't believe how much I missed this, Luke."

"Yes, I can," Lucas admitted, smiling into Jack's light blue eyes.

Jack buried his face in Lucas's nape. "I'm sorry I never came after you."

Lucas took Jack's head in his hands and forced him to look into his eyes. He realized his lover wasn't joking.

"I'm so sorry, Lucas." Jack had tears in his eyes.

"Jack, don't. I'm the one who ran away. When you were at your most vulnerable, I just left." He held Jack tighter in his arms. "It felt like the right thing to do at the time. I didn't want you to give up everything you ever worked for and then resent me afterwards."

"I wouldn't have," Jack answered, calmer now. "I would have gladly given everything up for you. I just wasn't very good at telling you that then, I suppose." He slowly kissed Lucas again. They were cozy now, both on their sides and facing each other, snuggled up together under the blankets, simply enjoying the closeness of their relaxed and naked bodies.

"We have to stay awake, so we're not too late to pick AnnElise up from Liz's," Lucas lazily told Jack in between kisses, but it was no use.

It was already dark when they arrived at Liz's house. Luckily she thought it was all very funny, making both of them feel incredibly self-conscious and she didn't skip a single opportunity to tease them about it mercilessly.

Chapter Twenty-Three

EARLY on in their renewed relationship, the decisions they had to make were easy. Lucas and AnnElise moved into Jack's apartment, because it was bigger, located in a better part of the city and closer to where they both now worked. More importantly, it didn't require paying any rent, though at some point Lucas remarked that what they had to pay in monthly expenses to maintain the elevators, their percentage of the building and the doorman, felt like rent to him!

Jack enrolled in the graduate program at Cornell just as he had said he would when he came back to New York, and even though he promised Lucas he wouldn't rush things, he did drive the four hours over to Ithaca a few times every month and spent countless hours behind his desk at home doing research and writing papers.

AnnElise was growing up happy, and Jack realized he really enjoyed being a dad. He blushed profusely, but was infinitely proud when AnnElise dragged him back into the U.N. day care center so she could introduce him as 'her other dad' to one of the new girls working there.

Most of their colleagues knew about their living arrangements and, to Jack's surprise in particular, it was usually met with everything from total indifference to the occasional 'well, good for you'. It was still strange to Jack to be matter-of-fact about Lucas, never sure if he should call him his boyfriend, lover, significant other or just partner, but whatever he called him, he was not hiding him anymore. In that respect, Liz was a great help, doing her very best to treat them no differently from the straight couples in her circle of friends.

Jack and Lucas's friends were an eclectic bunch of expatriates from a variety of countries, so by the time she was four, AnnElise was speaking French, Spanish and Italian with their children as if she had never heard anything else, and that was just the way her two dads liked it.

"REMEMBER when you asked me to marry you?"

Lucas had just put aside the press release he had been drafting all evening and was snuggled up to Jack who was reading 'Libération', one of the many foreign newspapers they subscribed to.

"I remember," Jack answered, narrowing his eyes as he fondly thought back to that night.

"Well, I accepted, right?" Lucas continued.

"Yes, you did," Jack said hesitantly and a little unsure of where exactly Lucas was taking this.

"Do you still feel the same?" Lucas asked, more seriously.

"Are you asking me if I still want to marry you?"

Lucas nodded.

"Honey, my feelings haven't changed; you know I still love you, probably even more now than when I asked you." Jack put his hand on Lucas's neck.

"But?" Lucas cut in.

"But what?" Jack could see the disappointment in his lover's face. "Luke, we don't need a piece of paper. Besides, here in the States it's not even valid."

"I know that," Lucas answered quietly, pulling away and creating some distance between him and Jack.

"Lucas, what's wrong? Why do I have to prove my love for you all of a sudden?" Jack put his newspaper down and turned in Lucas's direction.

"It's not about that. What if something happened to me? What if I had some kind of accident? I would want you to make decisions for me, and I would want you to take care of AnnElise."

"That's why I'm her legal guardian, and you had it written into your living will that I can make those decisions for you if you are no longer able to make them for yourself."

"I'm just scared that if something should happen to me, they will contact Lucy first."

Jack knew how much Lucas loved his daughter, but he also knew something must have happened to make him this worried.

"Just talk to me, Luke."

"She called, on the phone," Lucas cut in.

"Lucy?"

He nodded, and then the words came tumbling out. "She told me to leave her alone, that she didn't want to have anything to do with me or with 'the kid'. She doesn't even want to know her name!"

Lucas sat on the side of the bed, with his back to Jack, his head in his hands.

Jack waited for a moment and then moved behind his lover, scooting over so that he had one leg on either side of him and he could wrap his arms around the younger man's frame. At first Lucas pulled away, but Jack held him tighter and felt him surrender to the touch.

"Apparently they called her," Lucas eventually said, his voice thick with emotion.

"Who called her?" Jack softly asked, trying to calm Lucas down.

"The kindergarten school we filled out an application for. I handed them a copy of 'Lise's birth certificate and her adoption papers and I guess someone at the office got nosy and tracked down Lucy." Lucas sighed. "I mean, I don't have her phone number; I don't even know where she lives, but someone in that school had the nerve to track her down and call her to ask why I'm applying for a placement for AnnElise without her mother's consent."

"That settles it, Lucas. We enroll AnnElise in the U.N. International School. They don't need her mother's consent. Lucy signed away all her parental rights." Jack squeezed his lover tight.

Lucas leaned back into the touch. "That's what Lucy told me, too, and she said she told the man who called her as well."

"Must have been strange to hear her voice again."

Lucas nodded as Jack kissed his hair and rested his cheek against his head. "We could sue them for breach of privacy."

"No," Lucas whispered. "I don't want to sue anyone. I just want people to accept us for who we are. *We* are AnnElise's parents, Jack, you and I."

"So is that why you want to get married? To prove that?" Jack was trying to get to the root of it. He knew it would take more than a piece of paper for people to understand this.

"It's other things, too. If something happens to me, I want you to take care of 'Lise, Jack." Lucas was leaning against his lover, slowly caressing the strong arms that held him.

"You know I will."

"But it works the other way around, too. What if something happens to you, Jack? We'll be out on the street." Lucas turned a bit and lifted his legs over Jack's so he could face the older man. "Even if you put it in your will that we should get this apartment, I can't afford to inherit this. We're not legally a family so the inheritance tax will be enormous."

"You've really thought this through, haven't you?" Jack asked as he ran his hand through Lucas's soft hair.

"I can sort things out financially, Lucas. It had already crossed my mind that I should set up some sort of trust fund for AnnElise. That would help to resolve the tax problems and take care of you both. You and AnnElise are my family now."

"You would do that for me, for us, but you still don't want to get married?" Lucas looked at Jack questioningly.

Jack sighed. "I'm scared, Lucas."

Lucas straightened his back and turned towards Jack with an astonished look on his face. "Why on earth?"

"I can see the headlines now. 'Former U.S. Ambassador marries gay lover'," Jack pointed out. "I wouldn't want you, or AnnElise for that matter, to get any kind of backlash from this. We know they're okay about us living together, but it's only because we're fairly discreet about it. It's a delicate subject for a lot of countries, and I'm sure the U.N. is okay about one of their rising PR men living with another guy, but if we were to marry, while it's not yet legal in the state of New York, they might consider it 'drawing unfavorable attention'. I don't know if you've read the fine print of your contract, Lucas, but…"

Lucas rolled his eyes. "I know they can fire me if I do that."

"Listen." Jack squeezed Lucas tight in his arms and rocked him a little. "You know I love you and you know my brothers won't throw you out of this place if a Yellow Cab ran over me tomorrow."

Lucas shuddered, "Don't say that!"

"You know they won't, Luke."

Lucas turned some more to look his lover in the eye. "You better be careful not to get hurt. I want to dance with you at our daughter's wedding and I want you to bounce our grandchildren on your knee."

Jack looked at the serious expression on Lucas's face and couldn't help but laugh. "Who says she'll want to get married?"

Lucas smiled and grabbed Jack's hands while he moved to straddle him. "I don't care." He started as he placed a hard kiss on Jack's mouth. "I want to grow old with you, whether that means dancing at a wedding or not!"

Jack dropped to his back, allowing Lucas to continue the assault on his body. He knew that when Lucas didn't entirely get his way, he tended to take the lead in bed. It was one of the reasons why Jack liked to put up a good argument.

He liked to feel Lucas's bulge grinding against his, through their clothes, while his hands were pinned to the bed next to his ears. He liked how Lucas invaded his mouth with his tongue and then moaned, sending ripples through his entire body. He liked to watch the young man's eyes go dark as he said "just lie back and let me do all the work" while he struggled to get both of them out of their clothes. Jack would put up a silent argument, struggle a bit, but only because he knew it made Lucas's lust for him even stronger. Lucas would spoil him, let him suck on those long slender fingers of his while he had his mouth around Jack's swollen cock and the fingers of his other hand buried deep inside him.

Jack knew he would need all his resolve not to come right there and then. He knew that he would have to wait until Lucas was thrusting deep inside of him, nicking at his sweet spot every single time. Until they no longer knew where one ended and the other began, until he heard Lucas's low moan in his ear and his plea to "come with me, Jack". Only then could he let go, feeling all the sensations of lust and love course through his body and see them come out in Lucas's eyes.

"I promise that as soon as they make it legal, I'll ask you again," Jack whispered, his voice still a little unsteady.

"No, it's my turn to ask," Lucas rebutted, a lazy smile on his face as he pulled his lover closer in his arms.

Chapter Twenty-Four

LUCAS ran across the central hall, blue briefing folder in his hand, to pick up a Hollywood director and his security man at the courtesy desk. Apparently the director had been given the approval to film inside the United Nations building, which was normally unheard of. Lucas had been asked by the Secretary-General's aide to show both men around the 'backstage area' as well as the General Assembly Hall and the interpreters' booths. Since they were not in session today, both would be virtually empty.

Lucas vaguely recognized the man, but couldn't name any of his films off hand. His security expert was an old acquaintance, though.

"Mark! It's been….what? Four years now?" Lucas extended his hand and shook the rather subdued security man's hand.

"Mr. Carlton, if I remember correctly. Formerly of the British Embassy? And that would be closer to five years, sir," Mark answered, barely letting a smile break his stern exterior.

"United Nations now, and please, call me Lucas."

Mark turned to his employer. "Mr. Carlton and I go back to my Secret Service years when I was working for the American Embassy in Belgium."

"Ah yes!" the director answered, shaking Lucas's hand and then turning back towards Mark. "Isn't that where you got shot?"

Mark chuckled. "Yes, sir. Thank you for reminding me."

Lucas gave them their visitor's badges and took them through to the places they had been cleared to visit. He could tell Mark still had his eagle eyes. The bodyguard scanned his surroundings as if there were snipers on every overhang.

The director explained what the film they were going to shoot was all about and then asked if he could meet with one of the interpreters on staff.

"I think that can be arranged, sir. Why don't I show you around some more and then I'll make some calls and see what I can do?"

In the General Assembly Hall Lucas explained what happened when they were in session and then let the director take a walk around by himself to, as he put it, 'soak up the atmosphere'.

Lucas stayed to the side with Mark and picked up one of the internal phones.

"Jack? Are you really busy right now? No? Good. Can you come over to the General Assembly? I have some people here who'd like to meet you. Five minutes sounds good. Okay."

As Lucas sat down next to Mark, the man raised an eyebrow.

"Did I just hear you say Jack?" Mark asked with more amusement than inquiry in his voice. "Would that be Jack Christensen?"

"Yes. You know he no longer works for the State Department, right?"

"Are you saying he works here?" Mark asked, as he nodded towards the hall.

Lucas smiled. "Yes, as a senior interpreter. He'll be here in five minutes for the technical advice you wanted, and then I figure you might like to have the chance to chat with him as well."

"Well, he did save my life," Mark stated blankly.

"Strange," Lucas commented. "I thought it was the other way around."

"So the two of you are still together?"

Lucas was a little surprised at Mark's forwardness. "You don't waste any words, do you?"

Mark shrugged. "In tense situations, it's best to be direct. I'm sorry if that made you uncomfortable."

"No, it didn't. Not really. I just didn't think we were that transparent."

Mark looked at him sideways. "In my line of work, you learn to absorb any kind of information you can lay your hands on and use it to your advantage."

Lucas didn't quite know how to deal with that statement and realized he was speechless, which was highly unusual for him.

Luckily, Jack walked in at that very moment, nodded at Lucas and then grabbed Mark's hand to pull him into a bear hug.

Lucas watched a broad smile spread across the security man's face and caught himself noticing the handsome man behind the stern exterior. The fact that he and Jack obviously shared a great friendship made Lucas feel like an intruder. He knew there was no reason to be jealous, though and gave the men some space, walking towards the movie director, who was taking notes and no doubt already planning the upcoming shoot.

"**So** you're doing security for movies now?" Jack asked.

He and Mark agreed to meet that evening in a bar around the corner from the U.N. building. Lucas was invited, but Jack knew that he would want to be home for AnnElise and wasn't surprised when his lover declined.

"I got a medical discharge from the Secret Service so I had to do something," Mark answered, taking another swig from his bottle of beer. "This isn't too bad. A lot of it is consultancy work, you know, giving my opinion on who should be hired for what, securing movie sets and sometimes, like for this movie, I get asked to assess if the portrayal of Secret Service men is accurate."

"So who's going to play you in this film?" Jack asked, slightly amused.

"Sean Penn," Mark answered flatly. "He'll do okay. He's a good actor."

Jack sniggered. "He doesn't look much like you."

"Well, he doesn't have to, because he's not playing me, right? Besides, you know who's going to play you?"

Now it was Mark's turn to be amused and Jack wasn't sure if that was a good sign. He took a sip from his beer and shook his head.

"Nicole Kidman."

Both men started laughing. It was absurd, of course, but it felt good to rekindle the friendship that had grown between them in the weeks Jack had spent at his bodyguard's bedside after Mark's near fatal injury and Jack's career suicide.

Jack had realized in those dire times that real friends were rare, as many of the people he had known during his diplomatic career turned their backs on him. So, afraid to fall into a black hole after being a workaholic for so long, he spent his afternoons supporting the man who had saved his life by taking the bullet that had his name on it.

Mark had needed all the support he could get. The bullet had ripped through one of his lungs and nicked several large arteries in his chest. In fact, the doctors told him more than once that he shouldn't have survived an injury like that, but he did anyway. Jack's help in his recovery had been greatly appreciated, as both men knew that career-wise, they were facing an uncertain future.

Now four years later, the friendship was easily picked up again.

"I gather you and Lucas are still an item?" Mark asked glancing sideways.

"Yeah," Jack answered, surprised at his own hesitance.

"Good," Mark stated.

"Good?"

"Yeah, good."

Jack could tell Mark was having fun teasing him. "What exactly do you mean by that?"

Mark drank again and took his time answering, which made Jack a little nervous.

"It means that all those nights I spent in that cold uncomfortable car in front of his apartment were worth it."

"You…. You mean you actually stayed…"

"Not to mention all the times I told your wife you were in a meeting while I was sitting there, freezing my ass off."

Jack chuckled nervously and looked at Mark, who was still gazing out towards the rest of the bar. "Why did you?"

"It was my job to always know where you were. At all times," Mark answered.

Jack was confused, "I know that, but why did you lie to Maria? I'm sure it wasn't in your job description to provide me with an alibi for my extramarital activities."

Mark looked him straight in the eye. "Did you think you were the only guy in your line of work who slept around?"

Jack shook his head. "But I wasn't just sleeping around, was I?"

"I didn't get paid to form an opinion on whether it was worse that you cheated on your wife with another guy than with another woman. What mattered was that I knew where you were and that you were relatively safe. Plus, part of my job was also to protect your reputation and if that included lying to your wife…"

Jack didn't know what to say. "I'm sure you had your opinion on the matter?"

"And you had your opinion on the crises you were asked to mediate. We talked about it in the car from time to time, remember? It didn't stop you from defending something you didn't believe in. And let's face it, I wasn't trying to change the point of view of world leaders, I was just trying to make sure you could do your job, so my opinion was inconsequential."

The discussion was definitely turning serious, so Jack was surprised to see a broad smile forming on Mark's face.

"There's just one thing I've been dying to ask you, though."

"Shoot," Jack answered, glad to switch to some lighter banter.

"That day of the lock-down, when that madman was trying to blow up his car in the tunnels in front of the Embassy?"

Jack nodded, remembering the day well.

"Did you screw Lucas over your desk?"

Jack choked mid-swallow and coughed on the beer caught in his throat. He was speechless. How did Mark know? And if Mark knew, Gertje must have known as well. God knows how many other people had passed by his office door that day and wondered at the strange noises from within.

Mark was a good friend, even though they had lost contact after they both sought other employment. Could he just come out and say it?

Could he just admit that the tense situation had made both him and Lucas horny enough to have a quick shag in his office?

"I guess that's a yes, then," Mark stated as he emptied his bottle of beer and motioned to the bartender to bring them both another one.

"How did you know? I didn't think we were that loud," Jack tried as he regained his composure.

"Don't worry about it, Jack. I should call Gertje though, she owes me a hundred euros."

Jack buried his face in his hands. This was embarrassing. Here he was thinking he was totally comfortable in his relationship with Lucas, but Mark and Gertje's acceptance of that relationship almost five years ago made him blush like a school girl. The two of them had been relaxed enough about it to make a bet?

"I can't believe this," Jack shook his head, trying to will himself to stop blushing.

Mark laughed. "So you see, it's good that you two are still together."

Jack began to relax. "Were we really that loud?"

"Naah. I heard some, well, strange noises when I put my ear to the door, but what really gave you away was what I saw when you opened it."

Jack was almost afraid to ask. "What did you see?"

"Both of you, flushed, clothes a little rumpled and shirts badly tucked back inside your trousers. Your desk practically cleared, but papers all over the floor and Mr. Carlton... Lucas looked like a school boy who had been caught with his hand in the cookie jar. You were calm and collected though, as usual."

Jack nodded. He should have known Mark's eagle eyes would have been impossible to fool.

Chapter Twenty-Five

LUCAS was on the phone to Liz, trying at the same time to clear away some of the toys thrown all over the floor, when he heard the doorbell.

"Listen, there's someone at the door. Hang on while I go see who it is."

With the phone caught between his shoulder and his ear, he stuffed a teddy bear and a Furby under his arm and looked through the spy hole. He didn't recognize the woman with the blond ponytail standing with her back to the door, but since the doorman had cleared her, he opened it anyway.

The petite woman turned around to face him and he gasped. "Oh my God, Liz, I'll get back to you later." Lucas ended the call and dropped the phone on the hall table.

"Maria, I … I didn't expect you here. Ehm, Jack's not home yet; he told me you were meeting in town later tonight?"

"Yes, we are. Can I come in?"

Lucas moved away from the doorway to let her enter, not failing to notice that she looked amazing as she opened her warm winter coat to reveal tight jeans and a white turtleneck sweater.

"I didn't come here to talk to Jack; I wanted to see you." Her voice was calm, but Lucas could hear just a hint of nerves.

She looked around the apartment and smiled. "I like what you've done to the place. It feels very lived in. Not like when Jack's parents were still alive and this was only a place to spend Christmas holidays."

Lucas was unsure how to react as he stood there, still hugging his daughter's toys. "So why did you want to see me?" He was sure the coolness in his voice was clear to her. The last time they had spoken was at the hospital when she threatened to ruin Jack's career if Lucas didn't leave her husband alone.

"Listen, Lucas, I'm sure I'm probably your least favorite person on the planet, but…" All of a sudden she no longer looked like the women he had hated so much in Brussels. She was standing in his living room in her parka and he was seeing her as Jack had described her all along: as a kind, but very determined woman, who had her heart in the right place. What harm would it do if he was nice to her? Jack had told Lucas he was meeting Maria and had reassured him that she wasn't going to steal him back.

"Why don't I make us a cup of tea and we can talk?"

He gestured to her to give him her coat and they made their way to the kitchen. A few minutes later, they both held steaming cups of tea, and Lucas was apologizing for the mess.

"I was just clearing up around here. Three kids in the house doesn't make that any easier."

Maria's eyes went wide and as if by command, AnnElise darted into the kitchen, running behind the table and coming up behind Lucas's legs. She pulled on his trouser leg and whispered. "Who is this?"

Lucas smiled at her and picked her up. "AnnElise, this is Maria; she's a very good friend of Jack's."

"Is she coming to play with Jack?" The little girl asked seriously. Both Lucas and Maria had a hard time keeping a straight face. "No, she's going out to dinner with him tonight, while I stay home with you and Emile and Charlie. Will you be nice and say hi to her?"

AnnElise wiggled until Lucas set her back on the floor and then walked over to Maria, her right hand extended. "Hello, I am AnnElise Carlton. Nice to meet you."

Maria took the girl's small hand in hers and shook it. "Hello AnnElise Carlton, I'm Maria Donnelly."

The little girl giggled, retracted her hand, and ran out of the kitchen.

Lucas looked apologetic. "Well, she's four, we can't stop her giggling and running off yet."

"She's gorgeous, Lucas. How's Lucy? She is Lucy's, isn't she?"

Lucas was a little taken aback by Maria's reaction, but there was none of the reproach he had expected. "Yeah, she is. Lucy's fine; she's married to some heir to a supermarket chain, who doesn't know she has a daughter. Lucy gave me a lovely little girl and I'll always be grateful for that, but she wants nothing to do with AnnElise and as sad as that is, I can't help feeling it's for the best." He didn't want to elaborate on how Lucy had almost given his daughter up for adoption.

"Well, there's no mistaking her for anyone else but your daughter, she even acts like you. The way she introduced herself was just charming."

Lucas smiled softly. "Well, she's crazy about Jack, too."

"I always knew he'd make an amazing father," Maria stated enthusiastically, much to Lucas's surprise. "But you said three kids? Did you adopt two more?"

"No, no, they're Liz's sons. She's a colleague from work. AnnElise is crazy about the boys and Liz needed a weekend without kids, so… well, she helped me out quite a bit before… Jack came back." He didn't know why he was so uncomfortable talking to her about the kids. Was it because he felt he had taken this part away from Maria? That if it hadn't been for him coming along, she and Jack would probably have had kids by now?

Maria looked up at him suddenly. "I'm glad you gave Jack the opportunity to be a dad. I never had the nerve."

Lucas looked away from her for a moment, trying to gather his thoughts. "You're okay with this?"

She nodded. "It took me a long time to really understand, Lucas." She sighed. "I truly hated you. For taking Jack away from me. For pulling the rug from under my feet. In one swoop, you took away my husband, my career and the life, which I'd spent twenty years building up."

She looked at Lucas intently, making him uncomfortable. "It took me two years of living among people who didn't know where their next meal was coming from to realize it was all superficial. To realize that yes, I loved this man, but he didn't love me back, not the way he loved you!"

"He loved you too, Maria. He told me how hard it was to tell you about us. He kept putting it off. I'm sorry."

"No, you're not," she stated matter-of-factly.

Lucas couldn't help but chuckle. "You sound just like Jack. But... I *am* sorry. Not for loving Jack, I'll never apologize for that again, but I'm sorry that we hurt you."

Maria smiled softly. "I can't deny that. It's hard to see the man you've loved most of your adult life fall in love with someone else. It took me a long time to understand I could have a life beyond being his wife and to admit to myself that I liked seeing him happy, even if it was with you. It wasn't until I found my goal in life that I could see beyond my own jealousy."

Although deep down he still didn't trust her, Lucas realized he was starting to like her. "Jack told me you work for UNICEF?"

She nodded, smiling broadly. "Yeah, I coordinate relief teams. I just came back from Darfur. Sadly it was becoming so unstable there we had to leave, but we were building schools and setting up classrooms. You know, Lucas, I used to be a pretty good organizer, which made me every ambassador's dream, but it was all about the show. The perfect gala dinner, reception, luncheon. Show your face here; make a little speech there. Now I'm actually doing things in the field, things that actually change people's lives for the better, and I don't have to get all dolled up in expensive designer gowns with perfect hair and make-up. So I should really thank you for stealing Jack from me. I would never have realized what was making me unhappy if the two of you hadn't toppled my world."

Her eyes were wide and her face was shining. Lucas could tell she was genuinely happy with her life now. Maybe she was telling the truth; maybe she had forgiven them? Lucas was still not entirely comfortable though. Only time would tell if he could ever forgive her.

The tenuous mood was broken when they both looked up as the front door opened.

JACK walked in the door of his apartment to be met, as usual, by the excited chant of his name. He would never get enough of being greeted by AnnElise's voice ringing through the house. The door had barely closed and he was still holding his keys when she sprinted right into his arms, giving him a big hug and a smacker. No matter how tired he was after a day's work, she could always make him smile. She told him about Emile and Charlie being there and Jack smiled as he knew all too well who was boss in that playgroup.

He put his keys in the small bowl on the hallway cabinet and was hanging up his coat when AnnElise gave him a teasing smile. "There's a girl to see you." She giggled, obviously thinking that was a funny idea. "Her name is Maria."

He felt his heart stop. Poor Lucas. He could only hope Maria was nice to him.

Then his lover called out, "We're in the kitchen!" It didn't sound strained or too desperate. Maybe she had only just arrived?

With a "Why don't you go and play?" he sent AnnElise off to her boys again and walked over to the kitchen with a constricted feeling in his chest.

To his surprise, Lucas was sitting on the counter and Maria was leaning against the kitchen cabinets on the other side, both were drinking tea and smiling as they conversed animatedly. Maybe his apprehension was unnecessary?

Jack greeted Maria first with a kiss on the cheek and then realized he was uncomfortable kissing Lucas in front of her. He hesitated momentarily, and then saw in Lucas's face that he had felt it too. *Damn!* Why did she still intimidate him?

The atmosphere in the kitchen cooled a few degrees and Jack made his escape, telling Maria, "Listen, I'll just change my clothes, and we'll be ready to leave in about ten minutes, okay?"

LATER that night, Lucas went to bed early. Looking after three kids between the ages of five and three after a busy work day was tiring enough, but the additional stress of Maria arriving early and Jack's awkward response to her presence made it an exhausting evening indeed.

He'd noticed that Jack had hesitated kissing him on the mouth as was usual when he came home. Lucas didn't take it personally, since he hadn't been entirely comfortable with the situation either, but he wanted to know if it was just a matter of Jack feeling strange about being in a room with the only two people he'd had a serious relationship with, or whether there was something more to it.

Lucas shook his head and told himself there was no reason to doubt Jack's commitment to him. Really. Then why had things been so weird all of a sudden? Why had Jack disappeared into their bedroom and reappeared only minutes later, in different clothes, only to whisk Maria out of the kitchen and off to dinner in the city?

He turned off the light and snuggled under the duvet, knowing full well he wouldn't sleep until Jack was home even though there was no reason to be jealous. Jack had left Maria, gotten a divorce and changed his whole life around, at a time when Lucas wasn't even a part of that life. So why was he doubting Jack now?

He heard the front door open and the familiar clinking of Jack placing his keys in the small bowl. He could tell Jack was being careful not to wake up anyone and moments later heard him come stealthily into their bedroom, undress and slip underneath the covers.

In the darkness Lucas turned to face his lover.

"I didn't mean to wake you," Jack whispered.

"You didn't. I couldn't sleep," Lucas answered. "How was dinner?"

"Okay, I guess. Nice to talk to her again."

Lucas could hear the hesitation in Jack's voice so he moved closer and put his arms around his lover. "It's okay, Jack. You're allowed to enjoy catching up with an old friend, as long as it's just that." He sighed as he realized it sounded like the little green devil of jealousy was rearing its ugly head, so he added, "I know I can trust you, Jack."

Jack snuggled up close in his arms and kissed him tenderly.

"Damn! You had Thai food without me?" Lucas teased.

"How do you always do that?" Jack asked and Lucas could tell he was smiling, although it was too dark to see.

"It's the coconut milk and the lemongrass and the touch of coriander."

"You can taste all that?" Jack teased back.

"And more," Lucas answered as he pulled Jack even closer and all the feelings of jealousy waned to be replaced by something much nicer.

Chapter Twenty-Six

"**OH,** I almost forgot," Lucas said as he watched Jack bend over the table to wipe it, thereby finishing off the after dinner chores, "There's a letter for you. Big envelope, expensive paper, calligraphic handwriting and addressed only to Mr. Jack Christensen."

Jack threw him the wet cloth and walked into the hallway to retrieve the letter. As he returned to the living room, he opened it and read the formal invitation.

"Stacey's getting married. You remember her? My Junior Protocol Officer? In Antwerp, no less. And we're invited. Wanna go?" Jack asked while he was still reading.

"It's only addressed to you," Lucas answered sheepishly as he retreated to the kitchen, closely followed by Jack.

"It says Mr. Jack Christensen and partner," Jack rebutted as he wrapped his arms around Lucas, pushing him against the counter.

"That could be anyone," Lucas pouted, knowing Jack would fall straight into his trap.

"As I recall, I only have one partner." he kissed Lucas's hair, "boyfriend," and his neck, "lover."

"Will you two do that in your own room? Kids can just walk into this kitchen, you know." AnnElise was standing in the kitchen, her hands on her hips. She turned, grabbed a can of Coke Light from the fridge and exited before the two men, in each other's arms, could respond.

"Did we miss something? When did our daughter turn into a teenager?" Lucas asked, his mouth slightly open as he watched the little girl sashay out of the room.

"Last time I looked she was still six. She's reading *me* bed time stories now, but she still wants to be tucked in," Jack answered, also rather baffled by AnnElise's cocky remark.

"You think we should say something?" Lucas asked, raising his eyebrows.

"Naah, let it go," Jack chuckled. "She'll be worse when we get back from this wedding after she's been at Liz's for a week. I swear that hands-on-hips gesture is vintage Liz."

SIX WEEKS later, they arrived in the Antwerp Hilton for Stacey's wedding.

When they had called her to RSVP, she had explained that everything had been arranged, including hotel rooms the night before and after the wedding for all the friends and family flying in from all over the world.

When the receptionist handed them the keycard and announced that they had been given one of the executive suites, Jack turned to Lucas. "Luke, did you...?"

Lucas gave him an innocent look and shook his head.

The suite was the same room that held such special memories for both of them. After the porter had been given a tip and left, Jack looked at Lucas.

"Well if you didn't arrange this, then who did?" Jack asked, casually taking off his jacket. "I'm pretty sure Stacey didn't know about what happened in this room almost exactly seven years ago, Luke."

Lucas finished closing the drapes and shot across the room to Jack, throwing himself at his lover with such force they both ended up on the bed. "Happy anniversary, lover," Lucas moaned into Jack's mouth.

They kissed passionately, freeing themselves from most of their clothes and grinding their growing bulges against each other.

"The car will be here in about thirty minutes," Jack gasped as he came up for air, "to pick us up so I can get fitted for my dress suit."

"Fuck the car," Lucas answered, clearly desperate, as he pulled Jack closer to him again.

"Luke, we won't have time for a shower afterwards, if we..."

Jack watched in awe as Lucas turned around on the bed with a feral gleam in his eye. At the same time that he felt his young lover's hot mouth over his still clothed cock, he got Lucas's crotch pushed in his face. They were both panting; it would be over in a manner of minutes and it wasn't like he was going to be able to hold back anyway. Or wanted to, for that matter.

This was hunger and nostalgia. In this room, Lucas had shown him there was no way back, that he couldn't go on denying the feelings he had pushed aside most of his life.

Even now, after seven years, he still loved the taste of Lucas's leaking cock in his mouth and the feel of Lucas's mouth on his. He loved how what he was doing to this young man was making them both moan, loudly, sending the vibrations through their groins, making Lucas emulate the exact same motions, returning the little licks and gestures, the hungry sucking, until they were both bucking and thrusting into each other's mouths.

Lucas came first and Jack strained to look down to see Lucas's face, contorted with pleasure, as he tasted his white, hot cum filling his throat. Jack swallowed eagerly, feeling Lucas thrust out the waves of pleasure, then Lucas took his mouth from Jack's swollen cock, only to grab it with both hands, stroking it with surprising coordination.

The sight of his sated young lover, still trying to hold on enough to make him come, made the tingling feeling in his groin rise. He thrust hard into Lucas's hands and felt his orgasm overtake him as Lucas lazily opened his mouth to take the head in.

After a few moments of panting, Lucas crawled up, a lazy smile on his face as he moved closer to deeply kiss Jack, mixing up all the tastes in their mouths. Jack could still feel the aftershocks in his own body and the sensitivity of Lucas's as he stroked him so soon after their rushed climax. It was no surprise that they had time to spare before the car would come to pick them up.

Jack and Lucas chuckled with high spirits as they brushed their teeth together in front of the large bathroom mirror. Lucas had taken a quick shower and put on some jeans and Jack had gotten up from the bed only after Lucas dressed, fearing that if they took a shower together they would never leave the room. Now he too was freshly showered and they would be out of the door in a few minutes.

THE following morning Jack woke to the sound of someone banging loudly on the door. Lucas was sprawled all over him and he moved carefully so as not to wake the young man. When he checked the alarm clock by the side of the bed, it was 7:30.

Who would be knocking on their door this early? The wedding didn't start until ten o'clock, right?

He quickly pulled one of the complimentary white bathrobes around his naked body and went to the door. As he glanced at the bed he saw Lucas's deliciously naked body lying face down on the mattress. Quickly, he threw the covers over him before opening the door.

What he saw made him chuckle.

"Stacey? You okay, honey?"

Stacey stood in the doorway wrapped in a pink bathrobe with curlers in her hair and no make up. She was in a panic, something Jack had not seen before.

"One of my groomsmen stood me up!" she sulked pushing past Jack into the hotel room.

She covered her mouth with her hand like a child that has uttered a bad word. "I didn't interrupt anything, I hope?"

Jack gave her a toothy smile. "No, Stacey, he's sound asleep. And so was I, but what's your problem?"

"Well, Roy's brother, who's supposed to be his best man, got held up in Bahrain because of some diplomatic incident there. Now his best friend is here, so he can take over as best man, but that leaves me one groomsman short. You think Lucas could sub?"

She barely took a breath while telling Jack about this crisis.

"Sure, I don't see why not," Jack answered. "He doesn't have the right suit though and I'm sure you want us all to look the same?"

"Be right back," she told him, holding up her index finger before she sped down the hallway to her suite.

Moments later she was back, holding a hanger covered in see-through plastic. "Let him try this. If it doesn't fit, call the number on the plastic wrap and tell them it's an emergency."

Jack chuckled as he accepted the suit and watched Stacey run back down the corridor. He hung the bag on the coat rack and went back to the bed where Lucas was still sleeping. As he sat carefully on the edge, he let his hand wander under the covers, where he found Lucas's smooth soft skin. His lover moaned as Jack lightly stroked the back of Lucas's thigh, moving up toward his buttocks and the part of his lower back that sloped down in between the dimples. Lucas's skin felt warm from sleeping and he couldn't get enough of the smooth silken feeling.

"Lemme sleep some more," Lucas mumbled as he pulled the covers over his head. Jack lay down next to Lucas, who was now engulfed in sheets and blankets, and pulled the young man tightly in his arms.

"I have a feeling I can persuade you to get up," Jack teasingly tried to coax him.

"Noooo," Lucas sulked, keeping his eyes closed, "'s too early."

"No, it's not. We'll miss breakfast."

"Don't care."

Jack slowly tried to get his hand to find a way under the covers. "The wedding starts in two hours, we have to shower, get dressed into these nice grey suits and then walk over to the town hall. We'll never make it at this rate."

"*You* have to get dressed in a nice suit." the Brit moaned as he snuggled up closer to Jack, who was now rubbing his lover's stomach.

"You too. Stacey just brought a suit for you," Jack teased as he moved his hand from Lucas's stomach to his hips, carefully avoiding his groin area.

"She did?" Lucas asked, still keeping his eyes closed, but moving his body in the general direction of Jack's hand. "One of those nice grey ones like you tried on yesterday?"

"Yes," Jack murmured, burying his face in Lucas's neck, teasingly biting his shoulder.

When Lucas snuggled in closer, clearly having no intention of getting up, Jack started tickling him, soon making him break out in hysterical laughter.

Two hours later they would be rushing to get ready, just as Jack had predicted.

Fits of giggles and a ferocious tickling, followed by a pillow fight had ended up with Jack pushed face first into the door leading to the bathroom. Lucas had apologized for his roughness, but only half seriously.

"You're asking for it, Jack; you do realize it, don't you?" Lucas asked.

Not easily put off, Jack simply answered. "You're just happy that we don't have a daughter here who can listen in."

Lucas pulled down the plush white bathrobe that only just hung on Jack's shoulders and pressed his body against his lover's. "All the more reason to make you moan so loud that Stacey's going to be banging on that door again, asking what the hell I think I'm doing to you."

"Fuck," was all Jack could mutter.

"You think so?" Lucas asked teasingly as he offered two fingers for Jack to lick. "Better make them nice and slippery, because that's all the lube I have right here."

Jack took his time, tasting the slight saltiness of Lucas's slender fingers. He could tell Lucas was growing a little impatient, rubbing against his back, still he didn't rush. The young Brit was clearly getting aroused, but nowhere near as much as Jack. As Lucas placed his left hand flat on Jack's stomach, Jack realized he was glad he had the door to lean against. He moved his legs apart a little and opened his mouth to let out a low groan as one of Lucas's saliva covered fingers breach him roughly. They were so used to being quiet, always keeping in the back of their minds that just a few doors away, their daughter was sleeping. Only now they were half a world away from her and Jack didn't care who heard them as he felt the burn of Lucas's second finger subside and sheer ecstasy took over.

Lucas knew his lover's body well, knew just how much roughness Jack could take. He also knew he could get Jack off with just his fingers, but that they didn't dare do this with AnnElise in the other room, since all that twisting and pumping of his fingers made for a very loud response from his lover. Jack moaned with every movement, and this sent all Lucas's blood rushing to his cock. He curled his fingers slightly and brushed over the most sensitive area of his lover's body, making Jack shudder.

"Fuck, Luke!" Jack shouted as his breathing became ragged. Lucas pushed him against the door with more force, and then touched his sweet spot again, knowing that Jack's knees would give out eventually. Lucas felt his lover's stomach muscles contract and the ring around his fingers tighten. Jack was moaning almost constantly as Lucas stopped moving his hand and let the American set the pace, thrusting back onto Lucas's fingers and sending himself over the edge after just a few moves.

Lucas wrapped his arms around Jack and supported him as he slowly sank to the floor. He crawled on top of him and kissed him passionately, rubbing his own leaking cock against Jack's slippery stomach.

"You're not done yet," Jack whispered against Lucas's mouth.

"Want to watch me come?" the younger man asked seductively.

Jack nodded. "Always." He caressed Lucas's thighs as the Brit righted himself, then watched Lucas's teasing face as the young man stroked his cock with long determined pulls. Jack loved to watch Lucas pleasure himself, loved how he bit his lower lip, trying not to make too much noise.

"I want to hear you, Luke, I didn't hold back," Jack urged him on as he lifted his hand to touch Lucas's.

"Don't," Lucas replied, pushing away Jack's hand, "just… watch… just… see… what you do… to me."

His fisting movements became more uncoordinated as his breath grew ragged. "God… Jack…"

Lucas's face contorted, and he let out a low, throaty moan as he came, splattering all over his own hand and Jack's stomach.

The American reached up, cupping Lucas's head as he slumped down onto his lover's body. They remained wrapped around each other for some time, as Lucas caught his breath.

"We better shower if we want to look presentable at Stacey's wedding, honey," Jack eventually said.

"Mmmh," Lucas nodded, rubbing his face against Jack's neck.

"YOU look nice in that suit, Mr. Christensen," Lucas mentioned as he was helping Jack tie his cravat.

"Well, tails look good on you too, Mr. Carlton," Jack replied, prompting Lucas to step back and fall into an old fashioned curtsey. "It's surprising everything fits so well, since you didn't try it on yesterday."

"Well, it's a little on the snug side. Stacey's soon to be brother-in-law must be a real shrimp."

"Now, now," Jack mocked. "For beauty, one must suffer."

Jack moved behind Lucas to look at their reflection in the long hallway mirror. They looked very elegant, in matching grey coat tails with striped cravats. Stacey could be proud of her groomsmen.

"Marry me," Lucas asked, smiling at Jack in the mirror.

Jack put his hands on Lucas's hips and kissed his neck. "You know my answer to that, Luke."

"I want to hear it again… the short version," Lucas teased.

Jack looked up, seriously. "Yes, Lucas, I'll marry you. One day, I'll marry you."

STACEY'S wedding was a fun, informal occasion, with all the bridesmaids and groomsmen, family and friends strolling from one location to the next, since the town hall, cathedral, reception and banquet hall were all within walking distance of each other. The happy couple and most guests were decidedly tipsy by the end of the reception and rowdily drunk by the end of the sit-down dinner. This was partly because of the relaxed atmosphere, but the fact that almost all of the guests in the Antwerp Hilton dining room also had rooms in the hotel, was a factor as well.

Jack and Lucas woke up the next morning thoroughly hung over and not quite sure how they had managed to make it back to their room. They were grateful, however, that they had arranged to spend a few more days in Belgium before heading home again.

After their last night in the hotel room, as Lucas was brushing his teeth in front of the large mirror, Jack snaked an arm around his stomach like a thief in the night. Lucas had a hard time keeping a straight face at Jack's prowling look as the older man pretended to bite his lover's neck. They were both naked and Lucas turned serious when he felt Jack's erection rubbing against his backside.

Jack pulled Lucas's face around so he could kiss him, while his other hand strayed down over the young man's belly towards his already reactive groin. "You look good enough to eat," Jack growled against Lucas's lips. "I want to fuck you here, in front of the mirror."

"Fuck, yeah," Lucas responded, breathing more heavily. For a moment, he remembered Jack not wanting to do this with him on another occasion because it brought back memories of Maria, but that thought was quickly dismissed by Jack's strong hand on his cock, quickly stroking him to a full erection. He molded his body to Jack's, eager for as much contact as he could get, and wantonly rubbing his ass against his lover's arousal. There was an urgency to their movements, fueled by their hunger for each other and by the intoxicating picture reflected in the mirror.

Lucas leaned forward, holding on to the washbasin with one hand, the other clawing towards the complimentary bath oils and moisturizers in search of something that could be used as lubricant. He opened one of them and dropped it, the white, creamy fluid leaking out over the side of the basin. He was quick enough to catch the drops in his hand and he reached back to coat Jack's straining member.

Jack hissed at the cold fluid and then moaned as Lucas kept stroking him. Lucas couldn't help but gaze at the way their bodies moved together and he pulled Jack along so they were standing in between both basins, giving them a nearly unobstructed view.

"Do it now," Lucas whispered, his head turned towards his lover. "Fuck me now."

"Need to prep you first," Jack replied hoarsely, letting his movements be guided by the vision in the mirror.

"Forget prep," Lucas almost begged, "we've made love… three-four times a day since we arrived. I can take it." He knew he could and trusted Jack not to hurt him. Jack poured some more cream out of the fallen bottle, coating his erection again and rubbed his cock over the sensitive muscle inside Lucas's cleft. Lucas pushed back, wanting, needing to be penetrated, spreading his legs farther apart, giving Jack better access. Jack looked down and as the pressure against Lucas's guardian muscle increased, Lucas braced himself against the counter.

Jack pushed forward, one hand guiding his thick, dark cock and the other pulling his young lover closer. Lucas didn't feel the telltale pop and was a little disappointed when Jack moved to sit down on the covered toilet seat, pulling Lucas along with him.

"Ride me," Jack implored, "and watch yourself doing it. God, you look amazing!"

"*We* look amazing," Lucas corrected as he spread his legs, leaning on Jack's knees for leverage. With one hand, he guided his lover's cock to his entrance and sank down on it with a sigh, all the while looking into the mirror. Seeing the long, hard cock disappear into his body was almost too much and it was only the fierce burn that prevented him from coming. He was still hard though, so much so that the head of his cock nuzzled his belly and, as he rolled his hips, pearly streaks glistened in the light. The burn started to subside and he leaned back against Jack's chest while reaching between his legs to cup his balls. Before he could react, Jack grabbed his thighs and lifted them, exposing their union. Lucas could feel how his muscle stretched around Jack's thick cock and he rubbed it experimentally. The sensation shot sparks through his groin and judging from Jack's reaction, it felt good to his lover, too. Lucas was close and wouldn't need much to come, but he wanted more. "Let's move," he suggested. "I want you to fuck me hard." He reached behind to touch Jack and together they got up, careful not to break contact. Lucas braced himself, knowing the power his lover could bring forth.

Jack started moving, and Lucas moaned at the feeling of the large cock sliding in and out of his body. As he looked forward, he could see his own cock bouncing a little, creating a feeling that was familiar but that he had never really seen until now. He looked into Jack's eyes, now dark blue, staring at the perfect synergy with which they moved. It was an incredibly erotic sight, seeing how the slapping noises of their bodies colliding so intimately were translated to images in the mirror.

"Fuck you feel good," Jack exhaled more than said as his movements became more powerful and more accurate with each thrust. "So tight... so hot."

"Yeah," Lucas almost whimpered. "I'm close," he added as he tilted his hips slightly. "Oh fuck yeah... right there..." He couldn't touch himself, afraid that if he let go of the basins, they would crash into the mirror, but he could see his cock leaking with every thrust. "Oh yeah... don't stop now... make me come Jack... make me come... and come with me!"

Jack was hitting all the right spots, but the power of his thrusts and their accuracy was waning, alerting Lucas that his lover was close, too. He started pushing back, meeting Jack half way. Then Jack moved closer to him, whispering "aim for the mirror" and before Lucas could laugh, he felt his groin tingle and thick milky strands shot from his cock, splattering all over the pristine shiny surface in front of them. Jack thrust twice more, hard and accurate in the direction of Lucas's prostate, prolonging his orgasm and Lucas felt the heat spread throughout his body.

They stood clinging to each other and breathing hard as they stared into the mirror.

"Fuck, that was intense," Jack panted against Lucas's neck.

"Think we should get one of these for the apartment?" Lucas suggested, gesturing at the mirror.

"No way!" Jack chuckled. "I'd have to gag you to fuck you in front of it. There's no way we can do it quietly."

Lucas placed his hands over Jack's, watching his eyes in the mirror. "Guess we'll need to come back here at least once a year then."

Chapter Twenty-Seven

"**GERTJE!** Oh my God, it's so good to see you!" Jack held out his arms and hugged his former secretary tight. "Have you seen Lucas?"

Gertje was beaming and Jack realized she hadn't aged at all; she still looked like the vibrant, always busy and very motherly woman who had made his working life in Belgium a blessing.

"Oh yes! Well, he's doing what he does best. He's greeting all your guests, making them feel welcome. I'm so glad I was invited to spend New Year's Eve with your family, Jack."

"You look happy, Gertje."

"I am." She was blushing. "I miss my Eddy of course, but at least I get to travel around a bit now. Spend more time with my sister here in the States."

Jack nodded. "I heard about Eddy from Stacey. Why didn't you call me?"

Gertje smiled at him and tilted her head. "You were half way across the world, Jack. It was a private funeral. Anyway, we're here for you tonight."

Jack sighed and rolled his eyes. "You know I hate being the center of attention nowadays."

Gertje gave him an understanding smile. "I don't think you'll have to worry about who will be the center of attention. Not with Lucas and AnnElise around."

"I'm glad you're here tonight. It feels like the family is complete," Jack added.

She blushed. "I wouldn't have missed it for the world."

Jack knew this woman was a true friend, even though they didn't speak that often and he felt he should remedy that.

"You were always my big supporter, weren't you?" he asked, seriously now.

"One hundred percent, Mr. Ambassador." She winked at him.

"Why did you cover up for me with Maria when you knew I was sleeping around behind her back?"

"Oh, I didn't cover up for you especially, Jack. I didn't give her any other story than I would give other people. 'Mr. Christensen's in a late meeting. No, I can't disturb him. I can, however, give him a message afterwards.' I have to admit I knew that somehow you two were meant for each other."

Jack thought she looked like a proud mother when she said this to him.

"And seeing both of you here tonight, I know I was right."

There was that smug smile again.

"Yeah, I love him, Gertje, I really do."

"Oh, a fool could see that. I know. I knew it then. The way your face lit up whenever I showed him into your office. The fact that he was spending a lot more time with you than was strictly necessary. Even the fact that he took every opportunity to play diplomatic messenger. But I liked him from the moment he walked into the office. He's a special man, Jack. Like you, he's good with people, likes to make them feel at ease. Doesn't care whether it's the President or the doorman. And you have a wonderful daughter too. Perfect mix of the two of you."

Jack shrugged. "That's nice of you to say, Gertje, but she's all Lucas's."

"Don't believe it for a second, Jack. She may look like him, but I definitely see your hand in her upbringing. She's shyer than Lucas, a little more of a thinker. Smart kid, too, she knows what she's talking about. She explained your PhD thesis to me. Not bad for an eight year old, right?"

Jack smiled at her, not quite believing what she'd just told him. "You're joking, right?"

"No, no, she told me you always ran everything by her. She's an ambassador in the making, I think, and she'd be damn good at it!"

"Oh please, heaven forbid," Jack laughed as he hugged her again.

At that moment, Lucas walked in and Gertje made her excuses.

"Listen, I better leave you two and go back to the living room." Gertje kissed Jack on the cheek, then winked at Lucas and kissed him, too, before walking out.

"It's good to see her, Luke, that was a nice surprise," Jack told Lucas as he put his arm around his lover.

"Well, absolutely everyone is here. Stacey looks like she's about to pop any moment now. Sean came, too! He brought future wife number four, I think. She's nice, I talked to her, and she's younger than me." Lucas rolled his eyes, making Jack chuckle.

"Oh, and Mark brought a petite red head by the name of Zanna. Don't think we've met her before."

"Well, it's not like we see Mark every week," Jack answered quietly, enjoying how excited Lucas was about tonight.

"Before I forget, Liz asked me if we could look after her boys next week. I told her no problem, I think she's going to elope with Mr. Brazil."

"Well, he's a much nicer guy than Mr. Italy, who kept her running in circles all those years," Jack added.

"Yeah, I told her they never leave their wives."

"I did."

Lucas sighed contently. He looked at Jack and then kissed him firmly on the lips. "Don't know what my life would have been like if you hadn't."

"You would have found someone else. I'm sure you would have been happy."

Lucas shook his head. "Not like this, you and I were meant for each other."

Jack felt all warm inside. "Well, I've never regretted my decision."

"Good!" Lucas quipped as he smiled widely, "because Maria's here, too!"

Jack inhaled deeply, raising his eyebrows. "Next thing you're going to tell me Lucy made it, too, and then Santa Claus came down the chimney."

Lucas went silent. "You know she wouldn't come."

"Would you want her to?" Jack asked, pulling Lucas closer.

Lucas pursed his lips and shook his head. "Sometimes I think AnnElise would like to meet her."

"She probably will some day, but they both need to be ready for that. No use trying to force it. Now let's go in there before our guests wonder what we're up to. Besides, it's not fair to AnnElise to let her look after all those people alone."

Lucas snorted. "As though she isn't doing a better job than either of us."

"CAN I please have everyone's attention?"

AnnElise stood on a chair between her two fathers. She looked over at Liz, who gave her an encouraging nod.

She started hesitantly, clearly a little intimidated by the crowd, even though she knew most of them quite well. "Dad and Jack know I'm going to say a few words, but they don't know exactly what I'm going to say, so please listen."

Lucas heard Jack nervously clear his throat and admitted to himself that there was probably good reason to be nervous. Their full-of-surprises daughter was not to be trusted.

"First, some of you may already know this, but for those who don't: Jack handed in his PhD thesis a little while ago, and he was told last week that pretty soon we will have to call him Dr. Christensen. I told him 'fat chance'." A few people in the crowd laughed out loud, and she continued. "Please make him blush by clapping your hands for him."

Lucas saw Liz passing around the glasses of champagne as their guests applauded and cheered Jack loudly, making him smile uncomfortably.

"Secondly, Jack was asked by the President to become an ambassador again."

This too was met by cheering and Jack had to raise his hand to give AnnElise a chance to continue.

"After some heated discussions around the dinner table..." she looked at both her fathers, placing her hands on their shoulders. Both men were laughing nervously and looking at each other, "he decided to decline, saying they should ask him again when I was in college, which was really nice, because I really like my school here."

Aawws and ooohs sounded all around the room, but their friends still smiled.

AnnElise cleared her throat and Jack realized this was one of his nervous ticks she'd inherited. "Then lastly... and I may be sent to bed without dinner for this..."

AnnElise looked over at Liz who winked at her.

"Before I was born, Jack asked Dad to marry him and Dad said yes, only they couldn't then because Jack was still married." She rolled her eyes and Maria smiled at her in acknowledgement. "Then again when I was six, at Stacey's wedding - for those of you who don't know her, Stacey is the tall, beautiful lady with the red lips and the long dark hair, who looks like she's going to have her baby any minute now. Well, at her wedding, Dad asked Jack to marry him and Jack said yes, but not until they could do it in their own country. So now, finally, in the State of New York, two men can get married."

She turned to her two dads. "Could you two please get your act together already?"

Loud cheers rose from the group of people in the living room. They heard "Hear, hear!!" and "It's about time".

Jack blushed as he looked at Lucas and threw him a 'how about it' look.

Lucas bit his lower lip and nodded. "I guess there's nothing stopping us now," he whispered and leaned forward to kiss Jack. Their friends rose and as they looked around they could see raised glasses and happy faces everywhere, not one disapproving frown in the bunch. Even Maria was beaming, although she was no doubt explaining a few things to the handsome man, who had his arm around her shoulder.

Mark had a wicked grin on his face. "You're both going to need best men, guys!"

Which made Liz answer from across the room, "Who says the men should have all the fun here?"

"Well, you better go pick out your tux then, Liz," Lucas teased his best friend.

Jack and Lucas hugged with AnnElise between them. "Happy now?" they asked the young lady.

AnnElise ruffled both men's hair. "Yes!" she shouted. "I'll no longer be a child from a broken home! Now can we go check on dinner? I'm starving!"

Epilogue

"COME back to bed, Luke," Jack said lazily. He was stretched out on the bed they had spent the last six and a half years sharing.

"Can't," Lucas answered determinedly from the small balcony. He was gazing out over the city, sipping from the cup of tea in his hand.

"What's wrong?" Jack wasn't entirely sure if Lucas was joking or not.

"I promised myself nine years ago that I would never sleep with a married man again."

Jack chuckled. "Imagine how I feel. I told myself thirty years ago I was never going to sleep with a man and now I've fallen in love with one and married him, too!"

"So you're still in love?" Lucas asked as he casually let his bathrobe slide open, revealing his long legs and slender thighs.

Jack wanted to joke about being ruthlessly seduced by a beautiful body, but decided against it. Right now he wanted to get Lucas in his arms as fast as possible. He wanted it to be his hand rubbing Lucas's flat stomach and sliding down his treasure trail. "Yes, I am," he answered, lifting the duvet for Lucas to crawl underneath.

Lucas's skin was cool against his and they snuggled close together in each other's arms until it was time to get up.

THEY were married that morning at a friend's house in the Hamptons. It had been an informal gathering, a small ceremony with their closest friends barefoot on the beach.

Mark, now married to Zanna and with a baby on the way, was Jack's best man.

Liz had shown up in a tuxedo, complete with glittery top hat, looking deliciously androgynous except for her burgeoning stomach, a testament to the happiness bestowed on her by Rodrigo, a Brazilian/Portuguese U.N. interpreter, and with whom she had indeed eloped the weekend after Jack and Lucas's New Year's Eve party.

The six of them, along with AnnElise and Liz's two sons, celebrated with an elaborate picnic lunch on the beach, joined by Sean and his girlfriend and Maria and her 'Doctors without Borders' boyfriend. The atmosphere had been relaxed and happy with alcohol consumption at a minimum because of the pregnant female company, but with lots of speeches and ribbing from all the friends who had been party to the different stories that had shaped their lives.

Now in the early hours of the next day, they were making love in the bed that had always been their haven.

They took their time, slowly kissing, touching and rubbing up against one another. They each knew the other well, knew what felt good and what felt like heaven, all this familiarity representing warmth and safety.

Jack looked up at Lucas's dark lust-filled eyes as his lover impaled himself. He felt the deliciously warm tightness surround him as Lucas adjusted to the welcome intrusion.

As Lucas began to move, Jack could see the young man would not last long.

"Come for me, Luke; come for me, my husband."

Lucas smiled at the word 'husband', unable to respond in words as his movements became more urgent. He leaned forward, taking Jack's head in his hands and whispered, "Come with me, Jack. Please."

Jack had a hard time keeping his eyes open as the familiar bliss tightened his groin, but he didn't want to miss the beauty of his husband's face as they convulsed through the abandon of their mutual orgasm.

They woke up a few hours later, the rising sun shining in through the half drawn curtains.

"I'm glad you said no to the President," Lucas lazily admitted to Jack.

"I figured our lives were pretty perfect just the way they were," Jack whispered as he kissed Lucas's hair. "I like the anonymity; I like the fact that we could get married without causing a stir. I like the idea that AnnElise is growing up with friends she's known since nursery school."

Lucas just smiled as he snuggled up closer and drifted off to sleep again. Yes, life was pretty perfect just the way it was.

Zahra Owens was born in Europe, just before Woodstock and the moon landing, and given a much less pronounceable name by her non-English speaking parents. Being an Aquarian meant she would never quite conform and people learned to expect the unexpected.

She started writing fairy tales in first grade; the same year she came into contact with her first group of English speaking friends, a group which would eventually grow to include people from all over the world. On the outside she was a typical only child, accustomed to being with adults most of the time. On the inside, she sought ways to channel her wild imagination.

Becoming an Intensive Care Nurse only kept her interested for so long, the same was true for being a Computer Specialist. According to her mother, her hobby is collecting college degrees, but it wasn't until she was in her thirties that she realized what life was all about. By then she was making a decent living during the day and honing her writing craft at night. She wrote in English of course, which was also her preferred reading language. The final piece in the jigsaw of her writing career was provided when she met her editor, something she felt was essential for a non-English speaker.

The fact that the Internet has made the world a lot smaller, gave her access to readers from all over the world. And she couldn't be happier.

Visit Zahra's Website at www.zahraowens.com.

Other Novels from Dreamspinner Press

A Summer Place by Ariel Tachna   248 pages
Paperback $11.99   **eBook** $5.99
ISBN: 978-0-9795048-4-6   **ISBN**: 978-0-9795048-5-3

Overseer Nicolas Wells had been coming to Mount Desert Island for ten summers to help build cottages for the rich and powerful. Despite his secrets, he had grown comfortable in the peaceful little island town, getting to know its inhabitants and even to consider some of them friends. The eleventh year, however, he arrived to startling news: the island's peace had been shattered by a murder. At the request of the sheriff, Shawn Parnell, Nicolas agreed to hire Philip Hall, the local blacksmith and the probable next victim, in the hope that the secure construction site would be safer than his house in the village. He never expected the decision to lead to danger. Or to love.

Cursed by Rhianne Aile   232 pages
Paperback $11.99   **eBook** $5.99
ISBN: 978-0-9795048-2-2   **ISBN**: 978-0-9795048-3-9

Upon their grandmother's death, Tristan Northland and his twin, Will, come into possession of her Book of Shadows and the knowledge that their family is responsible for a centuries old curse. Determined to right the ancient wrong, Tristan sets off across the ocean to reverse the dark magic that affects the Sterling family to this day.

Benjamin Sterling might not be happy with his life, but it is predictable – at least until Tristan Northland shows up in his office, unannounced and with nowhere to stay. He has plenty of reason to distrust witches and Northlands, but instead of caution, he experiences two unexpected emotions: hope and love

To Love a Cowboy by Rhianne Aile   228 pages
Paperback $11.99   **eBook** $5.99
ISBN: 978-0-9795048-8-4   **ISBN**: 978-0-9795048-9-1

Seven years ago, Roan Bucklin left the family ranch for college, leaving foreman Patrick Lassiter with a mix of sweltering emotions: relief, regret, and nearly overwhelming desire. Afraid that Roan would regret giving himself to an older man, Patrick let him go without a word about his true feelings. But Roan took Patrick's heart with him.

Roan had harbored a crush on Patrick from the time he'd turned fourteen. He thought he'd gotten over it, grown up, moved on, but now he's back and home to stay. After one look, he knows he has something to prove to Patrick – that he wants to be claimed by the cowboy who has always possessed his heart.

www.dreamspinnerpress.com

Size Still Matters: Short Stories Still Long Enough to Satisfy
A Dreamspinner Anthology of Gay Erotic Novellas
Paperback $20.00   **eBook** $12.00
ISBN: 978-0-9801018-2-9   **ISBN**: 978-0-9801018-3-6

Sight Unseen by Shay Kincaid

Famous actor Jackson Prescott wonders if anyone will ever look past the glitz and glamour of his Hollywood persona and love the person behind the name. So after accidentally dialing a wrong number and feeling an instant attraction to Devon Forrester, the stranger on the other end of the line, he decides to test the waters ... using a different name. After getting to know Devon through their daily phone calls, Jackson starts to worry: Will the relationship they've built crumble when they meet face to face? Or will Devon be able to forgive Jackson's deceit?

Take My Picture by Giselle Ellis

Aaron has no idea what he's walking into when he shows up to pose for a famous photographer. Instead of being the focus of the camera, he ends up working as Jake's assistant. Five frustrating, thrilling and crazy years later, Jake discovers Aaron has become the focus of his life, a life that's threatened when Aaron finds someone else, and Jake has to set his beloved muse free.

Start From the Beginning by Chrissy Munder

A heart attack leaves Miles wrangling with a slow recovery and a quiet retreat ... just one cabin down from wounded warrior Drew. Although he's unhappy to have his solitude invaded, Drew finds himself fascinated with Miles, but he can't bring himself to push aside his skittish nerves. Both men fear rejection for different reasons, but what if they've instead found the acceptance they crave?

Evan's Heaven by Nicki Bennett

Actor MacAlester Kerr wanders into a whole new world of pampering and pleasure when his director sends him to *Evan's Heaven* for a pedicure. Right off, he meets *the* Evan and finds himself head over heels. Mac's on Cloud Nine when he finds out Evan feels the same.

www.dreamspinnerpress.com

Printed in the United States
126710LV00004B/184-186/A